MEET THE BENEDETTOS

ALSO BY KATIE COTUGNO

MEET THE
Benedettos

A NOVEL

KATIE COTUGNO

HARPER PERENNIAL

NEW YORK • LONDON • TORONTO • SYDNEY • NEW DELHI • AUCKLAND

HARPER ● PERENNIAL

HarperCollins books may be purchased for educational, business, or sales promotional use. For information, please email the Special Markets Department at SPsales@harpercollins.com.

FIRST EDITION

Designed by Jamie Lynn Kerner

Library of Congress Cataloging-in-Publication Data

Names: Cotugno, Katie, author.
Title: Meet the Benedettos: a novel / Katie Cotugno.
Description: First edition. | New York, NY: HarperPerennial, 2023. |
Identifiers: LCCN 2023014343 (print) | LCCN 2023014344 (ebook) | ISBN
    9780063324145 (paperback) | ISBN 9780063324152 (ebook)
Subjects: LCGFT: Domestic fiction. | Romance fiction. | Novels.
Classification: LCC PS3603.O873 M44 2023 (print) | LCC PS3603.O873
    (ebook) | DDC 813/.6—dc23/eng/20230414
LC record available at https://lccn.loc.gov/2023014343
LC ebook record available at https://lccn.loc.gov/2023014344

ISBN 978-0-06-332414-5 (pbk.)
ISBN 978-0-06-332900-3 (library edition)

23 24 25 26 27 LBC 5 4 3 2 1

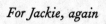
For Jackie, again

CHAPTER ONE

LILLY

It is a truth universally acknowledged that Lilly Benedetto drives the crappiest, most broken-down car in Southern California, which is how she finds herself sitting on a bench next to the valet stand outside Cecconi's in West Hollywood late Friday afternoon, waiting for her sister to come and pick her up.

"You realize there's a dealership like three blocks from here," June says when she cruises to a stop at the bright yellow curb, immaculate in a pair of high-waisted jeans and a tank top cropped just enough to show a sliver of tan, flat stomach. At twenty-nine, she's older than Lilly by two full years, though you'd never know it to look at her. She's been using a retinol serum since she was twelve. "You literally could have walked over, tossed your hair a little, and driven something new right off the lot."

Lilly shrugs, sliding into the passenger seat of June's cool, quiet Audi and cranking the air-conditioning, tilting the vents up so they blow against her damp, blotchy face. It's the end of October but still close to a hundred degrees in Los Angeles, and her stretchy black tank dress is sticking to the sweaty ridges of her spine. "My credit's bad," is all she says.

It's a bullshit answer, and they both know it, but it's a testament to June's sweet and mollifying nature—and, probably, to the fact that Lilly is the unequivocal boss of her four sisters—that she doesn't press. Instead she waggles her fingers at a couple of scruffy-looking photographers camped across the street as she pulls out into traffic; the guys wave back as they pack up their cameras, ambling off toward their black SUVs. "Did you call them?" June asks, nodding her curly blond head toward the window.

"Rude!" Lilly whirls on her, laughing. "What, so that they could all come down here and watch me get my shitty car towed? Of course I didn't call them."

June grins. "I'm just asking," she says easily. "You know Olivia tips them off every time she leaves the house."

"Olivia would tip them off every time she got a UTI if she thought it would get her picture in *Us Weekly*," Lilly counters, "but no. They were there to take pictures of Isobel. My vehicular difficulties were just a bonus."

"Lucky them," June says, glancing over her shoulder as they merge onto the 101 North toward Calabasas. Lilly leans her head back against the seat. She parked on the street specifically to avoid the embarrassment of the valets hiding her ancient Honda behind the restaurant with the rest of the undesirables, only to be rewarded for her foresight by a double-decker bus full of tourists gawking at the grim spectacle of the tow truck dragging it forlornly away. Isobel and the rest of her crew had left by then, thank god—not that it matters, since Lilly knows from experience that the whole debacle is probably already trending on Twitter. If there's one thing the internet can't get enough of, it's a Benedetto sister having a misadventure of any kind.

"I didn't even realize you guys were hanging out again," June says now, pushing her oversized sunglasses up into her hair as the late-afternoon light begins to fade. "You and Isobel, I mean."

"Oh, we're not," Lilly corrects. "It was just a brunch to launch her line of ugly purses, that's all. She only invited me like twenty minutes before it started, which means somebody must have gotten mouth herpes or something and she needed a seat filler."

June shakes her head, full lips twisting. "I'm sure that's not true."

"That's very loving of you, Junie," Lilly says, sliding her sandals off and propping her feet up on the dashboard. "Unfortunately, your optimism is undermined by the fact that my complimentary belt bag party favor was monogrammed for Addison Rae."

By the time they make it back to Pemberly Grove it's almost dusk, the sun slanting warm and pink and golden over the hills. They wave to Edgar, the octogenarian gate attendant, then follow the winding streets of the development past the long-shuttered clubhouse and the algae-covered pond before finally pulling into the long, curving driveway of their parents' sprawling faux colonial.

"You and your hobo wagon are already on the Sinclair," Olivia reports when Lilly and June muscle open the rusting gate into the backyard, fishing her phone out of her cleavage and waving it accusingly in Lilly's direction. She and Kit are draped across an enormous unicorn inflatable in the middle of the bean-shaped pool, the two of them wearing matching Valentino sunglasses and sky-high Louboutins. Their gangly, moribund friend Tony, who does all their photography—in exchange, so far as Lilly can tell, for the pleasure of their company rather than monetary compensation of any kind—snaps busily away. "Photos and everything."

Lilly bites back a grimace. That was fast, even for Hollywood's most notoriously salacious gossip blog; she supposes you've gotta be quick these days if you don't want to get scooped by a thirteen-year-old with an iPhone and a window seat on the star tour. "Just another day of breathless, fawning coverage, I'm sure."

"Shockingly, no." Kit reaches out with one intricately tattooed arm and plucks the phone from Olivia's hand, squinting down at the post. Of the five of them, Olivia and Kit are the two youngest and the ones with the most social media cachet, perpetually toasting each other with cronut-flavored vodka or filming cheery videos about how much they love their knockoff Vitamix. If their nascent careers as influencers haven't yet proven to be terribly lucrative in terms of actual American dollars, at the very least neither one of them will ever need to purchase their own flat-tummy tea ever again. "'Did Somebody Call for an Uber?'" Kit reads now, her plump, painted lips curling in dark amusement. "'Lilly B's Busted Beater Breaks Down Again.'"

"That's . . . alliterative." Lilly winces. "Sorry," she says, more to June than anyone else. She stopped caring what the Sinclair or anyone else had to say about her or the Honda a long time ago. Still, she doesn't like to embarrass her sisters.

"Don't worry about it." June sits down on one of the wobbly lounge chairs lined up on the patio. Then, suddenly realizing it's covered with a creeping fur of neon-green mildew, she sits on another one instead. "Could be worse."

"Could be better!" Olivia counters indignantly. "What is that, like, the third time in the last two months? Can you please just nut up and get a new car already? People are going to think we don't have the money to replace it."

"I mean, we don't have the money to replace it," Lilly reminds her. "Just ask Dad."

"It's not funny!" Olivia protests, though Lilly wasn't actually kidding. "Your whole"—she waves a hand in Lilly's direction—"*situation* is really dragging us down."

"Are you sure that's not the staggering weight of your fake eyelashes?" Kit posits sweetly. Olivia flips her the bird in reply.

"Dinner's here," Marianne announces then, sliding the patio door open and poking her pale, sullen face outside. At twenty-four she's the middleborn Benedetto, floating ominously at the center of their family like a haunted island in the middle of the sea. A couple of months ago she turned up in a supporting role in some random Lena Dunham mumblecore project none of the rest of them had the foggiest idea she was doing; if it turned out she was also breeding heritage pigs or running a high-stakes poker game out of the pool house, Lilly would not be the slightest bit surprised. "Mom says come inside if you want to eat."

Olivia sighs, dropping her head back so it's nestled in the crook of the unicorn's graceful white neck. She's got the same dark, wavy hair as Lilly, long enough that the ends of it are wet from trailing through the bleachy blue water. "Somebody needs to tow us in," she announces imperiously.

Lilly frowns as Tony sets his camera down and shuffles over to the skimmer, casting it into the pool like a fishing line so Olivia can grab hold. "What are you guys even advertising?" Lilly asks, holding her hand out to pull Junie to her feet.

"Nothing," Olivia replies, boosting herself neatly up onto the pool deck, heels and all. "We just look particularly good today, don't you think?"

They say their goodbyes to Tony and head inside the house, where their mother is standing at the kitchen island dressed head to toe in snow-white athleisure, pulling various Chinese food containers from a massive paper bag. "No, really, don't bother helping," she says, holding one manicured hand up dramatically. "I'm all set here."

"Sorry," Olivia says, leaning over to kiss her on one round cheek. "Were you slaving away over a hot stove all day long?"

Lilly nudges her mother gently out of the way, opening up the tubs and boxes. June rummages through the untidy cupboards, setting out plates and napkins as their father strides in from the pool house, where, following a massive heart attack a couple of years ago, he now spends the better part of his days listening to the This Is: Billy Joel playlist on Spotify and pedaling his recumbent bicycle. Whenever he comes upon all five of his daughters in the wild there's always a moment when his expression is the slightest bit befuddled, like they sautéed his vegetables in butter instead of olive oil at Spago and he's trying to recalculate the macros in his head.

Now he looks from the take-out cartons to Lilly's mother, then back again, frown lines furrowing his crispy forehead. "I thought you were going to cook."

Cinta shrugs. "I thought I was going to marry Mark Harmon," she tells him, thrusting a container of noodles into his hands and shooing him away from the island. "Looks like we were both wrong."

Her father catches Lilly's eye across the kitchen, raising his voluminous brows in exaggerated forbearance. Lilly winks at him in reply before grabbing a can of seltzer out of the fridge and following June into the dining room. They literally never ate together before the show started filming, when the network mandated a once-weekly family dinner in an attempt to maximize every available opportunity to get all seven of them in the shot—and, presumably, for somebody to say or do something inflammatory or offensive, though that was never explicitly mentioned in the production notes. In the end, the ritual outlasted the three seasons that *Meet the Benedettos* ran on cable, and they still wind up gathered around the table almost every Friday night.

"I'm serious, Cinta," their father says now, the light from the reproduction art deco chandelier bouncing off his head at the far end of the table. A few months ago he fired their housekeeper as a cost-cutting measure and signed them up for a meal delivery service instead, only he didn't realize it was the kind where you had to cook the food yourself, and since then the insulated cardboard boxes have begun to pile up in the pantry like a cursed tower of Pisa while their mother happily patronizes every take-out establishment in Los Angeles County, and a couple in San Bernardino besides. "We can't just be ordering dinner for seven people every night of the goddamn we—"

"It's rice, Dominic." Their mother waves him off. "I know that to hear you talk about it we're one order of General Tso's away from a life of penury on Skid Row, but I certainly think we can afford ri—"

"It's not just the rice," Dominic interrupts. "You know that. It's the rice, the house, the clothes—"

"On top of which, if you want someone to cook those damn meal kits so badly—"

"—not to mention the spa trips to Malibu—"

"—I seem to recall that there's someone in this family who loves to talk about how he went to culinary school—"

"—and the collagen injections—"

"—though I don't know that the certificate program at DeVry University is precisely what Escoffier had in mind—"

"Hey!" Lilly interrupts brightly, plucking a dumpling from its white paper carton as June casts her a grateful look across the table. "Here's a hard conversational swerve. Did you guys see somebody moved in next door to the Lucases?"

"About time," their mother sniffs. There are probably a dozen vacant properties in Pemberly Grove these days. The one on Netherfield Place has been empty for over a year, before which it was occupied by a couple of thirtysomething guys with slick haircuts who Cinta was convinced were using it as a set for adult films. "How do you know what the sets for adult films look like, exactly?" Olivia asked her once; Cinta's eyes narrowed before she huffed off to the aesthetician without condescending to reply.

"Not just somebody," Kit says now, reaching for the kung pao with the self-satisfied smile of a person who knows something. "It's Charlie Bingley."

Right away, everyone except their father whirls to look at her. "Charlie Bingley?" Olivia's eyes are wide.

"Like, *Charlie Bingley* Charlie Bingley?" Lilly is intrigued in spite of herself. In the last couple of years Charlie Bingley has transitioned seemingly effortlessly from second banana in a series of teenage gross-out flicks to a bona fide A-lister, the muscly star of a forthcoming comic book trilogy called *Major Fantastic* that promises to be both extremely loud and incredibly lucrative. *People* magazine recently declared him the nicest guy in Hollywood—a former high school football star turned Juilliard grad whose devotion to his mom back in Chicago is eclipsed only by how much he loves his rescue dog. Lilly has lived in LA long enough to know it's probably only a matter of time until he's unmasked as a pervert or a cannibal or, worst of all, a Scientologist. Still, it's not like she'd turn her nose up at the opportunity to get a gander at him washing his car in the driveway. "What the fuck is he doing here?"

"Excuse me," their mother counters immediately, the threat implicit in her voice. "This is a very exclusive neighborhood."

"Is it, though?" Kit tilts her head to the side.

"You're welcome to move out anytime, Katrina," their father reminds her, barely glancing up from the mountain of steamed vegetables heaped onto his plate. "Encouraged, even."

"There's another guy living there, too," Mari informs them, reaching for the carton of chicken and broccoli. "I saw him the other night."

"Through your telescope?" Kit asks immediately.

"What do you mean, another guy?" Their mother's eyes narrow. "A boyfriend?"

"If Charlie Bingley is gay I will literally fling myself into the ocean," Olivia announces.

"You should ring his doorbell and tell him that," Lilly advises, helping herself to another dumpling. "I'm sure he'd be happy to stop dating men for you."

"You should ring his doorbell regardless!" Cinta exclaims. "Honestly, I can't believe none of you have invited him over already. He's going to think we're all a bunch of low-rent inconsequentials with no manners."

"Oh," Marianne replies, "I'm sure we can all agree he probably thinks that already."

Their mother shoots her a murderous look, and Lilly ducks her head to hide a grin. After all, it's not like Mari is wrong: their family is steeped in the kind of cultural notoriety normally reserved for disgraced politicians or the emcees of beloved children's shows who later get caught masturbating in movie theaters. Lilly's father made a not-insignificant fortune a decade ago, rising to a campy sort of local celebrity with commercials for his small chain of red-sauce Italian restaurants, the Meatball King. They still run, occasionally—every once in a while Lilly will be flipping channels late at night and catch sight of her dad mugging like Luigi from *Mario Kart* in front of an enormous brick oven, crowing the King's iconic slogan: "You won't believe the balls on us!"

The business grew; they moved from a modest house in the Valley to Pemberly Grove when Lilly was sixteen. Cinta enrolled them all in a tony private school, where Lilly took AP Literature and Composition and also wrote the occasional paper for Isobel DesRoche, the famous hotelier's fashion model daughter. Isobel took her out to the clubs on Hollywood and Sunset; Lilly brought June, who caught the attention of the second-most-handsome member of a screamingly popular boy band, and suddenly there they were in their party dresses on the blogs and in the magazines, photographers snapping pictures while they drank their iced lattes at Starbucks and a camera crew running cables through their living room for the first season of *Meet the Benedettos*. Cinta hired a ghostwriter to pen a glossy paperback about parenting socialite daughters. Kit and Olivia launched a juniors' line at Kohl's. Their father licensed the Meatball King as a franchise, and if, all these years later, neither the restaurants nor their family's alleged celebrity—not to mention Lilly's friendship with Isobel—are exactly what one might call thriving, their mother still carries herself like a deposed queen stubbornly awaiting her golden jubilee.

Now Cinta sighs and reaches for her wineglass, visibly bored with all of them. "You're not the only one with exciting news," she tells Lilly. "Guess who I had lunch with today?"

"Lil Wayne," Kit fires back immediately.

"The Broadway Across America cast of *Jesus Christ Superstar*," Lilly tries.

"That lady astronaut who drove across the country in a diaper to confront her romantic rival," June puts in.

"I think she died," Mari says. "Didn't she die?"

Their mother rolls her eyes. "Oh, you all are hilarious. No." She pauses dramatically. "Joaquin Shannon."

Olivia frowns, plucking a noodle delicately from her bowl with two fingers. "None of us know who that is."

Cinta sighs impatiently. "The interior designer," she informs them. "Come on, girls. He just did Jennifer Aniston's art barn. If we're going to be hosting guests like Charlie Bingley and his friends—"

"Do you imagine we're going to be hosting guests like Charlie Bingley and his friends?" Lilly asks her, but before her mother can answer her dad puts down his fork.

"Cinta," he says, "we talked about this. And we agreed that now was not the time to undertake another reno—"

"We didn't agree on anything," Lilly's mom says crisply, then turns back to the rest of them. "Joaquin had some great ideas for blowing out the back of the kitchen—"

"Cinta—"

"—something really natural and organic—"

"Cinta—"

"—fully encased in glass—"

Lilly's father slams two meaty hands on the table with a startling thump. "Damn it, Cinta. What part of being ninety days from foreclosure don't you understand?"

All at once, the room gets very, very quiet. "Hang on," Lilly says, trying to keep her voice level. "Ninety days from what, exactly?"

"It's nothing," her mother says quickly, waving a paper towel like a hanky. "A paperwork snafu, that's all. Dominic, I already told you this isn't something the girls need to be worrying about."

"The girls are grown women, Cinta!" her father counters. "Look around, will you? They're certainly old enough to understand this family's extremely precarious financial situation. Who knows, maybe it'll light a fire under them to contribute before all seven of us wind up living in the basement of my mother's house back in Newark and selling zeppole out of a truck at the Saint Agrippina Festival!"

"We contribute," Olivia protests, looking wounded.

"I know you do, sweetheart," their father says. "But I am sorry to report the bank does not take loan repayment in the form of a lifetime supply of essential oils, no matter how compelling the health benefits might be."

Lilly swallows hard. The development was brand-new when they moved in eleven years ago, freshly constructed luxury homes nestled into the hills on the outskirts of Calabasas. She remembers sliding down the empty hallways, socks slipping on the gleaming hardwood floors. She thought this place was a palace—the biggest, grandest, most beautiful house anyone had ever lived in, with a copse of citrus and avocado trees in the backyard and enough bedrooms for each of them to have their own. It started falling apart more or less as soon as they unpacked their boxes, the sinks leaking and the doors coming off their hinges and the dining room chandelier crashing down into the cake at Marianne's fourteenth birthday party. Now, more than a decade later, it bears the scars of at least a dozen half-baked renovations her mother has undertaken and then lost interest in partway through, including a nonfunctional sensory deprivation chamber in the primary bathroom and a custom fresco in the entryway that looks for all the world like it belongs on the ceiling of the Cheesecake Factory at the Paramus Park mall.

Still, Lilly thinks, looking around at her sisters' lovely, stricken faces: it's their house.

"Well!" she says, clapping her hands together with practiced eldest-daughter authority, even though she's technically second in line. "Lucky for you all, I know an opportunity when I see one. Clearly the only option is to kidnap Charlie Bingley and hold him for ransom in the pool house until the producers of *Major Fantastic* roll over and agree to pay off the rest of the mortgage in exchange for his safe return."

"Or," her father counters pointedly, "you could all go out and look for jobs."

The five Benedetto sisters consider that for a moment: heads tilted in quiet contemplation, fingertips tapping their pink, glossy mouths. "Kidnapping," they decide unanimously, the clatter of their raucous laughter filling the dining room and drifting out the windows into the hot, breezeless yard.

* * *

After dinner Lilly takes her laptop out onto the second-floor terrace and props her feet up on the railing, the fan whirring softly like the purr of a well-behaved cat. Lilly's been writing her whole life, little plays for her sisters to put on and the overwrought short stories she used to post to her long-defunct LiveJournal. She actually got accepted into the creative writing program at USC back before the show got picked up, though she deferred at Cinta's urging—"College isn't going anywhere, is it? Your youth, on the other hand . . ."—and never actually enrolled. She thinks about what it might have been like sometimes, the workshops and the lectures, studying in the library late at night. She would have been bored, probably, would have missed the clubs and the parties and the vacations at Isobel's father's resorts.

Then again: maybe not.

Lilly tilts her head back, remembering a trip they took to the Maldives right after they wrapped the show's second season—the sea glittering endlessly down below them, the sky extravagantly, wastefully blue. She and Joe were newly engaged that winter, the diamond huge and heavy on the fourth finger of her left hand: Lilly remembers pulling it off to admire the tiny tan line underneath it, the mark it had already left on her body feeling almost more significant than the ring itself.

He found her on the uppermost deck their second night out on the water: "There you are," he said, sliding one familiar hand around her waist and pulling her back against him, his heart tapping hard and thready against her spine. Lilly glanced over her shoulder, frowning a little. It was still mostly party drugs at that point—at least, she was pretty sure it was still mostly party drugs—but his mother polished the pews at church on Saturday mornings. He wasn't built for the DesRoche family yacht.

Also, and even then Lilly hated the part of herself that thought this way: he was turning into a press liability.

"Here I am," she agreed anyway, dropping her head back onto his shoulder and tilting her chin up to watch the stars. He smelled like this afternoon's sunscreen and Lever 2000, cheap and slightly astringent: no matter how many fancy body washes she bought him, he always used the bars from CVS. "Everybody having fun in there?"

"Olivia just locked herself in the bathroom crying because

Anwar Hadid blocked her on Instagram," Joe reported, sliding his palms down over her stomach, "so probably that will require your attention at some point. Otherwise, I think everybody's doing good."

Lilly laughed, or started to: it turned into a gasp as his hands wandered lower, slipping up underneath her dress. "There are literally two dozen people right inside," she reminded him softly, nodding in the direction of the cabin. She could see June through the plate glass window, tall and luminous. She could hear Isobel calling for more champagne.

"So? What do they care?" Joe's smile was brilliant in the moonlight, nimble fingers sliding inside the elastic of her underwear. "We're getting married."

Lilly thinks there was always a part of her that knew what was coming. She thinks there was always a part of her that knew it couldn't last.

Now she fusses with some dialogue, deleting a couple of words and putting them back again five minutes later. The last few months she's been noodling on a screenplay about a lady vampire destined to outlive her one true love; she entered it into a blind contest over the summer and got to the very last round, but when she came in for the finalist meeting the team took one look at her, sent her out into the hallway for ten minutes, then brought her back in and explained as delicately as possible that having her name attached to a project made it virtually unsalable. "I read online that it's actually one of the few things both Republicans and Democrats agree on in national polling," one of the executives mused admiringly.

Lilly blinked. "How much they don't like me and my family?"

"Well." He had the decency to seem embarrassed. "Pretty much."

Eventually Lilly's eyes start to glaze over, so she gives up and closes the computer with a tidy click. After all, the problem isn't that she hasn't revised the damn thing. The problem is just . . . her. "If you ever wanted to develop something a little more on-brand," the guy offered as she was leaving, an assistant all but yanking her from the room with a shepherd's crook like something out of vaudeville. "A dating competition, maybe? Something with fun challenges! We could get your sisters in on the act."

Inside the cool, quiet house June's bedroom door is still open, the faint smell of gardenias and night cream hanging in the air. "Were you writing?" June calls, leaning back on her elbows and peering out into the hallway. She's already in her pajamas, one of the crisp matching sets that are all she sleeps in, like she's the sweet, plucky heroine in a Nora Ephron movie.

Lilly shakes her head. "Searching Craigslist for an honest living," she jokes. "Thinking about getting a job as a naked sushi girl."

"Do you think he was serious?" June asks, brow furrowing. "About the house?"

Lilly does, actually, but it's her job in this family to make it so her sisters don't worry, so instead she just shrugs. "Dad's scrappy," she promises, which is also what she said back when he was in the hospital undergoing an emergency triple bypass, the rest of them huddled in the waiting room at Cedars in their fuzzy slippers and robes. "He'll figure it out."

June nods, apparently satisfied. "You just missed Kit and Liv," she says, scooting over to make room for Lilly on the bed. "They were going to some tequila thing at Soho House, but they wanted to pick a theme for Rebecca's party."

"Pirates," Lilly says immediately. "The Bauhaus movement.

That alphabet poem by Edward Gorey about all the kids dying in unusual and gruesome ways."

June smirks. "I think they meant, like, jewel tones."

"Well, Junie, there's a real lack of imagination in this house, if you want my opinion." Lilly flops back against the pillows. "Is Rebecca's thing this weekend already?" Rebecca Barnes has the biggest, most over-the-top house in the entire development. She was a Hollywood sexpot back in the eighties and still dresses like it, is perpetually tottering down to the mailbox in a full face of makeup and three-inch heels, the morning sun glinting off her impeccably preserved décolletage. Every fall she throws herself an extravagant birthday party featuring acrobats or live emus or the entire cast of *Hamilton*; Isobel DesRoche would sooner be photographed perusing the clearance rack at Old Navy, but Lilly's mother has always believed the whole affair to be the very height of glamour, and lord knows none of her sisters have ever forgone an opportunity to increase their number of search results on Getty Images. "I swear that woman has like four birthdays a year."

"We could always skip it," June reminds her, but Lilly just hums noncommittally. After all, it's not like her social calendar is exactly groaning at the seams. She doesn't want to be remembered for all eternity as the straight man on *Meet the Benedettos*, maybe. But that doesn't necessarily mean she never wants to be remembered at all.

She says good night to June and pads through the bathroom they share, shutting the door behind her. She knows it's strange that they all still live here, five grown women all crammed into their parents' McMansion. She actually did move out for a while—she and Joe rented a place in a high-rise downtown right after the show got canceled, what was supposed to be a fresh start for them both—but after everything that happened there was no way she could stay there, all alone with their sleek, modern furniture, the city sprawling endlessly down below. Two years back home and Lilly barely even talks about leaving: "The rest of us would kill each other," her father said last time she mentioned it, "and I'd hope to be murdered first."

It's after midnight but already Lilly knows there's no way she's going to fall asleep anytime soon, so instead she slips on her sneakers and creeps out of the house through the mudroom, the blue night air cool on the back of her neck. She started doing this after she moved back to Pemberly Grove, wandering in loops through the mostly empty neighborhood—a way to spend her nights other than crying or staring blankly into the middle distance, trying to convince herself she wasn't about to fly off the face of the Earth. It's quiet out here, just the owls and the jacarandas and the soft, steady thud of her own two feet on the pavement. It's peaceful.

She's not consciously heading for Charlie Bingley's but she's also not completely surprised when she looks up and finds herself there, the house itself a faux-Mediterranean villa with arched doorways and a red tiled roof. There's a warm yellow light glowing in an upstairs window and a Land Rover parked in the drive; on the lawn a single tennis ball glows neon in the moonlight, presumably abandoned after a wholesome and healthful game of fetch.

Lilly thinks about her Honda sitting busted at the mechanic's. She wonders where her family will go if they have to leave Pemberly Grove. She imagines the last days of Rome, everyone washing their hair and pitting their peaches and falling in love while an empire fell all around them. Then she turns around and walks back home.

CHAPTER TWO

WILL

Will is lying on the couch in the living room, muttering to himself in iambic pentameter, when Charlie bounds down the stairs and tells him they're going to a party.

"What? No," Will says immediately—struggling upright, his dog-eared script still clutched in one hand. "Like, tonight?"

"Tonight," Charlie says cheerfully. "Like, now. Go get dressed."

"I am dressed," Will protests, though admittedly he's been wearing these particular sweatpants for longer than might be advisable. "And I can't. Filming starts a week from Monday."

Charlie clambers over the arm of the monstrous sofa, landing with a *whoof* at the opposite end. "Good thing I didn't say the party was a week from Monday, then."

"I'm not off-book."

"Nobody expects you to be off-book a week before you even start," Charlie tells him. "Also, don't say 'off-book.' It makes you sound like a dickhead from Juilliard."

"I am a dickhead from Juilliard," Will points out.

"So am I, but there's no reason to advertise it."

Will ignores him. "I'm gonna pass," he says, sinking back down into the dune of sand-colored throw pillows. Charlie rented this place sight unseen a couple of weeks ago, wanting a quiet place to crash while he did West Coast press for *Major Fantastic*. Will flew out from New York last weekend, the two of them staying up until four a.m. eating pizza bagels and watching shitty reruns like it's college all over again.

"Oh, come on," Charlie says now, undeterred. "A couple of hours. You gotta eat, right?"

"I'll eat here."

"There's no food here."

Will shrugs. "I'll order something," he says, but Charlie shakes his head.

"There's a whole weird thing with delivery drivers and this neighborhood," he explains, wandering into the kitchen and digging a beer out of the fridge. "Literally none of them can ever find it, and then if they do find it they have to, like, answer three riddles to get past Paul Blart at the gatehouse, and it's also entirely possible that fake pond thing is full of alligators. I'm still waiting for a burrito I ordered the night I moved in."

Will smirks. It didn't take long for it to become glaringly obvious that Pemberly Grove wasn't quite the exclusive luxury oasis promised by Charlie's real estate agent. In the short time Will has been here they've discovered a terrarium of mold in the dishwasher and a family of coyotes nesting in the pool house; two days ago the garage door nearly crushed Charlie's Land Rover like an empty can of Budweiser, stuttering up and down for the better part of an hour before finally grinding to a halt. Both Will and Caroline keep telling him to just find someplace new, but Charlie, typically, is adamant about making the best of it: "I signed a lease," he keeps explaining, like he's bargained his soul to Mephistopheles and has no choice but to soldier bravely on toward hell.

"I feel confident in my ability to feed myself," Will promises now, which isn't entirely true. He's been a wreck since he got here, anxious and itchy; he doesn't feel confident in his ability to handle much of anything, be it cobbling together a weird pantry dinner or making his major motion picture debut. He wavers for a moment, glancing back down at his script.

"Come on, bro," Charlie urges, sensing Will's hesitation as keenly as Ranger, Charlie's shaggy shepherd mix, sniffing out a half-eaten cheeseburger under a park bench from half a mile away. "You have the whole rest of the weekend to shuffle around the house in your bathrobe masturbating to Lady Macbeth, or whatever the fuck you've been doing. You've barely left the house since you got here."

"Not true," Will protests. "We went to that juice place literally yesterday."

"And you complained the whole time about how the sun was too bright and beets turn your pee red."

"It's not natural," Will says darkly. He tips his head back against the couch, gazing up at the double-height ceilings. "Also, I hate parties."

"You don't hate parties," Charlie counters immediately. "Nobody hates parties. Even people whose whole personality is saying they hate parties don't really hate parties." He finishes the rest of his beer in one long guzzle, lets out a jaunty-sounding burp. "On top of which, we're new here, and we were invited. It's the neighborly thing to do."

Will huffs the ghost of a laugh then; he can't help it. That's the problem with Charlie: he says things like *it's the neighborly thing to do* and sincerely means them. Will remembers him trundling through the door of their room the first day of freshman orientation fifteen years ago, all massive shoulders and broad Chicago accent. The first thing he wanted to do was get a hot dog off the street.

"It's not my whole personality," Will grumbles finally. "Saying I hate parties."

"Fifty percent," Charlie shoots back.

"Forty."

"Sold." Charlie grins. "Hurry up and get changed, will you? I don't want to miss the good snacks."

"Whoa whoa whoa," Will says, holding a hand up in alarm. "I didn't—"

"Gentlemen," Caroline says before he can finish, scuttering downstairs in a sleek black dress that makes her collarbones look very elegant, her lemon-mouthed friend Lucy in tow. Caroline is Charlie's half sister from his dad's first marriage; a couple of years ago she left the talent agency where she was a junior partner to handle Charlie's career full-time—which, not coincidentally, was three months before he got cast as Major Fantastic. Caroline is very, very good at what she does. "You ready?"

"Almost," Charlie reports happily. "Will just needs to put his face on before we go."

"Hang on one fucking second," Will protests. "I definitely never said—"

But Charlie waves him off. "You were getting there," he promises, already strolling toward the door to the mudroom. "I'm just speeding things along."

Will sighs. Charlie's the one who gave him the hard sell about taking the part in the movie, an undoubtedly ill-advised post-apocalyptic retelling of *Antony and Cleopatra*. "Dude, you'd be a dumbass not to take it," Charlie said when he called back in July, the connection crackling across three different time zones. It was a week after Will got out of Lenox Hill, his head like a balloon from all the meds they'd pumped into his bloodstream. That morning he'd looked down and realized, with a detached kind of wonder, that the hospital bracelet was still looped around his pale, skinny wrist. "You realize basically every actor in LA would cut off his left nut for a chance to work with Johnny Jones."

"I am not," Will reminded him, "nor have I ever wanted to be, an actor in LA." He wasn't an actor anywhere, actually. At least, not anymore.

"Not yet, maybe," Charlie countered easily. "Seriously, why not give it a shot? Come out here, get a little sunshine. Hang out with me." He cleared his throat. "Also, not for nothing, but a change of scenery might not be the worst thing to ever happen to you."

All at once, Will realized what this was about. "I'm fine, Charlie," he promised, deeply and abruptly embarrassed. "I mean, I'm not like, great, maybe. But you don't have to—I mean, this isn't some big thing where I need to be supervised by an adul—"

"For fuck's sake, Darce," Charlie interrupted. There was a raggedness in his voice that Will didn't want to examine too closely, that he did his best to pretend he didn't hear. "Just come the fuck out here, will you?"

Will booked his ticket the following day.

The party is on the other side of the development, so they drive over in Caroline's sporty little Mercedes, even though it's probably only about the equivalent of a dozen New York City blocks. Back at home Will walked everywhere, and since he got here it's like he can feel his muscles atrophying in real time, his entire body shriveling up like a California Raisin. "Go to the gym," Charlie suggested when he mentioned it. Charlie spends two hours at the gym every morning, which means he looks like . . . well, like Major Fantastic; it's not like Will needs help opening pickle jars, exactly, but something about living with a flesh-and-blood action figure makes him feel like maybe he ought to at least lift a couple of soup cans.

To drive through Pemberly Grove is to bear horrified witness to a long parade of architectural atrocities, fake Tudors next to faux Craftsman next to counterfeit Frank Lloyd Wrights, and the massive property they pull up in front of a few minutes later looks like something out of the English countryside—or, more accurately, like something out of the establishing shot of a movie *set* in the English countryside, a comedy of manners about British aristocrats who are cheerfully oblivious to the plight of the help. Ivy crawls up the imposing stone façade, oil lamps flickering in the blue and purple twilight. The parking attendants are wearing breeches, each and every one.

"I love LA," Caroline murmurs as they edge their way through the crowded foyer, cater waiters bustling by with trays of champagne and canapes while a string quartet saws inexplicably away at a cover of "Baker Street." Everywhere Will looks is another surface covered in toile. Caroline takes his hand and squeezes, tugging him toward the bar in the living room like she can sense him getting ready to bolt. "Let's get drunk."

Charlie gets swallowed up into the crowd more or less immediately, photographers swarming, and Will drains two consecutive gin and tonics while Caroline and Lucy provide him with a quiet dossier on the various residents of Pemberly Grove: a gaggle of teenagers who got famous for making off-color videos on a social media platform he doesn't understand and now all live together like *Lord of the Flies*, a set of extremely telegenic twin brothers who have a show on the home and garden network about building extravagant treehouses in Alberta. "Somewhere on the internet is a website devoted exclusively to dirty fan fiction about them performing depraved sex acts on each other," Caroline informs him.

"I mean," Will admits, gazing at them across the room, their identical Canadian heads tipped close together in murmured conversation, "I kind of get it."

Caroline grins, then waves at a willowy brunette in a stiff-looking black jumpsuit glumly nibbling a prawn. "Oh, good," she murmurs in Will's ear, "Anne Mulgrew is here. I think she's going to be Charlie's next girlfriend."

Will snorts. "Does Charlie know?"

"Not yet," Caroline admits. "But look at her. She's beautiful. She's a name, but not a bigger name than he is. And she's brilliant—she only does absolutely boring art house movies, I literally fell asleep three times trying to get through that thing about the lesbian war widow on the wheat farm—which I think will help neutralize our big dumb superhero problem."

Will frowns, unsure if the big dumb superhero in question is Major Fantastic or Charlie himself, but before he can ask he's distracted by the rumble of rowdy laughter from across the room. He turns and catches sight of a woman holding court on the arm of a damask settee, her elegant hands flying as she talks. He knows better than to ask Caroline who she is, but he can't help but watch her for a moment anyway, her slinky green dress and how sharp and canny her gaze is. Something about the way she's holding her body reminds him of the ballerinas from back at school, how they looked like they were dancing even when they were just walking around in the hallways between classes. Her hair is long and thick and dark.

Will looks away like she's caught him staring even though she hasn't, biting back a deep, reflexive scowl. He always instinctively hates people who know how to be the center of attention, how easily things seem to come to them both at parties and in life; still, it isn't a quality he particularly likes in himself, so he leaves Caroline talking to Lucy about a pair of former child stars who recently eloped to Las Vegas and gets himself another drink from the bar.

He weaves his way through the dense, teeming crowd, slightly dizzy with the heat and the noise and the cloying smell of perfume, trying to shake off the feeling that he wandered onto the wrong stage by accident and wishing he'd stayed home to work like he planned. He was lying when he told Charlie he didn't know his lines yet—of course he knows his lines, it's *Antony and* fucking *Cleopatra*—but he'd also be lying if he said he wasn't scared to death to screw it up and make a total fool of himself in a brand-new medium. He has no business being on this coast in the first place, let alone wandering around this ridiculous simulacrum of a manor house. He should have just stayed in New York.

Even if his career there is pretty much over.

As soon as Will lets himself think it he knows he needs to get out of here, the panic rising inside him like high tide rushing into a hole in the sand. He glances around for the closest exit, passing Charlie talking to a pretty blond who is definitely not Anne Mulgrew of lesbian wheat farmer fame and the social media kids doing what he's pretty sure is Molly before ducking out an unattended set of French doors at the rear of the house. When he steps onto the wide, capacious stone balcony, two things become immediately apparent: one, that this backyard is enormous, the acreage butting up against the rise of the hills in the distance, and two, that the bulk of it is filled with what appears to be a—a—

"You're not hallucinating," says a wry voice behind him. "It's a hedge maze."

Will turns around. The dark-haired woman from inside is leaning against the house with her ankles crossed, a strong-looking cocktail in one hand. "I . . . see that," he manages to reply. The thing is half the size of a football field, dense and green and impossibly labyrinthine. Just looking at it gives him the creeps.

"Rebecca had a couple of landscape architects come out from Yorkshire to install it for her after her second husband died," the woman explains, pushing herself off the exterior wall and coming to stand beside him. She smells like mandarins and basil, expensive and faint. "At least, that's the story she tells everybody? It's possible the guy is actually still just wandering around in there, drinking rainwater and eating small birds." She smiles; she has a good smile, warm and intimate and slightly mischievous. Her teeth are television-star straight. "Anyway, if you're trying to Irish goodbye, you're better off going through the kitchen."

Will frowns, weirdly offended. "I wasn't trying to Irish goodbye," he lies.

"Weren't you?" the woman asks, tilting her head to the side. "Because the way you darted out here like your underwear was full of beetles and you didn't want anyone to notice kind of suggests otherwise."

Will huffs a breath, feeling his face flame. There are two, *maybe* three people in this world by whom he can bear to be teased, and this random, garrulous stranger is emphatically not one of them, no matter how long-limbed and arresting. "I wasn't," he insists. "But also, excuse me for not wanting to spend a perfectly good Saturday night wandering around the set of a PBS miniseries about a scullery maid trying to get an abortion."

That makes her laugh, a surprised, full-throated cackle. Before he knows it, Will is laughing, too. "I'm sorry," he says belatedly, scrubbing a hand over his face as something loosens up deep inside him. "Your city does this to me. It's like I got off the plane and immediately turned into George Costanza. My second day here, I literally got heat rash. I had to lie in a cool room with a cloth on my forehead like a Victorian consumptive while I waited for my body temperature to regulate."

"I fell asleep in a tanning bed once when I was a teenager," the woman confides. Her eyes are an intelligent, complicated hazel. "I'm actually lucky I didn't burn alive. It took me all summer to recover."

Will is horrified. "No one came to get you?"

"They all thought I was going for, like, an especially deep bronze." She wrinkles her nose. "I used to go tanning kind of a lot."

"It's not good for your skin," he advises. "It can cause cancer."

The brunette looks at him curiously. "Shit, can it?" she asks. "I never knew." She grins at him again, like they're in on something together. "How do you know Rebecca?"

"Oh, I don't," Will says immediately. It feels important to clarify. "I'm staying with a friend in the neighborhood, and she invited him. He just moved here, so—"

"Oh!" The woman cuts him off, pointing with one accusing finger. "You're Charlie Bingley's hot boyfriend."

Will blinks. "I'm *what*?"

"Forget it." She waves him off, then offers her hand. "Lilly Benedetto."

There's something familiar about it, though it could just be that everyone he's met out here has a fake-sounding name, like they all were invented by Aaron Sorkin for a network pilot about young, earnest civil rights lawyers. "Will Darcy," he says as they shake.

Lilly nods. "So, Will Darcy," she says, taking a sip of her cocktail, "what are you doing in LA?"

"That . . . is a great question," he admits, tilting his head back against a faux-Doric pillar. Suddenly his name sounds fake, too. "Making an ass of myself, probably."

"Oh, we can't get enough of that here."

"You know, I am getting that impression." He smiles. "What about you, what do you do?"

Lilly's eyes narrow just for a moment, and right away Will feels like a twerp. Charlie and Caroline are always giving him shit about how he has zero pop culture competence; he once sat next to Jay-Z on the 2 train in New York and had no idea why everyone was pointing their phones in his direction until some little kid in a school uniform clued him in at Grand Army Plaza. Lilly probably won an Academy Award for Best Actress last year while he was sitting in his apartment like an ascetic, reading *No Exit* for the sixteenth time. Still, Will thinks, this is exactly why he hates Los Angeles. Everyone who lives here always thinks they're the most important person in the room, and screw you if you don't fall all over yourself with fear and trembling. "Sorry," he amends grudgingly. "Should I know—?"

"No, no." Lilly's expression clears then; she holds her hand up in sheepish surrender. "I just—sorry. I'm a writer."

"What do you write?"

"None of your business."

"How's it going?"

"Not great."

"Writer's block?" he guesses, taking a step. Every instinct he's got is telling him to go home to the safe, anonymous quiet of Charlie's janky rental house and hole up with his script like he planned when he ducked out here in the first place, but for some reason that eludes all understanding, he can't seem to make himself say good night. There's something about this woman that makes him want to stay a little longer. There's something about her that makes him want to break his own rules. "Creative ennui? Paralyzing fear of being unadulterated shit at the thing you want to do most in the entire world?"

That makes her smile. "Exactly."

Will nods. Fear, he's familiar with. Fear, he understands. Fear, if he's being honest with himself, is what landed him on a seventy-two-hour emergency psych hold at Lenox Hill, his throat red and raw from the charcoal, though that doesn't feel like the exact right anecdote to share at this particular moment. "Well," he says finally. "Screw your courage to the sticking place, et cetera."

"That's very wise," Lilly says seriously. "Is it the lyric of a Sara Bareilles song?"

"Back of a Chipotle bag."

Lilly smiles at that, the hint of a dimple appearing at one corner of her full red lips. "What about you, huh?" she asks. "What do you do?"

"I'm an actor," he tells her. "Theoretically."

"Huh," she says, like that's not what she was expecting. They've drifted closer now, the warmth of her thigh bleeding straight through his dress pants. "Say more about that."

"You know," he says, "I don't think I will."

Both of them are quiet for a moment. Will keeps on looking at her mouth. When he leans it's without ever quite deciding he's going to do it: their noses brushing, their foreheads millimeters apart. He's already closing his eyes when suddenly Lilly puts a hand on his arm. "Wait."

Will backs off almost before she gets the word out, pulling away so fast and hard he nearly winds up smashed like a watermelon at the bottom of the staircase. "Sorry," he says immediately, feeling his entire body prickle with horror. What the fuck was he thinking? This is how people wind up getting investigated by Ronan Farrow. "I shouldn't have—"

"No, no, no," Lilly interrupts. "You're fine, I just mean—" She glances over her shoulder. "Not, like, here." She takes him by the hand before he can put a reply together, then pulls him down the wide granite steps and into the hedge maze, turning left and right and left again until Will is fairly certain he'll never be able to make it back out on his own. Her smile, when at last she stops and turns to face him, is like a slice of moonlight in the dark.

"Okay," she says decisively. "That's better."

Will lifts an eyebrow. "Better for what, exactly?"

"Oh please," Lilly shoots back, all confidence. "Don't act for one second like you weren't about to—"

Will kisses her.

She kisses him back, thank god, her hands fluttering for a moment before fisting in his jacket, yanking him closer. Will breathes a quiet sound against her mouth. His palms skate up her rib cage, learning the dramatic S curve of her body; his thumb traces the underside of her breast through the fabric, and Lilly gasps.

It goes on like that for a while—his hips slotted against hers, rocking gently, her fingertips sneaking up underneath his shirt.

Will's blood thuds wildly in his ears. Exactly nobody would accuse him of being the kind of person who has ever been caught up in a moment, but still there's something about this woman—her mouth, her smell, her heartbeat—that has him forgetting all about the party still clanging on the other side of the hedgerows. That has him forgetting about everything he's lost. He's reaching up underneath her skirt, fingertips just brushing the smooth, hot skin of her thigh, when someone rounds the leafy corner beside them and stops so short they nearly trip.

"Whoops!" the guy says. In the moment before he turns around and scurries back off the way he came Will vaguely recognizes him as the host of a morning game show Charlie used to watch sometimes when he was hungover. "Sorry!"

"Um," Will calls after him, his voice sounding strangled, "just a second!"

Lilly starts laughing again then, her whole body shaking with silent giggles as her forehead drops down against his shoulder. "What?" Will asks, feeling himself flush.

"'Just a second'?" she mimics, looking up at him fondly. "It's not a bathroom."

Will laughs, too, he can't help it—one hand cupping the back of her neck, feeling her pulse tick underneath his fingertips. Her cheeks are warm and pink. "Oh, I'm sorry," he replies, trying to maintain a single shred of dignity. "What should I have said, exactly?"

"I don't know," Lilly says, still smiling. "Not that."

"No," he agrees softly. "Not that."

They look at each other, breathing. Will drops his hands to his sides. He wants to kiss her again, but he feels like maybe the moment is over. "Should we stagger our exits?" he asks finally, and he can't tell if the look that flickers across her face is disappointment or not.

"Oh, for sure," she tells him seriously, plucking a twig from his hair and twirling the stem between two delicate fingers. "That'll fool them." She grins. "Nice to meet you, Will Darcy," she tells him, then yanks his belt loop once, hard, before turning and disappearing into the darkness.

Will watches her go for a minute, dazed and dazzled, half expecting her to have left a glass slipper in her wake. He meant to get her phone number. He meant to ask her if she wanted to elope. It feels like he's been underwater for the last three months and only just finally surfaced, stunned and gasping, the sun bone-bleachingly bright on his skin.

He does in fact get lost in the fucking hedge maze, a combination of lust and alcohol and a general inability to navigate any cartographic system that isn't a grid. When he finally bursts back out into the garden he nearly crashes right into Caroline, who's standing on the grass with a glass of white wine in her hand, mouth slightly agape. "Were you just in there with Lilly Benedetto?" she accuses, pointing at him with one manicured finger.

"I—no. Yes?" Will confesses before he can think better of it. His head is still swimming pleasantly, which is why it takes him a beat to register the dark, vaguely dangerous hilarity in her voice. "Why, who's Lilly Benedetto?"

Caro laughs. "See, this is why I love you, William. You're like a weird homeschooled child who reads the book of Revelation for fun and thinks the devil lives in his boom box." Caroline grins. "The Benedettos are a bunch of reality show trash bags who got famous for being famous and now spend their one wild and precious life getting in drunken catfights at the openings of not-quite-exclusive nightclubs and shilling collagen powder on TikTok."

Will feels the horror blooming like black mold inside him. "I—what?" he asks. "No."

"Did I just hear something about Will fooling around with Lilly Benedetto in the hedge maze?" Lucy asks delightedly, hurrying up to them with a glass of champagne in one hand and Charlie at her heels.

"He didn't know who she was," Caro says, in his defense. "But now he's going to go dunk his penis in bleach as a precautionary measure."

"We didn't—I mean—" Will sputters. "My penis is fine."

"That's a relief," Lucy says. "Is Lilly the one who was married to the anti-vax football player for a week and then got an annulment? Or the one who had the skincare line and then all the products turned out to be made of ground-up animal bones from Mexico?"

"You guys are mean," Charlie protests. "I just talked to June for like half an hour, and she's a total sweetheart."

"Oh, *everyone* is meeting the Benedettos this fine evening, I see." Caroline shakes her head. "June's the one who threw the unironic Gatsby party where everyone got listeria and had to be hospitalized," she reminds Lucy. "Lilly is the one who had the tacky boyfriend, the Pepperoni Pirate or whatever from the dad's pizza place? The one who died from, like, doing whippets or eating Tide Pods?"

"Oh my god, I had forgotten all about that," Lucy says, shaking her head. "Better watch yourself around common household chemicals, Will."

Will bites back a grimace, but barely; if there's one thing he truly hates, it's drawing unnecessary attention to himself. *In that case, you picked a weird line of work*, Charlie always says, and Will never quite knows how to explain that for him acting is the opposite thing entirely, that the main appeal of the entire endeavor is disappearing into someone else—the knowledge that, if he does his job right, people will forget he exists altogether. The worst part of being in the hospital—besides all the other worst parts about being in the hospital—was the feeling of everyone looking at him all the time.

"Didn't she give them to him or something?" Lucy is asking now, pulling her phone out of her purse to confirm. Charlie has already been absorbed back into the party, charming a pair of washed-up sitcom stars across the patio. Will wishes he could evaporate into thin air. "The Tide Pods? I'm trying to remember the story."

"Did you guys have a chance to cover that during your time together in the hedge maze, Will?" Caroline asks teasingly. "Or were you otherwise engaged?"

Will scowls. "Can you lay off, please?" he asks, knowing he sounds peevish. His entire body feels like it's on fire, his skin burning with shame and regret. "I can promise you I wouldn't have gotten anywhere near her if I had known she was a reality show trash bag who killed her boyfriend with Tide Pods."

"It was heroin, actually," says a pleasant voice behind him. "And he got it all on his own."

Will feels the heat drain abruptly out of his body, his blood turning to seawater in his veins. When he turns around there's Lilly with her shoulders back and feet planted on the bluestone, her expression haughty and regal and—oh, fuck him—possibly just the tiniest bit hurt. Her lips are swollen from kissing. Will can feel that his are, too.

"That's not—" he begins, then completely fails to follow it up in any meaningful way. If he was ashamed of himself a minute ago it's nothing compared to the way he feels now: the nearly irresistible urge to find the nearest luxury vehicle and lie down directly in front of it. "I didn't—" He breaks off again. Lucy is staring down at the patio. Caroline clears her throat.

Lilly fixes them with a reality show smile that's nothing short of luminous, warm and winning and profoundly insincere. "Welcome to Pemberly Grove, neighbors," she tells them, then lifts her middle finger in their direction and stalks back into the house.

CHAPTER THREE

LILLY

"You didn't," Lilly's mom says later that night, her dark eyes wide over the bowl of her oversized wineglass. They're gathered around the kitchen island, a giant plastic clamshell of the Meatball King's signature garlic knots open on the granite. Kit and Olivia are perched on the counter. June leans against the fridge. Marianne lurks in the doorway, nibbling a piece of her hair while she peers down at the glowing screen of her phone. "What did he say to that?"

"I mean, nothing," Lilly admits, flexing her aching toes against the tile. Even as she's telling the story she knows she's making it all sound funnier than it actually was, turning the whole thing into a madcap comedy bit for everyone's entertainment. She likes to think she's developed a thick skin—you basically can't live your life as one of the five socialite daughters of the Meatball King of Southern California without at some point accepting the fact that people are going to say what they're going to say—but the truth is she was into him for a minute there, Will Darcy, with his smirk and his stubble and his rough, capable mouth. She hadn't kissed anyone since Joe. "It's not like I stuck around and put on my best Transatlantic accent so we could do a little Hepburn/Tracy back-and-forth."

"Well, that's a shame," June observes, reaching delicately for a garlic knot. "I for one love your Transatlantic accent."

"Thank you, darling." Lilly blows an imaginary ring of cigarette smoke in June's direction—trying not to notice the way her sister pulls the dough apart rather than actually eating it, or the way her wristbones have once again begun to jut. "You know I've always thought you're just divine."

"Can you focus, please, girls?" her mother asks irritably. She's wearing a flowered robe that Lilly knows she bought because she thought it made her look like Sophia Loren in *Yesterday, Today and Tomorrow*, though the total effect is closer to John Travolta in *Hairspray*. "Who even is this person? Will Darcy? *I've* certainly never heard of him."

"Well, in that case," Kit tells her, "I'm sure he doesn't even exist."

"He's the lead in that new Johnny Jones movie that's about to start filming, isn't he?" Olivia asks. For a person with virtually no interest in the art of filmmaking, Olivia has an encyclopedic knowledge of the industry, mostly on account of being on a first-name basis with every publicist and paparazzo in LA. "The weird fucking Shakespeare thing? He's a stage actor, I think, but apparently Johnny wanted him so bad that he flew to New York and, like, made him an offer he couldn't refuse."

"Sex stuff?" Kit asks hopefully. June snorts. Lilly raises an eyebrow, trying to affect disinterest; Johnny Jones is an auteur if ever there was one, an Oscar-winning eccentric known as much for his art house sensibilities and erratic behavior as his blockbuster budgets. By all accounts actors are falling all over themselves to work with him, not the other way around. Still, she refuses to be impressed.

"His father was Fitz Darcy," Marianne announces, and Lilly glances over at her in surprise. She didn't even think Marianne was listening, though she knows from experience that that assumption is made at one's own peril.

"Oh!" Cinta says in a decidedly friendlier tone of voice, just as Kit asks, "Who's Fitz Darcy?"

"Who's Fitz Darcy?" Cinta echoes, horrified. "Sometimes I swear it's like I've taught you girls nothing."

"You taught us how to wax our own bikini lines in case we ever get stranded on a desert island," Olivia reminds her. "That was very helpful."

"He was in a bunch of movies back in the late eighties and early nineties," Marianne reports, holding up her phone to display a Wikipedia entry. "Everyone said he was on track to be the greatest actor of his generation, but then he and his wife died in a car crash trying to escape the paparazzi after an Oscar party at the Beverly Hills Hotel."

Lilly blinks. "When was that?" she hears herself ask.

"Ninety-seven, it looks like?" Marianne frowns down at the screen. "They had two kids, Will and his sister." She's quiet for a moment, then keeps reading. "'There was speculation at the time that Darcy, who'd struggled with his mental health following a string of box-office flops, may have purposely caused the accident by driving into oncoming traffic.'"

"Oh." Lilly busies herself with a garlic knot, ignoring the sudden drop in her chest. *Losing your parents young doesn't make you a good person*, she reminds herself. *It just makes you unlucky.* And in Will's case, apparently, an enormous douche. "Well. That explains his East Coast hate boner for the entire state of California, I guess."

"From what I heard, that's not all he had an East Coast hate boner for," Olivia murmurs.

"What's a hate boner?" their mother wants to know.

"I don't want to talk about Will Darcy anymore," Lilly declares instead of answering, stuffing the garlic knot into her mouth and swallowing it in one pungent, slightly stale bite. "He sucks. I want to talk about Junie and Charlie Bingley." She turns to her mom, smiling wolfishly. "Not gay! Took her number."

Cinta is immediately and thoroughly distracted, just like Lilly knew she would be, and they debrief the rest of the party in relative peace before Kit and Olivia head out to meet some friends at a club in West Hollywood and Marianne wanders upstairs. Lilly follows not long after that—flinging open the window above her desk so that the warm breeze ruffles the curtains, the smell of bougainvillea and star jasmine drifting through the air. She watches idly through the open bathroom door as June does her going-to-bed routine: her dutiful flossing, the fourteen-step antiwrinkle regimen Lilly is always a little bit too tired to remember to do herself.

She tucks her feet under the covers and plucks her phone off the nightstand, typing Will Darcy's name into the search bar of her browser before she can talk herself out of it. She hits go and suddenly there he is: all dark, close-cropped hair and the faintest scruff of beard along his jawbone, the plush, sulky line of his frown. For fuck's sake, that frown! In every single picture! It's like someone has always and perpetually just shat in his sneakers. She wants to call him up and tell him to be careful or it will freeze that way, like their aunt Veronica used to say to her when Lilly was young and in a snit about the last of her Bomb Pop falling into the sand at Zuma Beach.

She clicks through the search results, allowing herself a quick, guilty romp through the last ten years of Will Darcy's career. He landed the role of Mercutio in Shakespeare in the Park when he was still at Juilliard, she reads with grudging interest; he won his first Drama Desk Award for a turn in *Long Day's Journey into Night* when he was twenty-five. "Ten Reasons Why Will Darcy Is the Thinking Girl's Newest Obsession," offers a New York gossip blog. Further down on the page are photos of him with the cast of *Uncle Vanya*, which premiered at the Public two years ago, alongside a shot of him ducking out of a Brooklyn bookstore in glasses and a leather jacket. There's also one of him eating lunch on an Upper West Side patio with a curly-haired brunette (unidentified, according to the caption), his face broken open into a smile so relaxed and surprising that Lilly gasps.

It's—well. It's a good smile.

He landed the title role in a star-studded production of *Hamlet* at the Hayes last spring, she reads on, though it doesn't seem to have run for very long. Lilly is just about to click on the *New York Times* review—it looks bad, which is promising—when Junie turns off the faucet and pads into the room, her hair freshly braided and her complexion as creamy and unblemished as an ingenue in an Icelandic yogurt commercial. "What are you doing?" she asks, nudging Lilly over and climbing into bed beside her.

"Nothing," Lilly says too quickly, closing out the app and feeling vaguely like she's gotten caught reading Treehouse Brothers erotica. "Just messing around."

June lifts an eyebrow, but she doesn't say anything as she makes herself comfortable, the two of them scrolling in silence for a long, quiet moment. Lilly has spent so much of her life in the same room as June that being with her is basically the same as just being with herself—the two of them breathing in tandem, the light from June's phone flickering out of the corner of Lilly's eye.

"So," Lilly says finally, rolling over and propping herself up on one elbow. "Charlie Bingley."

June snorts, scrunching herself down into the pillows. "You sound like Mom." Then, a little shyly: "He asked me to lunch tomorrow."

Lilly smirks. "I bet he did." She clocked the two of them at the party earlier tonight—June's expression gone pleased and rosy, Charlie's hand on the bare skin of her upper arm—and while June is notorious for being nice to literally everyone, no matter how boring or putrid, Lilly could tell as soon as she glanced in her sister's direction that her smile was sincere. June is a human sunbeam, warm and bright and steady; Lilly's not surprised that even Major Fantastic turned his face instinctively in the direction of her light.

"I mean, who knows if it's anything," June qualifies. "But he's cute, right?"

"He's very cute," Lilly agrees, her bare feet brushing June's under the covers. "It almost makes up for the fact that his friends are all horrifying garbage monsters."

June hums noncommittally. "About that," she begins, wrinkling her nose a little. "I mean, obviously you were there and I wasn't, but are you sure they were saying what you think they were saying? Because I talked to Caroline and Anne Mulgrew for a little while in the library, and they didn't seem so bad."

Lilly sits up so fast she gets light-headed. "Seriously?" she asks. All at once she can feel the garlic knot sitting barely chewed behind her breastbone, doughy and thick. "What do you think, I made it up?"

"Of course not," June says quickly, holding both palms out. "I'm just saying, with great love and affection: occasionally you have been known to look for a fight where there isn't one."

Lilly bites back a scowl, but barely. This makes her nuts about June, her preternatural willingness to give the benefit of the doubt to people who clearly do not deserve it. If there's one thing Lilly has learned from being not-quite-the-right-kind-of-famous, it's that it's better to judge first and ask questions later. "Often," she counters crisply, "*I'm* just saying, with great love and affection: there is in fact a fight."

"Well," June replies calmly, patting the pillow beside her, "not here, there's not."

Lilly holds her frown for a moment longer before feeling the annoyance drain right out of her. It is, and always has been, impossible to be mad at June for more than a second or two at a time. "I wonder if he'll let you hold his magic spear," she teases quietly, then lies back down in bed and rests her head on her sister's shoulder until she falls asleep.

CHAPTER FOUR

JUNE

⁓

"You're sure this is okay?" Charlie asks the following afternoon, his handsome face creasing worriedly in the brutal midday sunlight. "Because we really can—"

"No, no, no, this is great," June promises, reaching out as casually as she can to pluck a fat black water bug from the plastic tub of organic fruit salad. When he asked her to lunch she was thinking maybe Nobu or Little Dom's but instead he showed up at the house with an enormous bag from Erewhon and asked her how she might feel about a picnic. Thirty minutes later—once her sisters had gotten their gander at him, the quartet of them draped dramatically over the upstairs railing like old women on a fire escape back in Sicily—and they're sitting on the marshy bank of the man-made pond at the center of the development, an unsubtle whiff of sulfur wafting through the air. June wipes a bead of sweat from her upper lip as surreptitiously as possible, telling herself it has nothing to do with him not wanting to be seen with her in public. "It's perfect."

"Are you sure?" Charlie looks deeply unconvinced. "I had it in my head that this would be, like, romantic and unusual, but I also kind of didn't anticipate the . . ." He waves his hand, presumably to indicate either the heat or the smell, which seems somehow both fishier and more pungent than it did even a moment ago. "Whatever. We're good. We're good!"

"We're good," June assures him, trying and failing not to be charmed. He was like this at Rebecca's party, too—bashful and a little bit dorky, like he was surprised she'd be talking to him at all. She keeps waiting for the gotcha, the moment when he reveals that he has half a dozen cardboard cutouts of himself propped in various locations around his home or that he thinks showering is overrated and so just does his pits with a Clorox wipe every couple of days, but actually he's just sort of fun and cool and nice to be with—an easy and generous smiler, a good asker of questions. He talks a lot about how hard it is to find good deep dish in Los Angeles. He talks a lot about his dog.

"Four sisters, huh?" he asks now, handing her a tomato and mozzarella sandwich, balsamic vinegar soaking into the crusty baguette. June smiles—he must have googled her; she's been a vegetarian since she was twelve—then sets it down on the blanket, hoping he doesn't notice she doesn't actually take a bite. It's nothing to worry about this time, her diet. Like three more pounds and she's going to stop. "What's that like?"

"It's incredible," she says, which is mostly true. "And, you know, an occasional feral catfight. We contain multitudes."

"You're the oldest, right? Does that make you the boss?"

June shakes her head. "Lilly's the boss. Of all of us, including my parents. And maybe your parents as well, actually."

Charlie laughs. "I will be sure to let them know."

"It's possible she already sent them a certified letter."

"Sounds about right." He holds the bag of chips out in her direction; June shakes her head automatically, and he reaches in for a handful of his own. "I get it, though," he says, taking a bite of his sandwich—roast beef and Vermont cheddar, she notes, probably twelve hundred calories all-in. "The sister-in-charge thing. I mean, look at me and Caroline. It can be nice to let someone else handle the details, right? Especially if they're going to do it anyway." He sets the sandwich down then, brushing his palms off on his jeans. "Okay," he says, broad shoulders dropping, "real talk: that smell is, like, really bad, isn't it."

June wrinkles her nose. "I mean," she admits, "it isn't great? Also, I don't want to alarm you, but I'm pretty sure I just saw a rat the size of a cocker spaniel take a swan dive off the fountain."

"Do you want to get out of here?" he asks, getting to his feet and holding a hand out. Gazing up at his broad body silhouetted against the brilliant blue sky, all at once June understands why they cast him as Major Fantastic: He looks like someone who could leap tall buildings. He looks like someone who could snatch bullets clean out of the air. "Go to an actual restaurant? Somewhere indoors, even. Real big swing."

"Real big swing," June echoes with a grin, tucking her uneaten lunch back into its waxed paper wrapper. Lacing her fingers through his.

CHAPTER FIVE

LILLY

Charlotte hosts a supper club at her restaurant featuring a different up-and-coming female or nonbinary chef every month, so Lilly borrows June's car and stops by with lattes to help her arrange the flowers. They've been best friends since the Benedettos moved into the development when Lilly was a junior in high school; all of them used to carpool, Charlotte climbing cheerfully into the back seat of Junie's gleaming white Escalade five mornings a week. It was Charlotte who taught them how Saint Ann's worked, at the beginning, where the good bathroom was and which teachers were hard-asses or perverts and that the truly and effortlessly popular girls didn't wear their uniform skirts hiked quite so high. She was kind to them back when she had absolutely nothing to gain from it, and even at sixteen and spoiled, Lilly knew enough to grab tight and hang on.

"How did it go last night?" she asks now, perching on a stool at the scarred marble bar while Charlotte frowns intently at a half-finished arrangement of lupine and wild herbs. The restaurant is called Lodge, and Charlotte is deeply and lovingly fanatical about every detail, from the provenance of the salad greens to the hand soap in the bathroom, which is probably why even three years after opening celebrities are still ripping each other's throats out with claws and teeth vying for a table. "Didn't you say you had a date?"

"I may have said something like that, yes." Charlotte makes a face. She's wearing her uniform of dark denim apron over fitted black button-down, her riot of red hair pulled back with a stretchy cotton headband. "He was wearing a shirt with a dinosaur on it."

Lilly almost snorts her coffee. "I'm sorry, come again?"

"You heard me." Charlotte wiggles her fingers for more rosemary.

"I did," Lilly admits, pulling a fragrant handful from the bucket on the bar and passing it over. "I'm just wondering if he was also carrying a lunch box, or the place you guys went to was, like, the latest food and beverage offering from celebrity chef Charles Entertainment Cheese—"

"It wasn't *Barney* the Dinosaur," Charlotte protests. "It was, like, a cool dinosaur."

Lilly nods seriously. "So, like, a velociraptor."

Charlotte rolls her eyes. "Like, a Keith Haring dinosaur!"

"Would you call that a cool dinosaur, though?"

"Can you stop?" Charlotte laughs, tossing a purple flower in Lilly's direction. "I'm trying to talk myself into him, clearly."

"I can see that," Lilly agrees, tucking the bloom into her hair for safekeeping. "Did he have, like, an amazing personality or washboard abs or a gajillion dollars to invest in exciting new culinary ventures?"

"He—" Charlotte sighs, sitting down hard in one of the vintage bentwood chairs. "No, not really."

"So then what's the point?"

"You know what the point is!"

"I mean, sure," Lilly says, although the truth is she doesn't, not entirely. Charlotte has been preternaturally boy crazy since they were teenagers; she's on about a dozen apps, her phone buzzing with potential matches like a coin-operated bed at all hours of the day and night. Frankly Lilly would rather spend the rest of her life rattling around Pemberly Grove, listening to her mother perseverate on her skin tags, than subject herself to an endless parade of men who come recommended mainly by the fact that their opening salvo was anything other than a picture of their own crooked genitalia.

Charlotte sighs loudly, standing up and plucking the flowers from their vases before starting again. "I saw Junie and Charlie Bingley on the Sinclair," she announces.

Lilly lifts an eyebrow at the sudden change of subject. "Since when do you read the Sinclair?"

"I don't," Charlotte says immediately. "I mean, I do, clearly, I started looking at it when all that stuff was happening with Jamie Hartley going to jail and now I can't stop, but. I don't." She turns back to the flowers. "And speaking of romantic encounters that people in your family had at Rebecca Barnes's house that I had to read about on a morally gray gossip website: let's talk about Will Darcy."

"I hate Will Darcy," Lilly says immediately.

"Well, my darling," Charlotte tells her, "in that case, you're really going to hate that I invited him and Charlie Bingley to dinner tonight."

"Are you kidding me?" Lilly snaps to attention. "When did you even *meet* him and Charlie Bingley?"

"My parents are at a silent retreat in San Luis Obispo and their dog walker has bursitis," Charlotte explains with the exaggerated casualness of a person who has purposely buried the lede. "I came over to take him for a stroll, Will and Charlie were out for a run, et cetera." She grins. "You know how Arthur is with handsome men."

"I do," Lilly says grimly. Arthur is the Lucases' cranky old schnauzer, who's deaf in both ears and always smells like tempura batter. Most days Charlotte's mother can barely drag him out the door for a shuffle around the neighborhood, but last summer he slipped his collar and took off at a dead sprint upon spotting Channing Tatum at the Hollywood Bowl.

"Anyway," Charlotte continues, "I told you Charlie used to come in for brunch sometimes, back when he was still getting cast as like, Shirtless Bro in the direct-to-streaming production of *Cock and Balls 2*."

"So weird how they haven't added that one to the Criterion Collection."

"Well, it just wasn't as good as the original *Cock and Balls*," Charlotte deadpans. "Sequels never are. Anyway, he recognized me from here, so he stopped to say hi. It felt rude not to invite him."

"Oh, right," Lilly says, looking at her pointedly. "You were just minding your manners."

Charlotte ignores her. "Your pal Will runs shirtless, PS," she announces, fussing daintily with a handful of flowering thyme. "He's got that kind of happy trail, you know, when the hair goes from his belly button right down into his—"

"I know what a happy trail is, Charlotte, Jesus." She knows about Will's, too, remembers the feeling of her knuckles rasping against it in the hedge maze at Rebecca Barnes's ridiculous faux Edwardian estate. Remembers the hard press of his body, the surprising wiriness of him. The heat of his hands through her dress.

Also, she remembers the way the ground momentarily tilted underneath her when she overheard him talking about her to his snotty, elitist friends.

"I'm just saying," Charlotte tells her now, "if you wanted to wear something extra cute tonight, this is your advance notice."

"It's Halloween," Lilly reminds her. "I'm going to come in costume."

"Sexy nurse?"

"Sexy Chester Cheetah."

Charlotte nods approvingly. "Now that," she says, turning the finished arrangement for Lilly's inspection, "would kill on Tinder."

* * *

Lilly leaves Charlotte to her prep work and heads back to Pemberly Grove, rolling down the windows of June's Audi so it's too loud to think. She feels pissed off and set up, though it's not like she doesn't understand why Charlotte did what she did: as far as free publicity for the restaurant goes, Charlie Bingley at Monday Night Supper Club pretty much guarantees they'll be booked solid right through next spring.

She could just skip the whole thing, Lilly guesses, though the thought of it fills her with an immediate, visceral contrariness. She's been going to Charlotte's pop-ups since before Lodge even opened; she's certainly not about to get chased out of the dining room by some so-called serious actor who probably only owns one pair of shoes. Let him feel awkward about it, if he even has human emotions under that brittle veneer of smug superiority. She didn't do anything wrong.

Back at the house she opens her closet and stares frowning at its contents for a moment: the rows of jeans and heels and athlei-sure, the going-out clothes she hardly ever wears since Joe. Finally she sighs, then turns and pads barefoot down the long hallway to the guest room—or at least, it used to be the guest room. Now it's stuffed close and claustrophobic with unopened cardboard boxes, half a dozen rolling racks, and enough felt hats for some haunted creature with ten thousand heads. In the center of it all Kit sits pretzel-legged on the carpet in her underwear, daintily embroi-dering what appears to be a curse word onto a vintage silk hand-kerchief. She's the craftiest and most fashion-minded out of all of them, cares about things like color theory and diffusion lines and not just how her ass is going to look in a pair of pants; back when she and Olivia had their clothing line, Kit did most of the design work herself.

"Will Darcy is going to be at Supper Club tonight," Lilly an-nounces, crossing her arms and leaning against the doorjamb.

Kit looks up and raises one thick eyebrow, then sets the hanky down on the carpet and grins. "Step into my office," she replies.

CHAPTER SIX

WILL

Charlotte Lucas's restaurant is tucked away on a quiet, leafy side street in Silver Lake, the sky streaked pink and indigo through the dense, heavy branches of the mimosa trees overhead. Will is expecting some kind of echoing, gentrified macaroni factory but in fact Lodge is small and intimate and familiar in a good way, the walls painted a warm cream and votives flickering in tidy lines on the wide wooden tables. Out back is a courtyard, wisteria vining along the brick walls and tiny white lights strung up overhead. It reminds him of the kind of place you'd find hidden down at the end of a pee-smelling alley in the West Village back home, and for a moment he misses New York so much and so viscerally the inside of his head starts to roar.

Lilly and her sisters are already clustered around the bar when he and Charlie arrive, the five of them wielding champagne coupes like cudgels in their delicate, manicured hands. Will stops short at the sight of them, somehow startled even though Charlie explicitly told him they'd be here. Every time he thinks about the other night at Rebecca Barnes's party—Lilly's hair and her jaw and the sound of her laughter, the look on her face before she turned away—it's like trying to hold his brain against a hot stove.

Charlie heads directly for June, the two of them peeling off from the group and disappearing in the direction of the patio. Will orders a drink from a passing waiter and leans back against a wall near the door. He glances at Lilly—watching in spite of himself as she runs a distracted finger around the rim of her glass, tilting her dark head close to Olivia's—then glances away.

Glances back.

She catches him once, rolling her eyes a little before turning back to her sisters. When it happens a second time, she marches over like a nun in a Catholic school about to pinch his ear for masturbating under his desk.

"Look," she announces, grabbing his arm and hustling him around a corner into the short hallway that leads to the bathroom, "enough. You can either apologize to me or you can fuck off, but stop brooding in my general direction like you're Heathcliff on the fucking moors, will you? It's weird."

Will opens his mouth, then closes it again, heat flooding his face. "I'm not *brooding*," he protests finally.

"Oh no?" she asks, crossing her arms. She's wearing a slinky black dress that hits midway down her calves and a pair of sandals with a million fiddly straps, her hair in a long, loose ponytail over one shoulder. "What would you call it, exactly?"

"Standing," he says uselessly. "Minding my own business."

"Well." Lilly looks deeply dubious. "In that case, feel free to mind it elsewhere." She gestures toward the dining room, and when he makes no move in that direction, his feet dumbly rooted to the floor, she sighs. "Can I ask you a question?" she says, then doesn't wait for him to answer before she forges ahead. "Why are you even here?"

Will looks around at the warm bustle of the restaurant. "I . . . was invited?"

"Not *here*," she says impatiently. "Here. LA. Why come at all, if you hate it so much?"

For one preposterous second, Will almost tells her—about New York, about *Hamlet*, about Georgia finding him curled unconscious on the bath mat in his apartment, his skin gone waxy and blue—before, thankfully, coming to his senses. "To work with Johnny Jones," is all he says.

Lilly nods slowly, though he can tell she isn't buying it. "Right," she says. "Johnny Jones."

Will grits his teeth. "Look," he finally tells her, "about the other night at the party. I should apologize."

"Okay," she agrees. Then, when he doesn't say anything quickly enough: "Wait, was that it? Because you realize that saying you should apologize isn't actually—"

"Can you give me a minute?" he interrupts irritably. "Jesus." He scrubs a hand over his face. "I'm sorry," he tries. "I am. I handled that badly. I didn't know who you were—"

"Wait a second." She holds a hand up. "That's what you're sorry for? Not knowing I was—how did you so cleverly put it?—'a reality show trash bag who—'"

"That's not what I meant."

"Wasn't it?"

"No," he snaps. "Of course not. I didn't—what I'm trying to say is—there's nothing wrong with being famous for—for—"

"For what, exactly?"

"For being famous, I guess."

Lilly's eyes flash. "I knew it! See, that drives me up a tree when people say that, 'famous for being famous.' What does that even mean?"

Will feels his face get warm. "It means—"

"Because my father got famous for starting a chain of successful Italian restaurants that had a commercial that people found memorable," she interrupts, ticking the list off on her fingers. "My sisters Kit and Olivia are brand ambassadors, which is in fact an actual job, regardless of what you might think of it, and one that they're extremely talented and savvy at. June sits on the board of an animal welfare foundation that's raised millions of dollars for abused and neglected dogs and cats, not that anyone ever talks about that because she also likes to get dressed up and go to parties on the weekends. And Mari . . . well, fine, nobody really knows what Mari does, exactly, but that means that you don't, either, so. I would argue she should be exempt from whatever judgy bullshit you're putting on the rest of us."

Will sputters, cowed. "And you?" he can't help but ask, trying to recover. "What did you get famous for?"

Lilly fixes him with an expression of deep loathing. "You heard your friend Caroline," she says evenly. "I got famous for killing my boyfriend."

Right away, he feels about two inches tall. "Lilly—" he says, and he's about to apologize again—properly this time, he tells himself—when she cuts him off.

"Do not play with me about my sisters, Will. I will fight you, and I will win."

Will smirks at that, even though he knows it's only going to make her angrier. She just looks so *serious*, like she's fully intending to take him out to the parking lot and stab him in the carotid artery with a hairpin to defend the honor of a family whose principal contribution to arts and letters, so far as Will understands it, is a viral video of four-sevenths of them getting into a physical altercation with an Uber driver outside a Sweetgreen in Calabasas.

Her loyalty would almost be admirable, if he wasn't so annoyed. "You know, not for nothing," he tells her, "but you're awfully indignant about my failure to respect the many accomplishments of the Benedetto family for a person who purposely didn't mention she was one of them."

"I literally told you my first and last name, asshole!" Lilly looks incredulous; still, by the way her shoulders straighten Will can tell he's hit a nerve.

"And when you said you were a writer?" he presses. "I guess I didn't realize we were counting Instagram captions."

Lilly's eyes flash. "Fuck you," she says. "You don't know anything about me."

"Unlike the millions of social media followers who are privy to your every split end and cold sore."

"Wow." She barks a laugh. "You are really a miserable snob, do you know that?"

"I do, actually," he counters. "But at least I'm honest."

"Oh, is that what you'd call it?" Lilly fires back. "Because it sounds to me like you're too much of a tight-ass to admit you had a little itch for a Benedetto sister, so now you need to compensate by being a complete and utter dick. I'm working on a novel, not that it's any of your business. And my Instagram captions? They're works of fucking art."

Will opens his mouth, closes it again. Opens it one more time. He wants to keep fighting with her. He wants to back her up against the wall. She's not wrong, clearly—he does have an itch for her. He's got more than an itch for her, potentially, but he'll audition for the Whitney Houston role in a genderbent remake of *The Bodyguard* before he ever says that out loud.

They face off like that, neither one of them saying anything.

Both of them are breathing hard. Just for a second Will lets himself imagine doing it: wrapping a hand around her waist and pulling her even closer, pressing his mouth against hers. He can tell she's thinking about it, too—the way her lips have parted, her haughty chin just barely tilted up. He takes a deep breath, ducks his head—

—and catches nothing but the faint smell of citrus as she skirts neatly, nimbly away.

"Better luck next time, Birdman," Lilly tells him, then turns on her heel and slips back into the warm, crowded bustle of the dining room. Will stands and watches her go.

* * *

Back at Charlie's house there's a big, padded envelope waiting for Will on the doorstep, another package from his sister Georgia at home in New York. Ever since he came out here she's been sending him shit from Amazon what feels like every other day—sunscreen and undershirts and an expensive insulated tumbler for iced coffee even though caffeine gives him heart palpitations. He's not entirely sure what her deal is. Also, he's starting to run out of room.

Tonight it's an enormous box of PowerBars, like possibly she thinks he's going to climb K2 really quick before the movie starts shooting. Will dutifully puts them away in the kitchen cabinet, texting to thank her on his way up the stairs.

Georgia texts back immediately, just like always: *How was your dinner thing?* she wants to know.

Will frowns. *How did you know I was at a dinner thing?*

I saw you in the background in Charlie's insta stories. Then, a moment later: *You need a haircut.*

Upstairs in bed he tosses and turns for hours, throwing the

blankets off and pulling them on again. Telling himself he's not thinking about anyone in particular at all. Finally he gets out of bed, shivering at the blast of cold air piping in through the floor vent. Charlie's house, like everything else in California, is violently air-conditioned, and the chill of it always gives Will the uneasy feeling that his body is being forcibly preserved for some later purpose, like organ donation or a hungry giant's Christmas feast. He opens the window and sticks his head out, but all he smells is chlorine from the pool and the scent of some far-off burning.

Finally he picks up his phone, opens a new browser window. He's not supposed to do this—his therapist back in New York explicitly told him to stop doing this, actually, on top of which it's not like he doesn't have the whole thing memorized—but he types in the first few letters of the address for the *New York Times* review anyway, his phone autofilling the rest. "A Sea of Troubles for *Hamlet* at the Hayes," the headline reads, right below an enormous photograph of Will's pale, sweaty face.

He's halfway through the second paragraph when he's interrupted by a soft knock on his door; Caroline doesn't wait for him to answer before she eases it open and slips inside in leggings and a tank top, her hair combed out for bed. "I thought I heard you rattling around in here," she says, perching on the edge of the dresser and stretching her long legs out so her bright red toes just brush the edge of his mattress.

Will shakes his head, rubbing hard at the nape of his neck. "Couldn't sleep."

Caroline grins. "Poor baby," she singsongs softly, then slips like a cat off the dresser and stamps her mouth against his.

Will lets out a quiet *oof*, catching her weight and falling back against the pillows, his fingertips tangling in her silky blond hair. They haven't told Charlie about this. It's been on and off for almost a decade, since the summer Caroline's old agency sent her to New York to sign an up-and-coming director based in Brooklyn. Will was in *Coriolanus* in the park that year, grit and sweat and pollen creased into his elbows as they collapsed into her fancy hotel bed. It's friendly, their arrangement, both of them entirely free to see other people. There have been years when they met up every other weekend; there have been years they didn't meet up at all. "No strings attached," Caroline told him the morning after the first time they slept together, bending down to scoop her lacy underwear off the carpet, and he's never had any reason to think she didn't mean it. Still, it occurred to Will when he accepted Charlie's invitation to come stay here that possibly it was a bad idea for them to be living in the same place for an extended period of time.

Caroline, evidently, has no such reservations: in the half dark of his borrowed bedroom she slings a leg over his hip bones, planting a hand on either side of his head and leaning forward so that her hair makes a shampoo-scented curtain around his face. "Do you have a crush on Lilly Benedetto?" she asks.

Will freezes. "I—what?" he asks, his voice cracking a little. "Of course not."

"Because she's sexy, in a Victoria's Secret Fashion Show kind of way," she continues, sitting back so that her ass grinds against his dick. "I'm just saying, I would get it."

Will huffs out a laugh that sounds more like a wheeze. "Caro," he says, reaching for her hands and lacing their fingers together, his hips bucking up against hers, "there is nothing going on between Lilly Benedetto and me."

Caroline gazes down at him with great skepticism. "Prove it," she says imperiously, then reaches back behind her and pulls her tank top over her head.

* * *

Caroline slips out of his room sometime before dawn, Will stirring awake as the door snicks shut behind her. He lies there for a while, watching the light get gray out the window and trying to ignore the creeping feeling that he's doing something wrong or dishonest or sleazy. He meant it, what he said to Caroline: there's nothing going on between him and Lilly Benedetto. He barely even knows Lilly Benedetto.

He reaches for his phone on the nightstand one more time, scrolling news headlines long enough for plausible deniability before blowing a noisy breath out and typing the name of her show into the search bar. He has to subscribe to some obscure streaming service to get access to the episodes; the whole thing gives him the queasy feeling of paying for pornography—not that he's ever paid for pornography, for the record. Which isn't to say that he doesn't think sex workers deserve a living wage, or that he—oh, for fuck's sake. Will grits his teeth and hits play.

The show is . . . not good. The plots are farcical—one episode revolves entirely around two of Lilly's sisters going to war over an excruciatingly ugly dress both of them want to wear to a launch party for a vegan food product of their father's invention that is called, regrettably, WheatBallz—and the whole thing looks like it was shot on a flip phone and edited with scissors and tape. Still, he guesses it's not entirely without its charms—the way they talk and laugh and argue, the rise and fall of their voices like a chorus of sirens in a myth. He always thought it might be nice, to be part of a big family. All this time it's only been Georgia and him.

He watches all three seasons in one long feverish binge, morning turning to late afternoon outside the window. The theme song is so loud and jarring he's sure the whole house can hear it, and he frantically lowers the volume on his phone every time it jangles out into the room. The whole thing ends with no ceremony, a snoozer of an episode about a dopey, contrived family garage sale; at first Will thinks maybe there's something wrong with the website but a quick Google search confirms that that's all there is. *A spin-off of the show focusing on fan favorites Lilly Benedetto and her fiancé, Joseph Ianuzzi, was greenlit by the Tinseltown Network,* Wikipedia informs him, *though production was shut down following Ianuzzi's death by heroin overdose during the filming of the pilot. It is rumored that there is video footage of Benedetto discovering Ianuzzi's body in the couple's downtown Los Angeles apartment that was never released.* Will thinks of the look on Lilly's face the night of Rebecca Barnes's party—*It was heroin, actually*—and feels a little sick.

He throws back the covers and jumps out of bed, striding across the room and out the door to—do what, exactly? He stops short on the second-floor landing, dehydrated and dazed. "Television rots your brain," Charlie informs him cheerfully—jogging down the steps in his gym clothes, humming the *Meet the Benedettos* theme song under his breath.

CHAPTER SEVEN

LILLY

Lilly comes downstairs for breakfast on Saturday morning and finds June in the kitchen dressed head to toe in Lululemon, her golden hair in a sporty fishtail down her back. "Are you doing a partnership?" Lilly asks, peering at her curiously across the island. June, though tall enough that every gym teacher they ever had spent years trying fruitlessly to recruit her to play basketball, is hardly what one would call athletic. She once wound up in the ER with a sprained knee after tripping over a doll-sized windmill at a celebrity mini-golf tournament to benefit scleroderma research. Lilly hasn't seen her wear sneakers in years.

But June shakes her head. "Caroline Bingley invited me to work out with her trainer," she explains, yanking at one of the crisscrossed straps of her sports bra. "Be honest: do my boobs look like they belong to a JV volleyball player right now?"

"A little," Lilly admits. Then, trying to sound as casual as humanly possible: "Did you eat?"

June's gaze lingers on Lilly's just a moment too long. "I had a yogurt," she says at length, still rummaging around inside the bra. Lilly tries mightily to resist the urge to look in the trash for the empty cup: June has done inpatient treatment for anorexia on three separate occasions, and lately it's like Lilly can hear the sound of the fourth time coming closer and closer like the growl of a far-off engine in the desert. *Be careful*, she knows better than to say.

"She couldn't have invited you over to do something normal?" she asks instead, opening the fridge and pulling out a string cheese, biting off the end with a plasticky snap. It feels somehow suspicious, this olive branch from Caroline, though Lilly knows better than to say that out loud. "Like cocaine?"

June grins. "You should come," she says, reaching down and tightening the laces on her running shoes with the grim determination of a late bloomer suiting up for middle school dodgeball. "I'm sure she wouldn't mind one more."

"Can't," Lilly says immediately. "I'm getting my underarms depilated by Edward Scissorhands."

"Sounds invigorating."

"One can hope."

Once June's gone Lilly heads up to her bedroom in search of her laptop; she passes her father doing wall sits in the hallway, his calf muscles like a pair of genetically modified grapefruits bulging under the skin of his legs. "Elisabetta," he says, jaw twitching with exertion.

"Dad." Lilly can't help but smile. She's not sure when exactly she realized she was her father's favorite. She guesses she kind of always knew. Her earliest memories are of sitting on the counter at the original Meatball King with its revolving dessert case and red melamine bar, Dominic slipping her an extra garlic knot still hot from the oven when her mother wasn't looking. "Don't tell your sisters," he always said, and if occasionally in the years since then she's felt a little bit guilty about a certain lack of parental discretion on his part, she'd be lying if she said she didn't love him the most, too.

"Can I ask you something?" she says now, sitting down on the second step so they're more or less at eye level. "How much of what you said at dinner the other night about the house was real, and how much was you trying to put the fear of God in Kit and Olivia?"

Dominic grimaces, though she's not sure if he's reacting to the question or the exercise. "You realize I wouldn't need to put the fear of God in Kit and Olivia if they'd stop running their credit cards for thousands of dollars to celebrate the fact that it's Tuesday," he points out.

"Dad," she says again. "Come on."

Her father sighs. "I put the house up as collateral," he confesses, back still braced against the wall in his invisible chair. "Last year, right before the Six-Foot Stromboli debacle."

Lilly winces. "Oh, Dad."

"Six-Foot Stromboli was a good idea!" Her father bristles.

"Six-Foot Stromboli *was* a good idea," Lilly agrees, though if it had been up to her she's not sure she would have staked their family home on it. It's like this, with her father: the fact of his past success does suggest that at some point he knew what he was doing, even if lately it feels like he's operating his business in a world that no longer exists.

She waits for him to tell her he's handling it; she waits for him to tell her this isn't her problem to solve. She waits for him to tell her not to worry, but he doesn't, and after a moment she just squeezes him on the shoulder, feeling the muscle bunched belligerently underneath his skin.

Back upstairs she tries to work for a while, but Olivia and Kit are blaring EDM on the patio and her mother is down the hall in the primary bedroom consulting noisily with Joaquin Shannon regarding the feasibility of replacing her father's closet with a steam shower. Mari clomps inelegantly down the hallway in a pair of platform boots, a hiking backpack slung over her pale, narrow shoulders. "To sell my eggs," she replies when Lilly asks where she's going, which may or may not be the truth.

Still, it's no louder or more disruptive than any other day, and if Lilly is being honest with herself, none of it has anything to do with the real reason she can't concentrate. It's pointless, spending her days screwing around with the punctuation in a screenplay that's never going to go anywhere, that's never going to pay the bills or save the house or prove she's anything but a flighty, campy never-was. Nobody gives a shit about lady vampires. Not even Lilly herself.

She sighs and closes out the window, opening a new blank document. Staring at the empty page. She surprised herself at Charlotte's restaurant the other night, telling Will about the novel. She hasn't told anyone, not even June. Not that there's anything to tell, really—it's an idea, that's all, a few sentences scribbled in a journal in the middle of the night, and if there's a tiny part of her that wonders if it might blow her mind and her heart and her career wide open—

Lilly shuts the laptop. She's being ridiculous, that's all. Dreaming the goofy, grandiose dreams of a person who ought to know better.

Her phone trills on the nightstand just then, June's name appearing on the screen over a picture of the two of them as babies, sunning themselves in matching hats at the beach. Lilly picks up right away. "What's wrong?" she asks, heart already pounding. In her experience phone calls are for emergencies and emergencies only: Her father clutching his chest or Kit getting arrested on a drunk and disorderly. Joe's mother calling, her voice tight and formal, to ask if Lilly knew where he was.

"I fainted doing burpees," June reports now, sounding deeply miserable. "Can you come get me? I cracked my head on the floor."

"Holy shit," Lilly says, already springing guiltily to her feet. She *knew* it, she knew June hadn't eaten anything, but still she let her just—"Are you okay?"

"Probably?" June says. She sounds dazed. "I have a bump."

"Do you need to go to the hospital?" Lilly's heart stutters inside her chest. She thinks of Junie at sixteen, ninety pounds with no period to speak of. She thinks of Joe on the floor in the bathroom at their apartment, his skin gone cold and gray.

"No," June says immediately. "I mean, I don't think so? I just, like, probably shouldn't drive home."

"Okay," Lilly says, swallowing down a disproportionate panic. She feels like the worst sister in the world. "I'm on my way."

The Honda is still in the shop, so she jams her sneakers onto her feet and heads across the development, the sun warm on the back of her neck. She manages not to sprint, but barely; still, by the time she turns up at Charlie's front door twenty minutes later there's sweat dripping down her spine inside her T-shirt, her damp hair sticking to her neck.

"Did you . . . walk here?" Caroline asks when she answers the doorbell, her gaze flicking up and down Lilly's body.

"Yes?" Lilly replies, not entirely sure why that's relevant. She peers past Caroline into the house, knowing she's being rude and not particularly caring. She wants to put her hands on Junie's face. "How's my sister?"

"Better," Caroline says, still peering dubiously in Lilly's direction like she's here to sell vacuum cleaners or convince them to accept Jesus Christ as their personal Lord and Savior. She's wearing an immaculate white sports bra and a pair of spandex shorts that makes her ass look like two Royal Verano pears from Harry & David. "Come on in."

Lilly follows her through the light-filled living room and out to the patio, where June is sitting by the pool with a fancy electrolyte-replenishing drink on the table beside her. "I'm sorry," she says immediately, covering her eyes with both hands. "I feel like an idiot."

Lilly shakes her head. "You're fine," she promises, smoothing a palm over her sister's hair. She doesn't know why she feels like she's about to cry. "Why are you apologizing?"

"I wish you'd said something, Junie sweetheart," Caroline puts in, squeezing June's arm in a warm, sisterly way that makes Lilly want to growl. "Theo's workouts really aren't meant for beginners."

"Evidently," Lilly says, holding her hand out to pull June upright. "You ready?"

"Yup," June says. "My car keys are in my purse."

She gathers up her things and they say their goodbyes to Caroline; they're headed for the front of the house when the door from the mudroom opens into the kitchen and in walk Charlie and Will.

Lilly stops so short she almost trips over the tasteful marble coffee table. Will doesn't smile. He's wearing shorts and a Juilliard T-shirt that's been washed so many times it looks like it's made of tissue, the jut of his collarbone just visible at the stretched-out neck. In the moment before she puts the thought firmly out of her head, it occurs to Lilly that she would like to bite it.

"Hey!" Charlie says, his face breaking into the kind of open, radiant grin that nets him thirteen million dollars a picture. "What are you doing here?" Then, looking from June to his sister and back again: "Everything okay?"

"June had a little episode," Caroline announces, in a bright, astringent voice that positively invites a punch directly in the head. Being around Caroline reminds Lilly of the very first days after they moved to Pemberly Grove from the Valley, back before she met Isobel and learned how to stand for a photograph—the feeling of knowing she had the wrong kind of jeans and backpack and mother, of knowing she didn't belong. It makes her want to chew with her mouth open. It makes her want to pick a fight, feeling anxious to communicate the gravity of the situation, even if nobody else seems to think it's that big of a deal.

"It wasn't a big deal," June tells Charlie now; Will is still glowering in the corner like a bridge troll, water bottle dangling from his long, elegant fingers. "I think I was just a little dehydrated, that's all."

"She fainted," Lilly reports. "She hit her head."

"Holy shit," Charlie says, crossing the room and putting both hands gently on June's skull, feeling carefully around for the bump with the authority of a person who has played a doctor on three different nighttime soaps. "Are you okay?"

"I'm fine," June insists again—laughing, ducking out of his touch as her cheeks get pink. June is preternaturally shy about PDA of any kind. "Your sister has been taking good care of me."

Lilly blinks, stung in spite of herself, even though she knows June didn't mean anything by it. She should have tagged along this morning, even if it meant doing one-handed planks with Caroline and her trainer. She should have made June eat a Clif Bar while she watched. "We were just about to get going," she announces, not wanting Will to get the idea that she was lurking around here like some kind of weird Shakespearean fangirl hoping he'd show up, but Charlie is already shaking his head.

"No, no, you guys should hang out for a while," he says easily. "Have you eaten? We can grill."

Lilly opens her mouth to say they can't—meeting of the Reality Show Trash Bags of America, maybe, board elections, can't miss 'em—when June cuts her off. "Sure," she says, her cheeks still flushing prettily. "That sounds great."

Lilly frowns. "Junie," she says quietly. She feels jangly and nervous and twitchy to leave, like there's something she ought to be doing; she's thinking about Joe, about staving off disaster. About how to save people from themselves. "You should probably rest, no?"

But June shakes her head: "It's okay," she says, "I promise. I really am feeling a lot better."

June digs her heels in once, maybe twice a year, which is how Lilly knows whatever's happening between Charlie and her must be serious; still, she's about to keep arguing when a scruffy brown dog comes careening down the stairs, his nails clicking wildly on the hardwood. Ranger is smaller than he looked in *People*, a shepherd mix with a foxlike tail and freckly muzzle. He swerves at the last minute and heads directly for Will, who crouches down on the floor and runs his palms along his bristly back, the two of them wrestling for a long, unconscious moment. The dog rolls over and exposes his smooth pink belly, wiggling delightedly.

Finally Will looks up, noticing Lilly staring. "What?" he asks, his expression turning defensive.

"I—nothing," Lilly says, recovering a beat too late. "I'm just surprised, that's all. You didn't really strike me as a dog person."

"I didn't really strike you as a *dog* person?" Will laughs at that, though Lilly isn't sure if she's imagining that he looks slightly stung.

"Aw, he's cranky, Lilly," Charlie tells her, slinging a friendly arm around her shoulders and steering her and June back in the direction of the fully stocked bar out on the patio. "He's not a serial killer."

Lilly feels her cheeks get a tiny bit hot. "Can't be too careful," she manages to reply. Ranger butts his head against Will's hand.

In the end it turns into a little bit of a party, Caroline's friend Lucy showing up with a bottle of tequila and a couple of tech bros Charlie knows dropping over with some weed from an organic cannabis outfit they're hoping he'll invest in. Anne Mulgrew stops by, though it's unclear to Lilly who would have invited her; an Icelandic pop star named Sera Foye floats, happily stoned, across the length of the pool. Lilly remembers this, from back before her family's empire began to crumble: the way people come and go in houses like this one, the luxury and the largesse. More wine appears, seemingly out of nowhere. Charlie makes guacamole with avocados right off the tree.

The sun is just starting to set when Lilly ducks inside for more ice and finds Will standing freshly showered in the kitchen in jeans and a soft-looking Henley, gathering ingredients for a salad. "You need help?" she asks, surprised; she figured he'd disappeared entirely, off to quietly recite the *Aeneid* to himself in the original Greek or whatever it is he does for fun.

Will shakes his head. "I'm okay." She's just about to turn and head outside when he continues: "Caroline told me you walked here."

"Is that . . . noteworthy?" Lilly asks, lifting an eyebrow.

He shrugs. "To Caroline, it is."

"I walk a lot."

"Me too," he says. "Back at home, anyway."

"Where are you from again?"

"New York," he says immediately, then realizes a beat too late that she's screwing with him. "Oh."

"I'm teasing you."

"I realize that now."

"Welcome to the conversation."

"Thank you." He smiles then—a real smile, disarming. Before she can help herself, Lilly smiles back.

She sits down at one of the tall stools at the island, watching as he pulls a sharp-looking knife from the block. Lilly isn't much of a cook herself, but she can tell from years of being around Charlotte that he knows what he's doing, his hands quick and confident and keen. He adds walnuts and goat cheese and fat slices of peach to the big wooden salad bowl, working the fruit loose from the stone with the edge of his knife. "I have to say, Will Darcy," she tells him, plucking a blueberry out of the punnet on the counter and popping it into her mouth, "if I didn't hate you so much, I might be a little bit impressed right now."

Will's lips twitch. "If I didn't hate you so much, Lilly Benedetto, I might be trying a little bit to impress you." He shrugs. "I used to cook for my sister sometimes, back in high school."

"When the help was on vacation?"

Will makes a face. "Don't act like your family doesn't have help, too."

They don't, actually; not anymore, at least. She thinks of the stack of meal kit boxes listing in the pantry back at her parents' house, and decides not to mention them. No reason to add their dwindling fortune to the long list of reasons he thinks he's better than her. "Come on," she says instead, picking up a stack of plates and grabbing some napkins. It's only her and June left by now, the tech bros off to catch a flight back to San Francisco and Anne Mulgrew home to read the encyclopedia. Lilly has no idea what happened to Sera. She hopes she didn't drown. "Let's get out there."

Charlie grills some steaks to go with the salad, plus some vegetables for June, and they all sit around the long wooden table on the patio, the outdoor lights casting a warm white glow across the pool. Lilly's been in her share of nice backyards, but she can't help feeling a tiny bit covetous of the outdoor kitchen and capacious pergola, the lush garden teeming with native plants. The last landscape architect Cinta worked with convinced her to do some weird mood-lighting-and-vintage-lawn-furniture situation, and now their pool at home just kind of looks like the Playboy grotto.

"To new neighbors," Caroline says, raising her wineglass and clinking it against June's, "and old friends." She's had quite a lot to drink, which Lilly has to admit makes her marginally more tolerable. She's a pretty good storyteller, spinning yarns about the bad bosses she worked with at her old agency, the time she got rearended by the least of the Jonas Brothers on La Cienega Boulevard, the willowy art house ingenue whose rider was just one hundred individual serving–size bags of Doritos and nothing else.

"She never ate them, as far as I know," Caroline says, reaching for her wineglass. "I think she just liked to have them around her."

"To swim through," Will posits. "Like Scrooge McDuck," Charlie agrees.

Lilly smiles, sitting back in her chair as the warm breeze whispers through the hair on the back of her neck, the smell of citrus and chlorine and salt drifting through the air. She likes watching them together, Will and Charlie: the easy way they have with one another, their familiar back-and-forth. It reminds her of being with her sisters, the rhythms of their conversations creased and softened like a photo folded up in the back of a jeans pocket.

If the playlist he queued up for dinner is any indication, Charlie's taste in music swerves hard and unashamedly in the direction of Hall & Oates, but as they're finishing their steaks the opening bars of an old Stevie Wonder song pipe through the outdoor speakers, and all at once Caroline jumps to her feet. "I love this one," she announces, holding her hands out to Lilly and June and waggling her fingers. "We should dance."

Will's lips twist across the table. "So that Chuck and I can admire you?" he asks.

Caroline rolls her eyes at him. "I know this might come as a shock to your system, William, but not everything is about you," she chides, which is officially the most Lilly has ever liked her. It's possible Lilly's had quite a lot of wine herself. Still, there's a certain tipsy effervescence to Caroline right now that reminds Lilly of the girls she used to meet in line in club bathrooms sometimes, the ones who would drunkenly lend her a tampon or pass her a fistful of toilet paper under the stall door before disappearing back out onto the crowded dance floor.

"Sure," she agrees, getting to her feet and sliding one hand into Caroline's. Just for tonight, she decides, they can be friends. "Why not?"

They twirl around on the pool deck for a while, the sun sinking down over the trees to the west of them and the music changing from Stevie to Steely Dan to Fleetwood Mac. After a couple of songs Charlie gets up and joins them, his big dog-paw hands on June's waist; Lilly dances Caroline over to the other side of the patio, wanting to give them a little bit of room. If anyone deserves a big romance, it's June, who's so much better than all the rest of them. It's June, who is so sincerely good.

"I don't know, Will," Caroline calls over to where he's still slouched alone at the table, scrolling through Charlie's music with a despondent look on his face. "I don't think Lilly and I are feeling appropriately admired."

Will glances up, but barely. "You're admired plenty," he assures her. "You don't need me."

"He's watching," Caroline declares, raising her eyebrows mischievously. "He's just worried it'll make us vain."

"Too late for that," Lilly says with a shrug.

"I swear to god, Charlie." Will drops the phone on the table in defeat. "Do you have a single song on this thing that isn't just three and a half minutes of whammy bar? I feel like I'm growing a mustache just listening to it."

Lilly ignores him. She ignores everyone for a moment, closing her eyes as Stevie Nicks caterwauls away over the expensive sound system; when she opens them again she finds Will staring back at her across the still, dark expanse of the swimming pool, his gaze hot and steady and overt. Caroline is staring, too, sharp and canny, and the expression on her face is enough for Lilly to remember they're not actually friends after all.

Lilly clears her throat just a little too loudly. "You could dance, too, you know," she calls over to Will, trying to keep her voice light.

Will snorts, leaning back in his chair and stretching his long legs out in front of him. "Please believe me when I tell you that nobody here wants to experience that."

"He's right," Charlie calls helpfully. "He dances like an awkward guest host at the end of *Saturday Night Live*."

Will doesn't smile. Instead he gets up and abruptly starts clearing the table, assembling a tidy stack of plates in one arm and heading for the kitchen without further comment. Lilly moves to help him before she quite knows what she's doing, scooping up a couple of serving dishes and ignoring Caroline's watchful gaze from across the patio. Let her think whatever she wants to think, Lilly decides, following him into the cool, quiet house. She doesn't know anything.

The kitchen is dark but right away Will flicks a switch on the wall with one elbow, flooding the room with bright overhead light. So much for . . . whatever she thought they might do in here, Lilly guesses, unless his appendix suddenly ruptures and she needs to perform a quick DIY organ removal. "You know," she points out, setting a heavy ceramic bowl down on the granite counter, "if you want us to leave so bad, you could just say so."

"If I wanted you to leave, you'd know it."

"I—" Lilly breaks off. Every time she thinks she understands what's happening between them it immediately changes, like the flea market mood ring she had when she was fourteen that she accidentally left on the edge of the sink in the restaurant bathroom at Olivia's first communion dinner. Lilly loved that ring. She wishes she still had it, so that maybe she could name whatever it is she feels. "Okay," she says finally, turning on the tap and reaching for a handful of silverware. "Well, could have fooled me. Are you just that sensitive about your dance moves, then?"

"You think I give a shit about my—" Will blows a breath out, like she's the one who's being difficult. "I'll do that," he tells her, motioning to the plates.

Lilly shakes her head. She feels irritated and itchy, and she doesn't know why. She doesn't even like him, she reminds herself firmly. He's the actual, literal worst, except for the part where she can't stop looking at him, stealing quick hungry glances out of the corner of her eye. He has three tiny freckles on the side of his neck, like a constellation. His eyelashes are long as a girl's. "I got it," she says.

"No, really."

"It's fine," she says snottily. "I know you think I'm a useless, spoiled princess, but I promise I can rinse a dish."

Will rolls his eyes. "That's not—" He reaches for it, the full length of his body pressing against hers, and it's like she's an electric car that's suddenly been plugged in to charge after a thousand miles, everything inside her vrooming to life—dashboard flickering, a mechanical rev. Both of them freeze. They stay that way for a moment playing chicken. Lilly knows when she's staring down a dare.

"Can I ask you something?" he murmurs. His face is very, very close. "Why do you keep following me around trying to kiss me when you hate me so much?"

Lilly glowers, her cheeks getting hot. "First of all, who says I'm trying to kiss you?" she demands haughtily, turning back to the sink and shoving the plates under the faucet one by one. "For all you know, I could have come in here to change my tampon. I could have come in here to sit on the couch and stream the entire first season of *Glee*."

Will lifts an eyebrow, but barely. "Did you?"

"No," she admits grudgingly. "But second of all, stop crying. I don't hate you any more than you hate me."

"See," he says, "that's where you're wrong."

Well. Lilly doesn't know what to say to that, and Will doesn't say anything else, but when she glances up from the dishes there's that look on his face again, the one she seriously does not get. "Lilly," he starts, curling a hand around her waist, and the jolt of his touch is so hot and surprising that she drops the plate she's holding right into the enormous sink, where it shatters with a holy racket into a million tiny pieces. Lilly swears.

"Everything okay in there?" Charlie yells from the backyard.

"Everything's great!" they yell back in perfect unison. Lilly makes a face. She shuts off the water and turns around to face him, his fingertips just grazing her rib cage through her tank top. She can see his chest moving as he breathes.

"This is ridiculous," she announces, trying to sound like a person whose heart isn't slamming wildly against the inside of her rib cage, whose entire body isn't humming with frustration and want. "Let's just get it out of our systems already, and then we never have to see each other again."

"Romantic," Will comments dryly. He tilts his head to the side, interested. "Is that our problem here, you think? Am I in your system?"

Lilly scoffs. "Oh please," she says. "I think we know exactly who is in whose system."

"I mean." Will's eyebrows twitch; he takes a step closer, backing her up against the counter.

Lilly swallows hard. This close he's bigger than she thinks of him as being, all broad shoulders and solid chest, a full head taller than her. The palms of their hands brush down low at their sides.

"I keep thinking about you," he confesses quietly. He's got his fingers wrapped around her wrists now—his thumbs stroking over the thin, sensitive skin on the undersides, making tiny circles there. "I don't want to, but I can't help it. I can't fucking stop."

Lilly laughs at that, loud and genuine. "Oh," she teases, "now who's romantic?"

"Can you not?" Will growls. "I'm serious."

"I know," she promises. It's not like she doesn't understand the sentiment. It's a relief to have him say it, to know for sure she's not the only one. She looks up at him for a moment, her head thunking back against the upper row of cabinets. "What do you think?"

Will doesn't answer. He doesn't have to; the expression on his face is so nakedly, achingly specific that Lilly gasps. It reminds her of the wildfires that rip through California every summer—quick and uncontrollable and enormous, swallowing entire neighborhoods in the time it takes to call for help. Part of her wants to grab her valuables and run like her life depends on it. The rest of her wants to watch it burn.

"Come upstairs," he mutters finally, and it sounds like he's begging. "Lilly. Come upstairs with me."

Lilly hesitates for a moment, considering it. On the one hand, sneaking off to Will Darcy's bedroom in the middle of a dinner party would probably confirm her as exactly the kind of person Caroline Bingley goes around telling people she is.

On the other hand: fuck Caroline Bingley.

"Yeah." Lilly slips her hand into his and tugs him in the direction of the staircase, nodding. "Let's go."

That's when she hears a voice from the side of the house: "Yoo-hoo!" it calls, ringing out like a klaxon in the warm, still night. "Anybody home?"

Lilly freezes. She knows that voice. Will seems to know it, too, instinctive. "Is that—" he starts, but Lilly holds a hand up.

"Just—" She shakes her head, suddenly dizzy—desire or disbelief, she isn't sure. "Don't say anything for a second, will you?" She makes her way toward the patio on wobbly legs, sliding the back door open just as the gate swings wide at the side of the yard; Charlie and June are getting to their feet at the table, Caroline staring with naked disbelief.

"Mom," Lilly says, and her voice sounds like it belongs to someone else entirely. "Hi."

CHAPTER EIGHT

WILL

"We texted," Lilly's mother is saying when the two of them make it out onto the patio. Marianne, Kit, and Olivia are all standing behind her, three obedient ducklings in a fairy tale. "Didn't you get our texts?"

"I . . . guess I wasn't looking at my phone," Lilly says faintly. Her cheeks are still pink, her eyes bright and dazed-looking. Will had to adjust his dick on the way out.

"You could have let us know everyone was all right, Lilly sweetheart," Mrs. Benedetto huffs. "We were all worried sick about poor June, and then we thought maybe something had happened to you, too, so we decided to come over and investigate for ourselves."

"With wine?" Lilly asks, nodding at the bottle in her mother's manicured hand.

"Well, I didn't raise you all in a barn." She smiles coquettishly at Charlie, holding it out in his direction. "And we never properly welcomed you to the neighborhood, honey."

"Oh," Caroline mutters, so quietly that only Will can hear her, "I wouldn't say that."

"Have a seat, all of you," Charlie is saying now—getting up to pull extra chairs across the patio, every inch the gracious host. Back when he and Will lived together he used to keep a stash of chips under his bed—"In case we have guests!" he always reasoned, as if they might be called upon at any moment to throw an impromptu cocktail party, even though Will didn't really have any friends other than Charlie and also no one at Juilliard ate chips.

For four people who committed criminal trespass on the pretext of making sure June wasn't in distress, Will can't help but notice that none of them seem particularly concerned with her well-being; in fact, they're more or less only interested in Charlie, peppering him with questions about his workout regimen and his famous friends and how he's enjoying the warm bosom of Pemberly Grove. "Don't you have a movie coming out soon?" Kit wants to know, helping herself to a glass of vinho verde. From his deep dive into *Meet the Benedettos* Will knows she's the edgy one, tattoos and CrossFit and a well-publicized DUI.

"I do," Charlie says, shaking his head a little like he can't quite believe it, either. "Couple of weeks."

"You should invite us to the premiere," Olivia advises.

"Olivia," Lilly chides; Will can feel her wince from all the way across the table. "Jesus."

"What?" Olivia asks with a shrug. "I'm just making a suggestion."

"You definitely do not have to do that," June protests quickly, but Charlie is already nodding.

"Why not?" he asks, and Will isn't sure if he means it or if he's just very, very drunk. "I'd love to have you guys."

"And why wouldn't you?" Mrs. Benedetto asks brightly. "The more beautiful, vivacious, well-educated girls at a party the better, that's what I always say."

It goes on like that, Olivia pressing Will for Johnny Jones's phone number and Mrs. Benedetto casually inquiring how much

Charlie's paying in rent. The gaggle of them stay until well past midnight, ignoring Caroline's unsubtle yawns and Lilly's pointed attempts to get them all to pack it up and take off; once they finally say their lengthy goodbyes, Charlie and Will sink back down into the patio chairs like they've just run the New York City marathon without the benefit of any training.

"I cannot believe that just happened," Caroline says, setting three fresh shot glasses down on the table and emptying the bottle of tequila. "Like, you watch these people on television and you think to yourself, surely they're just edited in some hacky, ungenerous way that makes them seem like complete and utter clowns? But then you meet them in person and it's real! It's *real*."

"I like them," Charlie announces. He knocks back his tequila with nary a wince, his vowels loose and lazy. Will knows from a decade and a half of experience that they've got fifteen, maybe twenty minutes before he's either asleep in the patio chair or singing Lerner and Loewe at the top of his lungs.

"You like everybody," Caroline reminds him. "The point is, this is a cautionary tale. I invited June over here to try and get to know her better, and instead we wound up saddled with her whole ridiculous—"

"You invited June over here hoping she'd give you an excuse not to like her," Charlie corrects, "but by all means, continue."

"Can you blame me?" Caroline fires back. Will has to admit she's got a point. Charlie's taste in women has historically been nothing short of catastrophic: There was Alice, who cut off bits of his hair while he slept and sold them on the internet. Nikki, who lay down behind his car outside his condo when he tried to break things off. Lara, who conned him out of forty grand with some ginned-up story about opening a gallery, which turned out to be a small collection of erotic doodles tacked to the wall in the spare bedroom of her apartment in North Hollywood. He's a bighearted guy, Charlie; it's one of the things Will loves most about him. It also makes him an easy mark.

"Look," Caroline says now, her own diction crisp as England even though Will is pretty sure she's had just as much to drink as the rest of them, "this isn't some cute thing where you're going to do a couple of movies and maybe dabble in crypto and it's fine if your girl-friend is a D-list party girl whose mother is going to drop your name when she's trying to book late-night infomercials. You're on the cusp of something enormous, Charlie. This is the most important moment of your entire career. And if you honestly like June enough to risk that—to chance everything you've been working for since you were eighteen—then that's your business. But it's my literal job, as both your agent and as your big sister, to ask you to think it through." She turns in the moonlight, looking across the table. "Will agrees with me," she says, her tone faintly accusatory. "Don't you?"

Will almost chokes on his tequila. "I—" he says, then com-pletely fails to follow it up in any meaningful way. On the one hand, of course he agrees with her. The Benedettos are a sideshow: insatiable for every last greasy morsel of celebrity, hungry gears in the same ravenous fame machine that gobbled both his parents. He doesn't want Charlie anywhere near them. He doesn't want to be anywhere near them himself.

On the other hand—

Well.

He's saved from himself by a crash down at the other end of the table, the last dregs of the tequila seeping across the patio table. "Somebody dropped something," Charlie says, smiling guiltily. Caroline rolls her eyes.

CHAPTER NINE

CAROLINE

It's after two when she finds Will cleaning up the kitchen, Nina Simone turned down low on the stereo and his shirtsleeves rolled to his elbows. Charlie is passed out drunk in a lounge chair on the patio like a toddler who's had too much birthday cake, the cicadas shrieking high up in the trees. "You know I'm right," Caroline announces, padding barefoot across the tile.

Will raises one eyebrow at her reflection in the window. "I do, huh?"

"You do." Caroline plucks the dish towel from over his shoulder, nudges him aside so she can help. The whole place is a disaster, dirty plates stacked on the island and a precarious tower of empty wine bottles Jengaed into the recycling bin; there's a broken platter shattered like a mosaic at the bottom of the sink. "I'm not just being a cold bitch for no reason. You know as well as I do that when it comes to people who actually give a shit about him beyond what he can do for them at any given moment, it's basically you and me and that's it."

Will plucks the largest shards from the basin, tossing them carefully into the trash before going back for the smaller ones with a handful of paper towel. "I know."

Caroline glances at him out of the corner of her eye,

remembering the sound of the crash from earlier. Wondering exactly how the platter broke in the first place. "Okay," she says finally. "Well, glad we're on the same team, then."

The two of them work in silence for a long moment, moving methodically through the mess: wrapping up leftovers and wiping down counters, their wet fingertips brushing as he hands her the serving bowls that are too big for the dishwasher. They've cleaned up a lot of kitchens together, Thanksgivings and Fourths and the New Year's Eve party Charlie threw every year when he was still living in New York after college. One Christmas at Charlie's parents' house they ducked into the pantry and fooled around for ten minutes in the dark next to the Nutella and cans of green beans, accidentally knocking over an enormous canister of Quaker Oats in the process. Caroline used to think they were orbiting each other, waiting for the timing to be right for something more permanent. Lately, though, she's not so sure.

"Shit," Will says suddenly, pulling his hand from the soapy water. He missed a sharp piece of the platter; blood blooms in a long, startling red line across his palm. Caroline grabs a clean dish towel from under the sink, presses it tight against the wounded place. And see, this is what people like the Benedettos don't understand, Caroline thinks as they stand there in silence waiting for the bleeding to stop, surprised at the sudden depth of her own annoyance: That decisions, however small or stupid, have consequences. That people can get hurt trying to clean up the mess.

"You need a Band-Aid," she announces finally, peeking underneath the towel. He smells like tequila and like soap. "But I think you'll live."

Will nods, flexing his fingers. "So they tell me."

That stops her. Caroline takes a deep breath, knowing it's as much of an invitation as she's likely to get. "Can I ask you something?" she asks, pushing on before she loses her nerve. "Are you okay?" Charlie gave her the broad strokes, *Hamlet* and the *Times* review and the stint in the hospital, how quickly it all unraveled; she's wanted to talk to Will about it since he got out here, but she hasn't been able to figure out how. "Like . . . globally, I mean."

That makes him smile. "I'm fine," he promises, holding his hand up as evidence. "But thank you."

"I—all right," Caroline says, trying not to feel disappointed, trying not to feel like she's lacking in some fundamental way. She knows she's not the kind of person people come to with their sadness. Still, she thinks she would have listened to his. "For what it's worth," she says, putting her hands on the counter so she doesn't reach for him, "I'm looking out for you, too."

Will gazes at her for a moment in the dim light of the nighttime kitchen. They've known each other so many years. "It'll pass," he promises finally, and his voice is very quiet. "Charlie's thing for June, I mean."

"Will it?" she asks, and for a moment she's not sure they're talking about her brother at all. She thinks again of the broken platter. She thinks of Lilly Benedetto's long, dark hair.

Will nods. "It will," he says, more certain than he sounded a moment ago. It occurs to her to wonder which one of them he's trying to convince. "It always does." He looks around at the mostly clean kitchen, stifling a yawn with the back of his uninjured hand. "It's late," he observes, looking at the clock on the microwave. "I'm going to head up."

"You want company?" she asks, trying to sound like she

doesn't care one way or the other, like she isn't lurking around her brother's house waiting for his cute friend to notice her. Her mother would be appalled.

"I think I'm just going to crash," Will says, then lifts his hand one more time. "Try to keep myself from getting gangrene."

"There's some Neosporin in the upstairs bathroom," Caroline informs him automatically, then presses her lips together. It feels like she's scrabbling for something, lately. It feels like she's falling and trying not to hit the ground. "Sleep well."

"You too," Will tells her, pressing his cheek against hers before disappearing up the back staircase.

She finishes cleaning up by herself, taking out the trash and running the dishwasher. She scrubs the sink with a sponge until it shines.

CHAPTER TEN

LILLY

Lilly wakes up deeply hungover, mouth dry and a headache pulsing angrily behind her eyeballs. When she counts on her fingers she realizes she drank more or less a full bottle of wine last night, plus the tequila, which she never does anymore. She stands under the shower for a long time, scrubbing her fingers roughly through her hair and trying not to think about Will—the warm authority of his kisses, his narrow body slotted against hers.

She yanks a towel off the rack, shrugging into a robe and shuffling back into her bedroom. When she finally clomps downstairs she finds her mother standing in the foyer like a master of ceremonies at Barnum & Bailey, hollering directions at the cleaners in a way that makes Lilly cringe. "Who's coming over?" she asks, suspicious. Her mother only ever notices mess when she's trying to impress someone.

Cinta stares at her for a moment, like possibly she has no idea who Lilly is or what she might be doing here. Then she blinks and locks back in. "Didn't I tell you?" she asks airily. "Colin's flying in from Vancouver."

Right away, Lilly's entire body fills with annoyance and dread. "Colin?" she repeats, fully aware she sounds about thirteen years old. "Why?"

Her mother smiles at her with syrupy forbearance. "Because I invited him, Lilly. He's going to Joshua Tree to finish up his new screenplay, but his rental doesn't start until New Year's."

Lilly resists the urge to stamp her foot, but barely. Her cousin Colin once made her watch *Donnie Darko* twice, back-to-back when they were in high school; his sophomore effort, some masturbatory snorefest about an alcoholic lobsterman and his mean dad, got nominated for best screenplay last year. Lilly told herself the queasy feeling she had as she watched him walk the red carpet in a purple velvet tuxedo was revulsion, not jealousy, though if she's being honest with herself she knows it was probably a mixture of both.

"Did you know Colin was coming?" she asks June, who's padding down the stairs in ripped jeans and a loose-knit sweater, looking fresh as a newly picked lemon. Lilly doesn't know why she's the only one who seems to be hungover this fine morning.

"I . . ." June hesitates. "Might have heard something about it?"

"And you didn't say anything?" Lilly asks. "Or, you know, light the house on fire to collect the insurance money?"

"That would be a good solution to the mortgage thing, actually," Kit offers, coming in from the kitchen; Tony trails like a basset hound behind her, lugging a ring light in one arm. "You should mention it to Dad."

"I don't know what your problem is," Cinta puts in, poking one of the cleaners in the back with one finger and motioning to a smudge on the mirror. "Colin's a very successful screenwriter. I would think you of all people would be grateful for the chance to talk to him about your craft."

Lilly sighs. Sometimes she has a hard time reconciling this mother with the same one who used to get down on the floor with them to play Barbies when they were little, who held their hair back over the second-floor toilet in the little house in the Valley when they got sick. "Tell us your best story, Lilly-girl," she used to say, Lilly nestled into the crook of her arm at bedtime. "I'm listening."

Colin shows up in the late afternoon driving a Porsche and wearing a pair of aviators that make him look like a badly behaved detective on a spin-off of a spin-off of a police procedural that takes place in metro Houston. "Lil," he says, as if they're friends, which they aren't, and as if that's a thing her friends call her, which it is not. When he bends to kiss her on both cheeks he smells like a national park by way of Abercrombie & Fitch.

"Colin!" Kit and Olivia come thundering down the stairs, flinging themselves at him with the enthusiasm of puppies. Right away, Colin's ears turn pink. When they were kids he was always terminally awkward, dressed in cargo shorts and Star Wars T-shirts and deeply afraid of girls in general and her sisters in particular. From the look on his face Lilly is pretty sure he's still afraid of them.

"Since when are you guys pals?" Lilly mutters, grabbing Kit's elbow as they troop out to the yard.

"Since he got invited to Cannes," Kit says plainly.

They have dinner out on the patio, Colin tucking into the macrobiotic feast Cinta ordered him specially from a pop-up called the Grainforest and holding forth about his various successes, how he's working with Caitriona de Bourgh on his next film. "You all know Caitriona, right?" he asks.

"I think I might have heard of her," June says innocently. Lilly stifles a laugh. Caitriona de Bourgh is arguably the second-most-famous director in Hollywood, one of those women who is perpetually wearing a leather jacket and making movies full of unspeakable carnage just to prove that she can. She's famous for zipping around LA on a motorcycle, spewing a cloud of exhaust in her wake.

Colin turns to Lilly. "What about you, *cugina*?" he asks her. Colin isn't related on the Italian side of their family, not that it ever stops him. "How's the writing these days?"

"Oh, you know," Lilly says, biting back a grimace, swallowing down a weird rush of shame. "It's going."

Colin nods indulgently. "Let me know if you ever want me to take a look at some pages," he offers. "I'd be happy to let you pick my brain."

"That's tempting," she says, as politely as she can manage. "It's not really ready for that."

Cinta clucks. "Don't listen to her, Colin," she chides. "My daughter has been pecking away at that computer night and day for ages. I keep telling her that if she's not going to let anyone see what she's working on she should at least look into a brand partnership."

By the time Lilly wakes up the next morning and makes it downstairs Colin has already set up shop at the patio table, a vintage typewriter in front of him and no fewer than four different beverages at his side. He's halfway through what, from the sound of it, is an incredibly detailed, granular story about the time Ben Affleck asked him for a stick of gum outside a Sally Beauty in Santa Monica.

"Lilly!" her father exclaims. He's sitting across the table in his bathrobe, his voice sharp with the bright desperation of a sailor held captive by particularly garrulous pirates. "You're here!"

Lilly hides a smile, but barely. "I'm here," she agrees.

"Colin here is an early riser," Dominic reports. "He caught

me on my way to my workout and we have just been . . . talking ever since."

"That sounds lovely," Lilly says. "I'm sorry I can't stay and join you, but I've got—" What? A lobotomy? A Pap smear? "—another engagement."

Her father jumps up and takes her arm as she makes her escape back into the kitchen, lowering his voice to a mutter. "I am begging you, Elisabetta. Get this person out of my house. Take him to a horse race. Go shopping on Rodeo Drive. Bind his hands and feet, roll him up in a carpet, and leave him in an alley, it's entirely up to you. But he's gotta go."

In the end she rounds up her sisters—well, all of her sisters except Mari, who claimed to be attending an exorcism in Mulholland Heights—and Charlotte and they go to brunch at a vegan place near the development, splitting a bucket of champagne on the patio while Colin delivers a lengthy monologue about the death of the author and what he keeps describing, in earnest, as the *Annie Hall* Problem. Lilly is considering ordering a vodka tonic or possibly a gun when a couple of guys in extremely tight pants stop by the table.

"Olivia Benedetto," the taller one says. Lilly vaguely recognizes him as one of her sister's exes, all prominent cheekbones and a vaguely goth sensibility. Olivia's boyfriends always look like supporting werewolves on a CW show about a haunted town in the Midwest; usually they're deejays or club promoters or British pop stars with one hit that borrows heavily from the work of Black artists. "How you doing?"

"Oh, you know," Olivia says coyly, tonguing the straw in her green juice. "No complaints." She gestures around the table. "You remember my sisters."

"Of course," Tyler says with a smile. "How could anyone forget?" He nods at the guy next to him, who's nice-looking in a slightly scruffy kind of way, a chambray shirt rolled to the elbows and a tangle of bracelets looped around one elegant wrist. "This is my buddy Nick."

In the end they push the tables together, ordering another round of drinks while Colin lectures Charlotte on the benefits of intermittent fasting and Lilly eyes Nick across the table. "Are you a promoter, too?" she asks.

"Tyler is an entrepreneur," Olivia corrects huffily. "He just launched a bespoke women's lingerie disruptor."

"That sounds fascinating," Lilly lies.

Nick is a bartender downtown, though when Lilly asks him where he works he shakes his head bashfully. "You're definitely not going to have heard of it," he tells her, and sure enough she hasn't. Still, he says, "You guys should come by."

Tyler laughs out loud, not entirely nicely. "The Benedetto girls don't go to dive bars," he says.

"Fuck you!" Lilly says, though it's not like he's wrong. They went to one once on the show, but it was actually a new bar made to look old, with kitschy lamps repurposed from a Pizza Hut hung over all the tables and a palpable sense of smug superiority. The plot of the episode was Kit trying to convince the bartender to make her an Aperol spritz.

"Dude, I love a dive bar," Colin puts in. "So real, you know? Like, authentic."

She's just about to ask Nick if he likes working there when she spies Will and Charlie out on the sidewalk in front of the restaurant, Ranger pulling happily at his leash. Charlie spots them at the same time, his handsome face breaking open into a grin at the sight of her sister. "Hey, June," he calls, trotting over, seemingly oblivious to the stares from other tables, the way people reach for their phones. Will trails behind him, an expression on his face like he's being made to walk a plank with a sword at his back.

"William," she says, taking a sip of her cocktail.

"Elisabetta." She's surprised to hear him use her full name. It sends a weird little shiver through her, though she couldn't say exactly why. She thinks of his thumbs ghosting over her hip bones. She thinks of his lips grazing over her throat. She smiles—she can't help it—but to her small surprise Will doesn't smile back; in fact, he's barely looking at her at all, staring instead across the table at Nick, whose own expression is suddenly a little bit seasick. Lilly has no idea why they'd know each other—Will also does not strike her as a regular at a dive bar in DTLA—but they certainly seem to. Lilly files the question away in her pocket to consider at a later date.

In the meantime she takes Will's arm, tugging him over to the far side of the patio. "Look," she says quietly, "about the other night at Charlie's."

But Will only looks at her blankly. "We got it out of our systems, didn't we?" he asks. "Just like you said?"

Lilly blinks. "I mean, sure," she says, trying not to feel stung. It's not like she was about to suggest they shack up for the weekend in Malibu; still, she'd be lying if she said she'd been expecting to be brushed off quite so hard. "I guess we did."

"Okay," he says, nodding distractedly. It still feels like she's only got a sliver of his attention, that he's looking at something or someone over her shoulder. "So, I guess that's all there is to talk about, then."

"Um, yup," Lilly agrees crisply. Her whole body feels like it's on fire. "I guess so."

She follows him back to the table, ignoring June's quizzical expression; Will and Charlie take off not long after, Charlie waving gamely at the paparazzi who've materialized outside. Lilly asks their waiter for the check, praying that Colin will pick it up and feeling both miserable and furious without quite knowing why or in which direction. She wants to punch someone in the face and go to bed. She can't believe she'd actually started to like him, Will Darcy with his boring hair and neutral wardrobe. She can't believe she let herself be charmed.

"So what's the verdict?" Nick asks as they're leaving, and for a moment Lilly honestly hasn't the faintest idea what he's talking about. It must be obvious, too, because he grins. "About drinks later. You guys going to come hang out with me tonight?"

"Oh!" She looks in the direction Will and Charlie took off in. She looks back at Nick's open, curious face. "Tonight," she says with a grin. "We'll see."

* * *

Nick's bar is in fact an actual dive, all warped linoleum floors and fraying leather booths and a neon Budweiser sign glowing like a beacon in the tiny front window. The smell of mildew hangs faintly, though certainly not imperceptibly, in the air. Lilly spent the better part of an hour after dinner trying to decide on an outfit before finally settling on ripped jeans and a tank top Kit designed, sheer and mostly backless; at the very last minute she added a pair of sky-high heels—you can take the girl out of Calabasas, et cetera—the soles of which are now sticking ever so slightly to the tile.

Still, the whole scene is significantly less grim than she expected it to be when she bullied her sisters into coming with her: Kit and Olivia are playing the naked photo hunt game in the corner. Mari is posted up at the pool table, where by all appearances she's taking Colin for everything he's worth. And Junie is perched on a stool at the corner of the bar, sipping a bottle of Amstel Light and, judging by the small, secret smile on her face, texting with Charlie. Nobody in here seems to give a shit about them one way or the other, and if Lilly has never quite been able to decide whether she wants that kind of anonymity or she doesn't, for tonight at the very least it's nice to just be herself.

She sits back on her barstool, nursing a vodka and water as Nick dumps a five-gallon bucket of ice into the cooler. She'd be lying if she said she was completely uninterested—his shaggy hair and the dimple in his chin and his plaid shirt rolled to his elbows, his scarred-up, capable-looking hands. He did an actual double take when they all strolled through the door earlier tonight, then threw his head back and laughed a shocked, booming laugh, visibly delighted at the sight of them. "I underestimated you, clearly," he told her when she bellied up to the bar, shaking his head in bashful amusement. "I won't make that mistake again."

Lilly raised an eyebrow, sliding onto a stool and nodding at the dusty bottle of Ketel behind him. "See that you don't," she said primly, then grinned.

Now it's an hour later and she's pleasantly buzzed, her whole body warm and loose and humming. She watches as Nick opens a couple of Heinekens for a pair of grizzled guys in Dodgers caps down at the end of the bar, then pours two shots of Jameson and sets one down in front of her. "What's this?" Lilly asks, lips quirking in a smile.

"Just, you know." Nick winks at her. "Token of my esteem."

Lilly nods seriously, running her thumb around the edge of the glass. "That your love language?"

"Cheap alcohol?" Nick shoots back. "Absolutely."

"How long have you been a bartender?"

"Since before I was old enough to drink," he confesses. "My uncle owned a couple of Irish pubs in New Haven back when I was growing up. I used to stock the coolers and sneak shots of Fireball next to the dumpsters in the alley with my cousins."

"Charming."

"Well." He grins. "We can't all be as terminally fancy as your buddy Will Darcy."

Lilly feels herself perk up like a prairie dog at the Los Angeles Zoo, holding up one finger to stop him. "A," she says immediately, "he's not my buddy. And B, can I ask you something? What the fuck was going on with you guys at brunch today?"

Nick makes a face at that, lets out a sheepish sigh. "You noticed that, huh?"

Lilly laughs. "The two of you grilling each other like a pair of prize golden doodles about to go at it over a Milk-Bone?" she asks. "You were not what I would call subtle, no."

Nick clutches his heart in mock outrage. "Is that the vibe I give off to you?" he asks, leaning over so his elbows rest on the bar and his head is tipped close to hers. He smells like beer and drugstore aftershave, piney and sharp. "Golden doodle?"

Lilly smiles sweetly. "*Prize* golden doodle," she corrects him.

Nick smirks, straightening up again. "We knew each other back in New York, a little. We were . . . also not buddies."

"You're kidding." Lilly picks up her shot, daring him to say more. A swig of disgusting whiskey feels like a small price to pay for the chance to listen to someone else shit all over Will Darcy. "Care to elaborate?"

Nick hesitates. "I don't know," he says, crinkling his nose up in a way that makes him look like a little kid confronted with a heaping plate of broccoli. "I don't want to talk smack about a guy when he's not here to, like, defend himself."

Lilly rolls her eyes. "A little bit you do," she counters, and Nick grins guiltily.

"Fine," he agrees, lifting his shot glass and clinking it gently against hers. "Twist my arm."

They drink; Lilly winces at the burn of it in her throat and sternum, pressing the back of her hand to her mouth. "Back in New York," Nick begins, "when Darcy was at ballet school or whatever the fuck, he and his artsy-fartsy buddies used to be regulars at this bar I worked at on the Upper West Side. And, like, they were fine, or whatever—I mean, they didn't tip for shit, but you get used to that—but one night, I don't know if he didn't get the lead in the school play or what, but he was hammered. Just belligerent as all hell. Grabby with my waitresses, rude to the other customers, you name it."

"Seriously?" Lilly frowns. Will is a douchebag, 100 percent, but he's never struck her as a handsy drunk—and if there's a tiny voice in her head that reminds her that possibly that's because she's usually the one drunkenly groping *him*, well, that's nobody's business but her own.

"Yeah." Nick grimaces. "Anyway, I cut him off and told him he had to go home, and he definitely wasn't happy about it, but that's what bouncers are for, right? So he left, and I'm thinking that's that, but the next day when I showed up for my shift, my manager said that one of our regulars had come to him and told him he'd seen me take a handful of cash from the register. And the guy fired me right there, no questions asked."

Lilly's eyes go wide. "Are you kidding me?" she asks. "Will did that?"

Nick shrugs. "I mean, I can't prove it," he concedes. "But it's one hell of a coincidence, if not." He reaches for the bottle of Jameson, pours them each another shot. "Anyway, some friends of mine were moving out here around then and asked me to tag along, so it's not like I didn't land on my feet in the end. But I definitely wasn't expecting to run into him three thousand miles away."

Lilly's mouth drops open. "What an absolute schmuck," she says quietly, every single rude, obnoxious detail of Will's shitty personality suddenly thrown into searing relief. Not for nothing, but he's got a lot of nerve to accuse other people of being trash bags. She's hit with the nearly physical urge to call him up and tell him so. "I mean, just like, the entitlement alone! And don't get me wrong, I am saying this as a deeply entitled person." She shakes her head. "I am really, really sorry that happened to you."

"Yeah, well." Nick's full mouth twists, like *What can you do?* "Like I said, it all turned out okay. Led me here, didn't it?" His smile changes then—warm and slow and private, the intent in his expression unmistakable. "I don't want to talk about Will Darcy anymore."

Lilly tilts her head to the side, a feeling like a desert flower blooming deep inside her chest. "Oh no?" she asks as casually as she can muster, reaching out and grazing one finger delicately over his knuckles. "What do you want to talk about?"

"I don't know, Lilly Benedetto." Nick turns his hand over on the bar top, laces his fingers through hers. "You tell me."

CHAPTER ELEVEN

DOMINIC

The goddamn accountants want to meet again on Wednesday, which means that by the time Dominic fights traffic all the way to Culver City and back again the entire afternoon is shot, he's missed two workouts, and all he's heard all fucking day is bad news. "You really ought to consider bankruptcy here, Dom," one of them told him, some self-satisfied teenager in a slim-cut suit and Clark Kent glasses. Dominic didn't pop him directly in his Ivy-educated nose, but it was a near thing. Since the bypass he tries to keep his temper.

He sails by the exit for the original location of the shop, in Sherman Oaks, then changes his mind and turns around. He'll say hello just for a minute, he tells himself. See how things are going. It's the only Meatball King he still visits with any regularity; it's also the only Meatball King he still technically owns, but that's just semantics, that's all. Back when they first started expanding he used to like to drop in on all the other locations—mug with the customers, say the line—but after a while it was suggested to him by certain parties that perhaps the individual franchisees might not appreciate the imposition with quite such frequency. "I'm the face of the goddamn company," Dominic reminded them, but what can you do? Times change.

He yanks open the glass door and sucks in the familiar smell of garlic, the dual hum of air-conditioning and industry audible in the background. Right away he feels his blood pressure drop. Dominic likes business. More than that, he *believes* in business in general and in his business specifically, in the honesty of a hard-earned dollar and the viability of the American dream. He's had a job since he was ten years old, sweeping floors at Pathmark back in Newark; how he somehow failed to instill any sort of work ethic in at least three-fifths of his offspring remains a mystery he is unable to solve.

He looks around at the mostly empty tables—well, it's not quite dinnertime yet—frowning at a half-empty Parmesan shaker, a smear on the dessert case at the front. Above the register is a faded picture of the girls from a beach trip back when they still lived in the Valley—June with her head ducked, digging for sea-shells; Lilly and Marianne in a fight; Kit and Olivia still in dia-pers, their rear ends thick with padding underneath their ruffly swimsuits. When Dominic thinks of his daughters this is always the image that comes to him: Five little girls with dark hair and sunburned shoulders. All of their faces turned away.

He's used to a big hello from whoever's working the counter but the girl back there today is one he's never seen before, her ex-pression devoid of any recognition whatsoever. "Can I help you?" she asks dully, no intonation at all.

Dominic frowns. "Who are you?" he asks, his voice coming out small and peevish. He feels old all of a sudden, doddering; there's a moment where everything tilts and he's worried he's go-ing to wind up demented in St. Monica's like his father in New Jersey. *Can you help me?* he wants to ask her. *Can you* help *me? I'm the fucking Meatball King!*

Luckily his manager comes out of the back just then, a dark-eyed kid named Carlos who's been with him for ages. "Hey, Mr. B," he says with a smile, lifting a hand in greeting. "How you doing?"

Dominic feels himself relax. Ninety-two locations in fourteen states at the height of the business, he reminds himself, throwing his shoulders back. That's hardly nothing. That's something to be proud of, in the end. "Never better, Carlos," he says cheerfully. "No complaints."

CHAPTER TWELVE

LILLY

When Lilly gets downstairs two mornings later she finds Colin sitting at the kitchen island in a pair of glasses that are almost certainly not prescription, a thick stack of pages on the table in front of him. "*Cugina!*" he greets her. "What's up?"

"Not much." She glances at his manuscript as she heads for the coffee maker; then, actively feeling all the blood drain out of her body, she glances at it again. "Is that—" she asks, then finds she sincerely cannot make herself finish the sentence.

Colin takes care of it for her: "Your screenplay!" he reports happily. "I'm almost done."

Lilly opens her mouth, then closes it. Tries one more time. "Where did you—"

"Oh, your mom gave it to me," he confesses. "She said you didn't want to take advantage of our relationship, which I think is really decent of you. But seriously, you should have just asked me. You know I'm always glad to help you out."

"Help me out?"

Colin smiles. "It's honestly not bad," he says, tapping the pages with one finger. A signet pinky ring glints in the warm morning light. "A tiny bit self-indulgent, maybe. A little sure of its own cleverness. But the love story, all that stuff about her sister?

That's good work." He takes a swig of his kombucha. "I'd love to mentor you."

"Mentor me?" Lilly echoes. It feels like it's possible they'll be here all day, her helplessly parroting everything he says until finally her head explodes and they have to call in one of those crime scene cleanup companies to scrape her gray matter off the ceiling.

"Why not?" Colin asks mildly. "I mean, let's be real, people ask me all the time, and I always say no because frankly it's a giant drain on my creative resources, but we're family, right?"

"Allegedly," Lilly murmurs.

"You could send me pages every few weeks," he suggests, "and I'd mark them up for you. Offer feedback, you know. Speaking of which, can I just say one more thing?"

Can I stop you? Lilly doesn't reply—not that it matters, since Colin forges right on ahead without waiting for her to answer. "And really, this isn't a comment on the quality of the work product. But it kind of feels like you maybe . . . don't care about this that much."

Lilly feels her whole skeleton straighten up, like someone injected her bones with titanium. "What does that mean?" she asks, her voice a full octave higher than normal. Who the fuck does he think he is, sitting here in her house and presuming to tell her—

"I'm not saying it as a knock on you," he clarifies quickly, and the worst part is that it doesn't actually seem like he is. He actually just seems . . . curious. "And I don't mean writing. You obviously care about writing. I just mean, like, this particular story."

"I care about it," Lilly tells him, but even as she's saying the words she knows they're not entirely true. After all, wasn't she just thinking the same thing in the privacy of her bedroom? Hasn't the other thing—the real thing—been scratching at her door? "I care about it plenty."

"Okay," Colin says, and his voice is so gentle she immediately wants to drown them both in the shallow end of the pool. "Fair enough. You'd know better than I would. But you're a talented writer, Lilly. So if there's something you'd rather be writing, and it kind of seems from what I've read here that maybe there is, I guess I'm just saying . . . I think you should write it."

"Well," Lilly manages. Her face feels like it's on fire. "I will definitely keep that in mind."

She marches back inside and up the stairs to her mother's bedroom, where Cinta is lying in bed drinking coffee and watching Turner Classic Movies, seemingly oblivious to the fact that it's ten thirty in the morning. "You gave Colin my screenplay?" she demands.

"I did!" her mother exclaims, setting her cup down on the nightstand and clapping her hands delightedly. "Did he talk to you about it?"

"How did you even *get* my screenplay?" she asks. Her mother can barely log in to her email; back when the show was airing she briefly ran her own Instagram account, but she kept accidentally posting badly lit selfies taken at unflattering up-angles and offensive memes she didn't actually understand, so finally Olivia took her phone and changed the password.

"Mari helped me," Cinta says now, her voice airy. "It was in the cloud."

"I can't believe you," Lilly says. "Not only to just invade my privacy like that—that part actually doesn't surprise me that much, I have to say—but to turn the thing over to Colin, of all people—"

Cinta's mouth drops open. "Colin is an Academy Award nominee who knows a lot of influential people!"

"Colin is a total blowhard!" Lilly counters.

"I thought you'd be grateful."

"Why would I be grateful?"

"I thought you were too shy to ask him yourself!"

"When have I ever, in my entire life, been too shy to do anything I wanted to do?"

There's a moment of recognition on her mother's face then, like possibly that particular wrinkle hadn't occurred to her. Still, "I was trying to help you," she argues. "You've been moping around this house doing a fat lot of nothing ever since Joe died. If you're going to spend your most beautiful years slouched over your computer giving yourself wrinkles and a hunchback, at least you ought to get something for it."

Lilly opens her mouth, closes it again. She has no idea where to start. "This has nothing to do with Joe," she finally says.

"Doesn't it?" her mother asks archly, turning her attention back to the television. "You're in my way," she announces, flapping her hand in a way that indicates Lilly should move over. After a moment, Lilly does.

* * *

She and Nick go for a walk in Topanga Canyon the following day, wandering the rocky trails while the mockingbirds call to each other in the trees high above them, the smell of grass and salt and sunshine thick in the air. They've seen each other a couple of times since that night at the bar, long rambles through the West Hollywood farmer's market and the quiet, leafy neighborhoods of Pasadena, iced coffees sweating pleasantly in their hands. He's easy to talk to, full of jokes and good humor and stories that might or might not be wholly accurate. Lilly finds she actually likes him quite a lot.

"The twisted part," she says now, pulling Nick out of the way as a woman with two enormous poodles prances by in the opposite direction, "is that she really did think she was helping me."

"I mean." Nick glances at her sidelong, full lips quirking. "She kind of was, wasn't she?"

"What?" Lilly whirls on him. "No!"

"Really?" He shrugs. "I mean, don't get me wrong, I hear you, she went behind your back and you hate him and he's a stuck-up loser and all of that."

"He is a turd," Lilly says witheringly.

"Noted," Nick agrees. "Total turd. But so much of being successful in this town is about knowing the right people, isn't it? And it seems like if you want to be a screenwriter, then your cousin's not a bad guy to, like . . . know."

Lilly bites her lip. He's got a point, obviously. And it's not like she hasn't thought about it; in fact, she spent the last twenty-four hours stewing, loudly, until even Junie reached the limits of her patience and told her she had to let it go. But what Lilly doesn't know how to explain—to Nick, or to her family, or to anyone else—is that accepting help from Colin is as good as acknowledging she isn't talented enough to make it happen. It's like admitting she's been kidding herself this whole time, that maybe she really will only ever get by on luck and connections. That everything everyone ever said about her is true.

"No, of course," she says finally—hoping she sounds like the kind of person who doesn't take any of this too seriously, who hasn't built the entire scaffolding of her identity on a cheerful delusion. "You're right."

"But you're definitely not going to do it."

"Oh, yeah, absolutely not."

Nick laughs at that—loud and full-throated, throwing his head back. "A woman who knows her own mind," he says. "I can appreciate that."

They walk for a while longer without saying anything; the back of his hand brushes hers. He's wearing what Lilly assumes are his gym clothes, a T-shirt with the sleeves cut out and a New York Rangers hat turned backward. She can only imagine what Will Darcy would say about a grown man walking around in public wearing a backward hat like an extra in a Julia Stiles vehicle from the early aughts, which is only one of a great many reasons why it's a good thing she doesn't care what Will Darcy thinks.

"Anyway," Lilly says finally, "who knows. Maybe I'll do that dating show after all, let a dozen guys beat the shit out of each other with those big foam Q-Tips for the pleasure of my company."

"Now that I would like to see."

"I'm sure you would." Their shoulders bump, just casual, and she feels the contact sing all down her arm. "What about you?" she asks. "What do you want to do?"

Nick stops walking for a moment, tilting his head to the side. "Like, when I grow up?"

Lilly feels herself blanch. "I—no," she amends quickly, feeling her face flush. *Big talk*, she thinks with no small amount of shame, *from a woman who's never had a proper job*. "That sounded terrible. I didn't mean—"

"A little bit you did," he says, but he's grinning. "I don't know." They've reached an overlook and he sits down on a large, flat boulder, stretching his long legs out in front of him. "I guess I'm so used to scraping a living together that I've never really had that much time to think about it. Like, I'm grateful to be out here where the weather is good and I meet interesting people. I don't know that I have much of a plan other than that."

Lilly raises her eyebrows—unsure of whether or not to take him at face value, if maybe he's protecting his dreams from her in return. "How very Leonardo-DiCaprio-in-*Titanic* of you," she teases. "And that, I meant exactly how it sounded."

Nick laughs. "Screw you." He reaches for her hand, pulling her down onto the rock beside him. "You want me to fight eleven other guys first?" he asks her quietly, then doesn't bother to wait for an answer before he presses his mouth against hers.

* * *

When she gets back to the house she finds her family in the dining room in the middle of a séance—at least, that's what it looks like, Cinta and Kit and Olivia all sitting sullenly in the dark. "What's wrong?" Lilly asks, frowning out the window. There's an unfamiliar sound and it takes her a moment to realize it's silence, no low humming drone of the A/C. "Did we lose power?"

"Something like that." Olivia's voice is ominous.

"It is possible," their mother says crisply, "that we are a tiny bit behind on the bills."

"Did anyone call the company?" Lilly asks, three blank, cranky faces staring back at her. "Does anyone even know the *name* of the company?"

In the end it's Lilly who does it, crossing her fingers as she recites her credit card number to the bored-sounding customer service attendant. The lights flicker on, then off, then back on again. Lilly holds her breath.

CHAPTER THIRTEEN

WILL

Georgia calls on Thursday—or, more accurately, Georgia calls pretty much every night, and Thursday is when Will finally answers the phone. "I'm sorry," he tells her, instead of hello. He's making himself a bowl of spaghetti, the water boiling cheerfully on the stovetop in the empty house in Pemberly Grove. Charlie's doing *Jimmy Kimmel Live!* tonight. "I'm an asshole."

"You truly are," she agrees amiably. Georgia is four years younger than Will; she was six when their parents died, with scabby knees and riotous dark curls that made her look like a character from *Peanuts*. Now she lives in a doorman building on the Upper West Side and spends her days building custom portfolios and conferencing with Hong Kong. "Did you get my package?"

Will looks around at the half dozen unopened boxes on the counter; in the last week alone she's also sent a three-gallon tub of pretzel nuggets, a travel humidifier, and a candle that purports to smell like freshly cut grass. "Which one?" he can't help but ask.

"Yeah, yeah." He can hear her rolling her eyes all the way across the country. "Sorry for giving a shit about you. I know it makes you want to barf."

"It does," Will says, "but thank you."

"You're welcome," she says primly. "So how's the movie going?"

"It's . . . going," he allows. They've been filming for nine days and are hopelessly behind schedule. Johnny Jones spends most of the day in his trailer drinking gin before periodically emerging in a burst of alleged genius and keeping them all on set until three a.m. Still, it's not like Will isn't grateful for the distraction. He's been itchy and tense ever since the party at Charlie's, Lilly at the house and Caroline in the kitchen and then Nick Harlow of all fucking people squatting on the restaurant patio like an alligator in a New York City toilet. Will's been busy; sure, maybe. But that's not the only reason he's been avoiding Georgia's calls. "It's good."

"Wow," she replies now, her voice even. "What an evocative description. I really feel like I'm getting the full Hollywood experience."

Will sighs. It's like this with Georgia, it always has been, the knowledge that she deserves a different kind of brother lining the walls like lead. "I'm sorry," he says again, poking at the pasta with a wooden spoon.

Georgia sighs. "Don't be sorry," she instructs. "Just—" She breaks off, the silence stretching out for three thousand miles between them. "How are you doing?" she tries. "Like, for real."

Will huffs a laugh. "Now you sound like Charlie."

"Charlie is literally your only friend," Georgia points out. "He's also surprisingly emotionally intelligent for such a hot and famous person."

"He's the full package," Will agrees.

"I'm serious," Georgia presses, her voice a full click lower than he's used to hearing it. "We never really . . . you know. Talked. After."

Will swallows, watching out the window as a grackle builds a nest in Charlie's patio umbrella. He doesn't want Georgia to worry about him. He doesn't want anyone to worry about him, ever, but especially not her. "There's nothing to talk about," he promises, banging his head softly against the wall even as he says it. "Everything is fine."

By the time he hangs up the pasta is overdone and mushy, past the point of saving. Will dumps the entire pot in the trash.

* * *

"Hold on one fucking second," Will says two nights later, grabbing Charlie's arm and yanking him away from an MTV reporter with a microphone as they walk the red carpet for *Major Fantastic*. Well, Charlie is walking it, anyway, his face movie-star luminous beneath the neon marquee of a glittery art deco theater in West Hollywood. Will shuffles along behind him like a weird, spidery manservant, trying not to trip in his fancy shoes. "You actually invited them? I mean, like, all of them?"

Charlie turns and follows his gaze to the black SUV idling at the curb, watching as Lilly and June climb out of the back trailed by the rest of their sisters, all of them tumbling out one after another like a family jug band or members of a religious cult come to look for vulnerable young outsiders to conscript into agrarian servitude and sexual deviance. Their mother brings up the rear in a sequined floor-length gown. "I did." Charlie shrugs, pausing to sign an autograph for a squealing girl behind a barrier. "I said I would, didn't I?"

"I mean, sure," Will concedes. "But people say things all the time without actually following through on them."

"Not me," Charlie says happily, waving to a gaggle of photographers.

"You would never," Will agrees.

"Anyway," Charlie continues as they head toward the doors of the theater, turning his body slightly so that the flashbulbs catch his good side, "you should be thanking me. After the way you crashed and burned with Lilly the other day, somebody had to run your damage control."

Will whirls on him. "Who says I want you to run—" he starts, but Charlie is already gone, swallowed by the teeming crowd like a prop plane disappearing into the Bermuda Triangle. Will frowns, glancing back to watch as the Benedettos work the rope line. He once saw a picture of a flamboyance of flamingoes crowded into a bathroom at a zoo during a hurricane and he thinks of it literally every time he sees them all together: long necks and extravagant pink feathers and the knowledge that, working in tandem, they could probably eat the flesh right off his bones. He hasn't talked to Lilly since that morning on the patio, and he cringes at the memory of it: the proud, panicky way he brushed her off, his brain shorting out so fast and hard he's surprised he didn't pull a muscle. It was all too much, her smile and her sisters and Nick lurking over her shoulder, the palest hint of a smirk on his smug, self-satisfied face. He'd never want to see him again, if he was her.

She's here, though. She's here.

Will tucks his hands into his pockets, trying not to stare—or, at least, trying not to look like he's staring. Lilly's dress is blue tonight, a long slit up one leg and a back that shows off the sharp wings of her shoulder blades. He wonders again what it must be like, to feel so perfectly comfortable everywhere you go.

He falls into step beside her before he can talk himself out of it, trying to walk with the confidence of a person who doesn't get nervous and sweaty in crowds. "So, here's a question," he says, tipping his mouth toward her ear. "What do you think is the over/under on the number of exploding spaceships in this movie?"

"Cute." Lilly doesn't smile—or, she does, but not at him, waving over her shoulder to a couple of paparazzi. "Too bad we can't all be as smart and sophisticated as you, I guess."

"Weird," Will jokes, still hoping there's some way to brazen his way through this. Women like that sometimes, don't they? Brazen men? "I say the same thing to myself in the mirror every morning." Then, when she still just stares at him, utterly stone-faced: "It's three, for the record. Exploding spaceships. I've got an inside source."

"Charlie, right?" Lilly nods seriously. "Your friend whose house you live in and whose food you presumably eat even though you don't respect the work he does or think he's a serious actor?"

Will blinks. He's used to her being rude to him—he *likes* her being rude to him, if he's completely honest with himself—but this feels . . . different than that. "Ouch."

"Oh please," Lilly snaps. "Don't act for one second like I'm hurting your feelings."

"I'm not—" Will breaks off, confused. "Okay?"

Lilly ignores him. "Speaking of friends," she continues, "I've been spending some time with one of yours lately."

Will frowns. "Oh?" he asks. "Who's that?"

"Nick Harlow."

Will flinches at the name before he can quiet the impulse. "Nick Harlow," he manages, "is not my friend."

Lilly raises one eyebrow. "Well, no," she says sweetly. "I guess he wouldn't be."

"I mean it, Lilly." He tries to keep his voice even, his fingers flexing once at his sides. "He's not a good guy."

That makes her laugh. "Meaning what, exactly?"

Will opens his mouth, closes it again. "Meaning," he tries, struggling to think of how to explain it to her, here in the lobby at *Major Fantastic* while her sisters don't bother to pretend not to watch. "Meaning—" He breaks off.

Lilly smirks. "Yeah," she says, reaching out and chucking the underside of his chin with one polished fingernail. "That's what I thought."

Will reaches for her as if by instinct, grabs her hand out of the air. There's a jolt between them, sharp and electric; he's pretty sure she feels it, too, judging by the way her whole body stills for a moment like a fox in the woods. "Let's go somewhere," he murmurs, before he can stop himself. "I mean it, Lilly. Fuck the movie. Let me take you somewhere."

He's not sure which one of them is more shocked. "What the fuck, Will?" she asks—laughing a little, her lush red mouth making a perfect O. "You don't even *like* me that much."

"I don't," he agrees miserably, running a hand over his beard. "I don't! You're entitled. You talk too much. You're, like, a full click too confident in your own cleverness—"

"And you're a sanctimonious snob nobody has ever even heard of!" Lilly interrupts, temper flaring in her eyes as she yanks her hand back. "I cannot believe you, truly. Two seconds ago you're asking me to bail out of here and go to bed with you, and now you're telling me I talk too much?"

"I still want you to bail out of here and go to bed with me," he says, too far gone to bother denying it, "and I don't even know why. I mean, look at us, Lilly. You don't like me, either. There are literally not two people on the planet less romantically compatible."

"Post Malone and Phyllis Schlafly," Lilly counters, like possibly she can't help herself. "Nancy Reagan and Lil Nas X. My parents, conceivably."

"Your parents," Will groans, suddenly remembering. "God, your entire family is like something out of a nineteenth-century German farce. And, like, yeah, fine, conceivably you're a marginally more serious person than your sisters—"

Lilly rounds on him, baring her teeth. "Fuck you," she says. "I am exactly as unserious as my sisters."

"No, no," Will amends quickly, holding both hands up. "You don't understand. I'm saying it as—"

"I know exactly how you're saying it!" She pulls away for real then—color rising in her face, her dark hair wild. "Nick was right about you, Will, you know that? You're an asshole."

"Nick told you that?" Will blinks, stung and stupid, though he guesses he shouldn't be surprised. "What else did Nick tell you?"

Lilly shakes her head as the overhead lights flicker. "Forget it," she says—already turning away from him, the smell of mandarins faint in her wake. "I'm going to find my seat."

"Lilly," he says again; it comes out like *Wait*, but Lilly doesn't, disappearing into the crowd without another word.

CHAPTER FOURTEEN

LILLY

❧

Will was wrong about the movie, actually: in fact it features four exploding spaceships, plus an intergalactic car bomb and an extended slow-motion sequence of Charlie catching half a dozen fireballs to prevent them from hitting an orphanage. Also, it is three hours long. By the time they make it back to the house, all Lilly wants to do is shuffle upstairs, peel her dress off, and crawl directly into bed: Her head hurts. Her feet are killing her. And her neck and shoulders are crunchy and aching with a weird, black anxiety she can't shake. She has no idea what Will was after with her tonight, sidling up to her in the lobby with his dopey jokes and interested expression. She was expecting it to make her feel good to be a jerk to him, and it did for a minute, but then he fixed her with that wounded, baffled look, like a dog who'd been locked outside in a rainstorm, and just like that Lilly wasn't having fun anymore. *Leave it to Will Darcy to be one of those people who can dish it out but can't take it*, she thinks darkly, except for the part where that didn't actually seem to be what was happening.

Ugh, she hates him. She hates him!

But also, he did not look completely terrible in that suit.

She fully intends to climb under the covers with an episode of *Golden Girls* and forget this night ever happened, but when she detours into the kitchen to pull an eye mask out of the freezer she spies Colin out on the patio. He declined Charlie's invitation to the premiere tonight, standing in the upstairs hallway outside the dressing room and subjecting them all to a lengthy monologue about the scourge of superhero franchises and the flattening of the cinema landscape as they slithered into their shapewear on the other side of the door. From the looks of things, he's still going at it, clutching a tumbler of whiskey and gesturing wildly at—

"Charlotte?" Lilly asks, sliding the door open and stepping out into the warm blue night. "What are you doing here?"

"Hi to you, too," Charlotte says with a laugh. She's curled in a lounge chair with her legs tucked underneath her, her red hair loose and lovely; she's holding a glass of white wine in one hand. "I drove over to borrow my mom's old *Silver Palate Cookbook*—"

"And I was practicing my crow pose on the front lawn," Colin pipes up.

"Like one does," Lilly agrees immediately, ignoring the chiding look Charlotte shoots her from across the patio. *It's fine*, she wants to explain; *Colin has never registered a snarky comment in all his days on this miraculous green planet*. His own lack of self-awareness is thicker and more impenetrable than Major Fantastic's nuclear shield.

Sure enough: "We got to chatting," he continues, cheerful and oblivious. "I don't know if you know this about me, but I'm a huge foodie."

"You know, I might have guessed that." Lilly turns to Charlotte. "It's great that you came by, actually. I'm having a girl talk emergency."

"You are?" Charlotte asks, looking at her a little oddly. "Right now?"

"Uh, yup," Lilly says. "I just remembered. Sorry, Colin, do you mind if I borrow her for a minute?"

"Not at all," Colin says magnanimously, pulling his phone out of his pocket. "Charlotte, I'm going to text Caitriona and get the name of that Korean barbecue place she was telling me about so you can check it out. She always knows all the best spots."

Charlotte always knows all the best spots, actually, on account of being a highly regarded chef and restaurant owner, but she doesn't tell that to Colin and somehow Lilly manages to resist pointing it out on her behalf. "I'd love that," is all Charlotte says, then gets up and follows Lilly into the kitchen, Arthur heaving his furry little body up off the slate and trotting dutifully along. "What's up?" she asks Lilly, once the door is safely shut behind them. "Did something happen at the premiere?"

"What? Oh no," Lilly says, taking the bottle of wine out of the fridge and topping Charlotte's glass off; then, on second thought, she pours one for herself, too. "Well, I guess so, kind of, but that's not why I wanted you to come in here. I was just rescuing you."

"Rescuing—what, from Colin?" Charlotte laughs. "He's not actually that bad, you know."

Lilly makes a face over the bowl of her wineglass. "Oh, please."

"He's not!" Charlotte insists. "I mean, he likes to talk, clearly, and he did just use the word *foodie*, but he's really kind of sweet once you get to know him."

"I've known him my entire life," Lilly reminds her immediately, "and I can say with confidence I have not found that to be the case."

"That's . . . not really the same thing."

Lilly shakes her head. "You're losing your edge," she accuses.

"I'm not like you," Charlotte counters. "I don't have an edge."

Lilly isn't sure what that means, exactly, but suddenly she's too exhausted to parse even one more weird social interaction this fine evening. "Okay," she concedes around a yawn, holding a hand up before draining her wine in two long gulps. "I'm going to bed. You're on your own, old friend."

"You know," Charlotte promises with a grin, "I think I will somehow survive."

"I don't doubt it," Lilly says, blowing her a kiss as Charlotte heads back outside onto the patio; still, she glances behind her one more time before she pads up the stairs to her room.

CHAPTER FIFTEEN

WILL

As soon as the movie premieres Charlie has about ten thousand places he needs to be in rapid succession: New York and London and Tokyo and Beijing. Will gets back from set close to midnight and finds him packing a suitcase the size of a conversion van, listening to a guided meditation on his phone. "Shouldn't you get an assistant to do this kind of thing for you?" Will asks, standing in his bedroom doorway eating a bowl of ice cream while Matthew McConaughey gently encourages them to imagine themselves as trees.

Charlie dumps an armful of socks into the bag. "I had one," he says mournfully, "but then all my underwear started disappearing one pair at a time."

"Fair enough." Will stands there for another moment, shifting his weight uncomfortably. Caroline cornered him in the bathroom this morning, waving her phone in his face: "Literally every piece of press about this movie mentions June Benedetto in the first paragraph," she seethed, sleek blond hair beginning to frizz a bit around her temples. "Every single article, William! You need to talk to him."

"*I* need to talk to him?" Will spat a mouthful of toothpaste into the sink. "Why me?"

"You know why," Caroline shot back immediately. "You're his best friend. He trusts you. It sounds different when you say it." She shrugged. "Also, he's mad at me for sending those flowers to Anne Mulgrew and signing his name to the card."

Will wiped her mouth with the back of his hand. "Can't imagine why."

"I'm serious!" Caroline wailed. "If there's one thing those women know how to do, it's bottom-feed. Her mother is already on the Sinclair doing that winking, purposely coy no-comment bullshit. It's tacky. It makes Charlie look tacky." She caught his gaze in the mirror then, lifted her sharp, elegant chin. "He's better than that, don't you think?"

Now Will grits his teeth, watching as Charlie packs his jeans and his running shoes, the expensive vintage watch he bought when he booked *Major Fantastic* and then ruined in the pool by mistake. He still wears it, the thing winking uselessly on his wrist in the pages of *People* and *Us Weekly* and *In Touch*. If he needs to know the time he checks his phone. "Look," he begins, "about June."

Right away, Charlie shakes his head. "Don't," he says, turning his attention to the half dozen bottles of cologne on the dresser. "Seriously, dude—"

"I'm not!" Will protests immediately. "I'm not. But if I was . . ." He thinks of Cinta Benedetto plotting her reality show comeback across the development. He thinks of Lilly's face as she turned away from him at the premiere. He thinks of New York and of *Hamlet*, of letting himself want something—letting himself believe he could have it, even—only to realize the joke was on him the entire time. "It isn't worth it, man."

Charlie smirks at that. "What," he asks, "love?"

Will shrugs. "I don't know," he answers honestly, and it comes out a lot quieter than he means for it to. "Any of it, maybe."

Oh, Charlie doesn't like that. He straightens up quick as if someone has pinched him, dropping a couple of undershirts on top of the suitcase. "Hey," he says, taking half a step in Will's direction. "You all right?"

Right away, Will realizes his mistake. "Yeah, of course," he says, "totally. I didn't mean—"

"Because I can cancel this trip. I don't even really understand what a press tour is, to be completely honest with you. Probably they can just do it without me. Or maybe I can Skype."

That makes Will smile. "Pretty sure they need you on-site, brother," he says, trying to sound as sane as humanly possible. He is sane; at least, he's pretty sure he is. He's just . . . lonely, or something. Sometimes it feels like everyone he meets knows how to be a person except for him.

"A hologram, maybe," Charlie muses, reaching for a pile of T-shirts. Will laughs all the way down the stairs.

* * *

Charlie tells Will to stay at the house in Pemberly Grove for as long as he wants to, and there's technically no reason for him to find a place of his own, but once Charlie and Caro decamp to the East Coast it starts to feel a little bleak—Will shuffling around like Miss Havisham down the quiet, empty hallways, testing out line readings for the benefit of the artificial plants. He eats a lot of waffles. He hangs around on set. Georgia sends him a book of knock-knock jokes from Amazon, and he reads it cover to cover in a single go.

The longer he sticks around the more apparent it starts to become that the builder of this place should probably be on the receiving end of legal action or at the very least a dead fish in his glove compartment: On Monday the microwave door comes off in Will's hand while he's heating up a frozen bean burrito. On Tuesday, the A/C conks out. On Thursday he discovers a bright green fungus blooming under the sink in the downstairs bathroom, and by the time the weekend rolls around the urge to leave is starting to feel immediate, like he ought to make his escape before the whole place collapses around him and he finds himself standing in a pile of rubble in his boxers like something out of a comic strip.

On Sunday he runs out of shampoo, so he gets in the car and drives to Target, where he spends the better part of an hour wandering the pitilessly bright aisles wondering if he needs an Instant Pot or a Forgettle. He thinks he might stay there forever, subsisting entirely on Frappuccinos and cake pops from the Starbucks kiosk up by the registers, but his phone vibrates in his pocket as he's staring hypnotized at an endcap display of multipurpose cleaner arranged in rainbow order. "There are a lot of different kinds of Swiffers," he says, instead of hello.

"What are you doing?" Georgia asks.

"Having a dissociative episode in a big-box store."

"Big night," Georgia replies. He can hear the rustle and hum of the city in the background, horns honking even though it's close to midnight on the East Coast. Will resists the urge to ask if she's being safe. "I'll look for you on the Sinclair."

"'Will Darcy's Hollywood career ended before it began this weekend, following a psychotic break in the parking lot of a Los Angeles–area Target.'"

Georgia snorts. "Just get whatever you went in there for," she advises. "I'll order anything else you need."

"You don't have to do that," he protests, even as he feels the relief flowing through him. "You've gotten me like a hundred things already."

"And yet," Georgia teases. "Families look after each other, right?"

Will blinks, surprised. It's a thing one of their dad's friends told them at their parents' memorial service, Will and Georgia sitting side by side on the boat of a leather couch at their old house in Toluca Lake: "Families look after each other," he intoned, leaning over them like an omen. "And from now on, your family is the two of you." They used to use it as a joke when they were teenagers, covering for each other after curfew or passing the peas across the table at their aunt Marcy's apartment on East 63rd Street. Neither one of them have said it in years.

"Yeah," Will agrees softly. "I guess so."

He almost tells her then, standing alone in housewares: That the movie is a farce and he should never have come out here to begin with. That he misses New York so much he can barely breathe. That he's sorry and grateful she's the one who found him that morning, slumped over the toilet in his bathroom. That he doesn't think he actually wanted to die at all.

Instead he says good night and loads his eleven bags into the trunk of the Land Rover, then gets lost twice on the way back to Charlie's. It's not until he's about to climb into the shower that he realizes he forgot the shampoo.

CHAPTER SIXTEEN

LILLY

Charlie takes off for a press tour a couple of days after the movie premieres, promising June he'll text between interviews. "How long is he gone again?" Lilly asks, finding her out in the backyard later that week. Colin is still camped in their guest room showing no sign of vacating, but a few days ago Kit realized he goes out of his way to avoid seeing any of them in bathing suits, and since then they've all been spending a lot of time by the pool.

"I didn't ask," June reports with a shrug that's not quite careless. "I didn't want to be, you know—" She breaks off, waving her hand in a gesture presumably meant to indicate *vulnerable in any way.* "Now I feel like an idiot, though, because he's in New York partying with the guys from *Saturday Night Live* and I'm here fielding calls from *Celebrity Hot Dog Showdown*—who didn't even want me, PS, they wanted Olivia and got the contact mixed up." She sighs, tossing her phone onto the lounge chair beside her. "I haven't heard from him, in case that wasn't abundantly clear."

"You know," Lilly says, sitting down on the lounge chair beside her, "you were kind of giving off that vibe."

"Yeah." June picks up her phone again, scrolling for a moment before holding the screen up so that Lilly can see Caroline Bingley's Instagram page. The latest post is a picture of Charlie in a swanky-looking bar, his arm slung around a tall, smartly dressed brunette who Lilly doesn't recognize until the moment she does—the same glossy, unidentified woman who was in the photo of Will from that New York gossip blog.

"Who is that?" she asks, ignoring a weird flare of jealousy.

"Will Darcy's sister," June reports immediately. Then, off Lilly's raised eyebrows: "I may have sleuthed a little."

That makes Lilly smile. June has always been too good for any kind of internet detecting, has never known the searing mortification of accidentally liking a post seven weeks back in the feed of an ex's casual female acquaintance. If she's stooping to common social media snooping, she must be at least half in love.

"Let me see," Lilly says. She takes the phone from June's outstretched hand, squinting at the screen over the top of her sunglasses like her mother pretending not to need readers to decipher the menu in a fancy restaurant. Will's sister looks like him, a little—all thick dark eyebrows and haughty expression, that same full mouth and arrogant chin. She's also bonkers pretty, though that doesn't seem like a particularly helpful thing to point out at this particular juncture.

"Well," Lilly says at last, her stomach sinking as she scrolls through Caroline's photo stream. It's a private account, friends and family only, but even the most candid and casual of the images—Caroline and Charlie drinking wine on some European patio, Charlie and Will grinning on the glossy deck of a boat—reveal a kind of sleek, effortless glamour, the kind of life where it's always the magic hour and nobody ever gets a poppy seed stuck in their teeth. Even at the height of *Meet the Benedettos*, Lilly always knew they would never be the same kind of fancy as people like the Bingleys or the Darcys; still, looking at these pictures she can almost smell her own family's desperation sticking to her clothes and hair like red sauce and oregano at the end of a busy restaurant shift. Their money was too new; their clothes were too flashy. Their house wasn't built to last. "They're all friends, right? We knew they were all friends."

The patio door slides open before June can answer. "What are you losers doing?" Olivia wants to know, poking her head out into the yard.

"Stalking Charlie Bingley on social," Lilly replies—straightening her shoulders, waggling the phone in Olivia's direction. "Want to help?"

Olivia's face lights up. "Always," she says, holding her hand out as she skips happily across the flagstone. "Why didn't you text me?"

Kit gets home and joins them a little while later, dragging a couple of lounge chairs together to make a bed big enough for them all to sit on; even Mari comes outside in the end, and if she doesn't exactly help, she doesn't make disapproving noises and talk about the Patriot Act, either, which is almost the same thing. Looking around at the four of them, listening to the familiar rise and fall of their voices, Lilly feels a quick prickle of shame for betraying them, even if it was only for a minute and only in the most secret part of her heart. Maybe they are a little desperate, herself included. But she'd rather be desperate than cold.

"Is Will still in the house?" Kit asks, leaning her head on Lilly's shoulder. She's got Junie's feet in her lap, Olivia curled up beside them; they used to snuggle like this all the time when they were little girls, though they do it less than they used to. Their dad used to call it a Jersey Turnpike Pileup. "Now that Charlie and Caroline are in New York?"

"He sure is," Mari says, before Lilly can answer. "All by his lonesome. What?" she asks when they all turn to look at her, something that's not quite a smile flickering across the pale screen of her face. "I notice things."

"Evidently," Lilly says, surprised by the warm flood of relief rushing through her. She's gotten used to running into him around the neighborhood, she guesses. Probably she's just sensitive to change. Still, she lets herself imagine him alone in the house for a moment, restless and wakeful. Lets herself imagine knocking softly on his door.

Her own phone pings just then, Nick's name appearing on the screen: *Drinks tonight?* he wants to know. Lilly bites her lip, turns her phone facedown on the lounge chair without replying. Tucks the phone underneath her thigh. Not a good person, Will said, and maybe he really does know something scandalous she doesn't; on the other hand, Will probably doesn't think she's a good person, either, and she's not about to let him ruin a perfectly nice time.

Sure, she types, after pulling the phone out again, her thumb flying over the keyboard. *Drinks sound great.*

She turns back to her sisters then, watching idly as Olivia peruses the long-dormant Facebook page of Charlie's high school girlfriend with all the investigative gravitas of Carl Bernstein about to break Watergate. They stay out there, heads ducked close around the glowing screen of June's phone like a coven of witches consulting an oracle, until the sky turns from blue to black and their mother yells at them all to come inside.

CHAPTER SEVENTEEN

KIT

"I have news," Kit announces at Thanksgiving dinner; Cinta put in a catering order, mashed potatoes pooling with butter and stuffing studded with sausage and thyme. Lilly is buttering a dense-looking brick of cornbread while June frowns down at her phone, ignoring her own untouched plate. Mari eschewed the holiday altogether in favor of what she claimed was a two-day poker tournament in Las Vegas, which seemed suspect but not, in all honesty, completely impossible. "I sold two dozen hankies."

He mother looks at her blankly, reaching for the cranberries. "I don't know what that means."

"The ones I've been working on," Kit explains. Probably she should have led with that. "With the embroidery?"

"What, with the swear words on them?" Olivia asks, coming in from the kitchen and flopping down into her seat. "I thought that was just, like, a weird creepy hobby you were doing."

"I mean, it was, at first," Kit admits. "But you know Louie Rowes, the boutique in Beverly Hills? A friend of mine is friends with the buyer there and they liked the look of them, so they ordered a bunch."

"What, to sell?" Her mother frowns.

"Yeah, Mom." Kit frowns back. "To sell."

"Perhaps that will be the thing that saves this family, Katrina," her father says cheerfully, holding his hand out for the tofu. "Snot rags decorated with tiny obscenities. Could be the start of an empire."

Kit tries not to sag in a way that any of the rest of them will notice. Of course she knows the only one her father has ever taken seriously in their entire lives is Lilly; still, every once in a while she forgets. "Could be," she echoes, trying to keep her voice playful. "Never know."

She slips out of the dining room before pie—driving around for a long time listening to the radio, the moon full and heavy overhead. She knows it's stupid—that she's never going to have some second act as a serious designer, that in all likelihood she'll be hawking appetite suppressants on social media for the rest of her life. She's proud of those hankies, though, their details and their intricate stitching. The quiet zip of her needle and thread.

It's after midnight by the time she gets back, letting herself into the darkened foyer and padding barefoot up the steps to her room. On her sewing table is an enormous bouquet of flowers, jasmine and peonies, fat and round and fragrant. The card is signed by all four of her sisters but the message is written in Lilly's familiar scrawl:

Congratulations, you spectacularly bright light, you.
The rest of us can't wait to catch colds.

Kit smiles, glancing out the door and down the hall at the rooms where the rest of them are sleeping, wondering where in the entire city of Los Angeles Lilly found an open florist at nine p.m. on Thanksgiving night. She sits down at the table and plucks a handkerchief from the pile, threads her needle with floss the color of blood: *Sister*, she embroiders, the quiet of the house all around her. *Love*.

CHAPTER EIGHTEEN

LILLY

"I'm a simple man, Lilly Benedetto," Nick says a couple of weeks later, raising his rocks glass in a toast. "But I will admit it is, on occasion, nice to eat dinner at an establishment where one is not worried about accidentally touching old gum underneath the table."

Lilly laughs. "They should put that on Yelp," she says as they clink. They're at Charlotte's for the December pop-up, Sharon Jones being piped through the sound system and the hum and clatter of the dining room all around them. It's the last dinner before the holidays, the restaurant cozy and candlelit and smelling of citrus and cedar. Lilly loves this time of year—the whole city full of palm trees decked with twinkle lights and Santas wearing board shorts outside the Salvation Army, the cheery incongruity of celebrating Christmas in a desert.

She likes being here with Nick, too: how at ease he is with everyone around him, making fast friends with a pair of hipster jewelry designers seated beside them and joshing around with the waitstaff. He's wearing a thermal pushed to his elbows, a leather bracelet wrapped around one wrist. The hair on his arms is golden in the light from the tiny votives lining the long tables. They've been seeing a lot of each other lately, grabbing lazy breakfasts at

Little Dom's and going for long walks in Griffith Park; he's the kind of person who can talk to anyone, who makes friends wherever he goes. He's also an incorrigible, indiscriminate flirt, making eyes at the middle-aged housewives walking their doodles in Malibu and flashing his most charming smile at the bellman outside the Ace in DTLA, and if it can sometimes feel the tiniest bit tedious to wait around while he chats up the pixie-haired barista at Coffee Bean about the provenance of her fair-trade French roast, well, Lilly thinks there are worse qualities in a person. Better to like everyone than to like no one at all.

Tonight Charlotte's featuring a Chinese American chef who grew up in Monterey Park, and the air is redolent with ginger and lemongrass and the cocktails spiked with star anise. Lilly and Nick split an enormous bowl of fried rice topped with duck eggs, their sunny yolks flecked with tiny black sesame seeds. The whole effect is bright and festive, the kind of showing that will have Charlotte and Lodge on every food blog in town come morning, but Lilly can't get over the jangly, unsettled feeling that something—someone—is missing. She tells herself it's just because her sisters aren't here—Kit and Olivia begged off in favor of a launch party for some dubious NFT platform, June is nursing a cold, and Mari is Mari; Colin is here, somewhere, though thankfully he seems to have found someone else to pester for the night—and she always feels a little at sea without them. Still, the truth is she keeps catching herself glancing at the door, hoping in useless secret for . . . well.

"You didn't happen to invite Will again, did you?" she whispered to Charlotte the other morning at yoga, tying to sound as casual as humanly possible.

"I did not," Charlotte whispered back, fixing Lilly with an

extremely skeptical expression as she pressed her thumbs against her third eye. "Should I have?"

"No!" Lilly said, too loudly; up at the front of the room, the instructor glanced disapprovingly in her direction. "Of course not. I just wanted to be . . . prepared. You know. For like. Whatever."

"Mm-hmm," Charlotte said, dropping down into a deep forward fold. "Eyes on your mat, Benedetto."

Now Lilly nibbles the edge of a sparerib, listening with one ear as Nick engages the waiter about some gruesome-sounding Netflix series and clocking with some interest his smooth, warm palm creeping higher on her thigh underneath the table. They haven't slept together yet, not that she's necessarily opposed to the idea. The opportunity just hasn't presented itself, on top of which she has the sneaking suspicion that his bedroom is likely going to be of the mattress-on-the-floor variety, and she's trying to put off that moment of reckoning for as long as she can. Still, the last couple of days she's been thinking she ought to just get on with it already: it's been two years since Joe, and if it's true that Nick doesn't make her feel like her very skin is on fire the same way Will did that night in Rebecca Barnes's hedge maze, at least he's not a pompous, self-satisfied jackass who goes around getting people fired from their jobs for no good reason.

She waits until the waiter has trotted back off to the kitchen, then laces her fingers through Nick's. "Hey," she says impetuously, ducking her face close to his. "Do you want to get out of here?" Charlotte won't miss her, Lilly reasons. Even if she does, she'll understand. "Like, now?"

Nick grins at that, one eyebrow arching. "Like now, huh?" he teases. "I mean, yeah. I could probably be convinced."

"Good," Lilly says, glancing a kiss off the side of his mouth.

"Let me just run and powder my nose, and then I'll, you know. Do the convincing."

Nick laughs, raising his glass in her direction. "I honestly cannot wait."

She gets up and threads her way through the maze of long wooden tables, heading for the ladies' room; when she rounds the corner into the dim, narrow hallway, she stops short at the sight of Charlotte with her back to the door of the storage closet. Colin—Colin?—is looming over her, suddenly taller and more intimidating than Lilly thinks of him as being; one hand is braced on the wall beside Charlotte, and the other very much on her ass.

The panic and rage surge through Lilly like a riptide, some earthquake in the middle of the Pacific sending a tsunami of cortisol through her veins. "What the fuck?" she demands, booking it down the hall in two huge steps and whacking Colin on one arm. God, she should have known. Guys like him are like this: they get one speck of acclaim and they think they can just go around taking whatever the hell they want, putting their grubby, entitled paws on asses as far as the eye can see. Where are those women from the *New York Times* when you need them? They'd grind him up in a Vitamix and eat him with a Tostito. "Get the fuck away from her."

She's so intent on giving Colin a piece of her mind that it takes her a second to register Charlotte's hand on her arm, the way she's pulling Lilly away from Colin and slotting herself in between them. "Lilly," she's saying. "Lilly Lilly Lilly, stop. Stop."

Lilly turns to look at Charlotte, breathless. "What?" she asks, blowing a strand of hair out of her face.

"It's not what . . . I mean, we were . . ." Charlotte trails off. "This," she tries again, reaching for Colin's hand and lacing their fingers together, "is like . . . a thing that's happening."

"Wait, what?" Lilly repeats. She's hallucinating, she must be. There's no way Charlotte could have been fooling around with Colin, of all people, because she wanted to. "No it isn't."

Charlotte shoots her a look. "I was going to talk to you later tonight," she says quietly. "The two of us have been . . . you know."

"I don't!" Lilly exclaims, looking frantically back and forth between them. "I definitely do not."

"Lilly," Charlotte chides. "Come on."

"No, no, I get it," Colin says, completely misreading her horror. "Foods touching, et cetera." He grins. "The foods, in this situation, being Char and me."

Charlotte laughs at that, her hand still tucked into his for safekeeping. Lilly only stares.

* * *

Charlotte gets called into the kitchen before Lilly regains the ability to make compound sentences. Back in the dining room she sits down hard across from Nick, who's chatting animatedly about blockchain with the second lead from a Starz show about a pod of sexy mermaids who do organized crime. "Hey," he says. "Ready to go?"

"Why?" she asks, momentarily forgetting, then remembers and shakes her head. "I just caught Charlotte fooling around with my cousin in the hallway," she announces, reaching for the bottle of wine on the table and splashing a generous amount into her glass.

"Whoa." Nick smiles crookedly, slinging an arm around the back of her chair. "Good for them."

"What? No! Not good for them," Lilly corrects him. "Not good for her, especially. Colin, you might recall, is the worst. He's one of those guys who calls himself a sneakerhead. His favorite writer is Jonathan Franzen."

Nick looks at her blankly. "I . . . don't know who that is."

Lilly tries not to roll her eyes. "It doesn't matter," she concedes. "The point is, she's amazing and hilarious and successful, and he's a total chump with exactly zero redeeming qualities."

"Didn't you say he was nominated for an Academy Award last year?"

"That is emphatically not the point!"

It comes out louder than she means for it to, and the merman enforcer looks over curiously; Nick shoots him a look that pretty clearly communicates *Women, am I right*, and Lilly briefly considers stabbing him with a fork. "Relax," he says, patting her arm conciliatorily. "The heart wants what it wants, no?"

"Can I ask you something?" Lilly snaps, draining her wine in two big, unladylike gulps. "Has anyone, ever, in the history of the universe, been calmed down by someone telling them to relax?"

Nick's cool-guy attitude falters then, just a little. "Easy," he says, which is even worse than *relax* as far as Lilly is concerned, but she doesn't say so out loud. "I guess I just don't understand why you're getting so worked up about it, that's all."

"Because—because—" Lilly breaks off. She wants to tell Nick that Charlotte deserves a soul mate. She wants to tell him she's tired of watching Colin get things he hasn't earned. She wants to tell him that sometimes the gulf between how she knows things should be and how they actually are is enough to make her crazy, but she doesn't know how to explain that to Nick, or to anyone else, really, so she's left sitting at this table with an empty wineglass and enough potential energy roiling inside her to run clear out to the desert and back.

The server appears just then, setting dessert down in front of them: tiny, intricate ginger cakes topped with fresh whipped cream and edible flowers. "Forget it," Lilly says finally, lifting her fork and taking a bite. She can tell objectively that it is very delicious. Still, it tastes like sand in her mouth.

* * *

She sticks around the restaurant until the last of the stragglers have finished their nightcaps, turning down Nick's offer of one last drink at a bar he knows nearby. "Next time," she promises, though if she's being honest with herself the zing of excitement she felt when she thought about going back to his apartment has already fizzled, fading like a cheap pair of jeans. "I'll text you."

Once he's gone she finds Charlotte cleaning up in the back, wiping down the prep station with a kitchen rag while Aretha Franklin wails on a little Bluetooth speaker and tonight's featured chef packs up her knives. "Dinner was incredible," Lilly says, reaching out and touching the woman's arm; she can't be more than twenty-two or twenty-three, her glossy dark hair in a thick rope down her back and her expression equal parts dazed and elated. "Whenever you open a place of your own, I'll definitely be first in line." She looks over at Charlotte, who's scrubbing at a crusted patch of sauce on the industrial range like it's personally offended her. "Can we talk?"

Charlotte exhales, dropping the rag on the counter. "Totally," she says, washing her hands and leading Lilly back out into the dining room, untying her apron before sinking onto a stool at the bar. "Do you want to go first, or should I?"

"I mean, you should, right?" Lilly shrugs. "Explain yourself, et cetera."

"*Explain* myself?" Right away, Charlotte straightens up. "Lilly, I thought you stuck around so you could apologize."

Lilly stares at her blankly. "For what?"

"Are you serious?" Charlotte laughs, though in truth she doesn't sound particularly tickled. "For being a horror show at my place of business, to start with."

Lilly thinks back on the scene in the hallway, considering the possibility. "To Colin, maybe," she concedes after a moment. "Not to you."

"Lilly!" Charlotte says, in a voice like maybe Lilly just isn't paying attention. "Colin is my boyfriend."

"Oh my god," Lilly says, dropping her head into her hands, "please don't say that."

Charlotte sighs loudly. "Can you stop?"

"No!" Lilly fires back. She doesn't understand what's happening here; it feels like she's talking to a stranger, not a person with whom she's been sharing a stall in a public bathroom for the better part of a decade and a half. Charlotte and Colin? It's like when June was hooking up with Pete Davidson, only worse. "Also, I'm sorry, he's your boyfriend? Since when?"

"Since recently!"

"I mean, it would have to be pretty recent, since you literally just met five minutes ago."

Charlotte rolls her eyes. "We *literally* met at your high school graduation, Lilly. And again at your mom's fiftieth, and another time at Kit's wedding weekend, and then also in the ER after Junie's Gatsby thing—"

"Okay fine," Lilly interrupts, throwing her hands up. "Whatever." She's flailing, she can feel it, like she's tripped at the top of a mountain and is scrabbling for purchase as she somersaults her inelegant way down. "You guys are childhood sweethearts and your love for him has been simmering in secret since puberty. That didn't seem like something you wanted to mention to me?"

"No, actually! Because I knew you were going to react like this."

"I'm reacting appropriately!"

"You're reacting like a psycho!" Charlotte shakes her head. "Can I ask you something?" she says, then presses ahead before Lilly can respond. "Has it ever occurred to you that it's possible your objections to Colin have a lot more to do with you than they do with him?"

"Of course it has," Lilly says, feeling her face heat up. "And I can assure you, my objections to Colin are a direct result of twenty-eight years of tolerating his smarmy, entitled, largely talentless—"

"He's not talentless, Lilly!" Charlotte shakes her head. "He's not. He's smart, and he's kind, and he's actually been really good to me so far, and I've gotta tell you, to the outside observer it sort of seems like maybe you're jealous that he's doing what he set out to do instead of hanging around his parents' house waiting for something to happen—"

"And to the outside observer it sort of seems like you're settling for the poor man's Zach Braff because you're afraid you're never going to find a guy who isn't a total loser!"

Both of them are quiet for a minute, the air between them strained and sludgy. Lilly digs the heels of her hands into her eyes. She's spent the last few years worrying she's never going to be anyone but a reality TV footnote, destined for nothing but casual mockery. It sucks to know Charlotte thinks so, too.

"Look," she says finally, "it's late. Obviously we're both tired, and—"

"Yeah," Charlotte agrees, not quite meeting her eyes. "Of course."

Lilly picks her purse up off the table. Neither one of them says good night.

* * *

She stomps out into the parking lot, unlocks the Honda. She only finally got it back from the mechanic a couple of days ago, and she mutters a quiet thank-you to Joe, wherever he is, when for once the car starts up as soon as she turns the key in the ignition. She feels uncomfortable and exposed, like she's walking around in public with a visible panty line. She has no idea why Charlotte blew up at her like that—after all, what is a best friend even good for, if not to save you from romantic shame and degradation at the hands of their loser cousin? Lilly's, like, seventy-five percent sure she's not the asshole here.

Sixty-five.

Fifty at least.

She idles in the parking lot for a minute, head back against the seat. She used to imagine this car still smelled like Joe, his skin and his laundry detergent and the wintergreen gum he always chewed, the zing of it behind his teeth whenever they kissed. Now it kind of just smells like rust. It's starting to feel this way lately, like maybe he never actually existed. Like he was a character on a show that got canceled two seasons ago.

When she gets back to the house June and Olivia are sitting at the kitchen island in the half dark, passing a pint of low-calorie dairy-free frozen dessert back and forth. "How was dinner?" June asks, waving her spoon in greeting.

"It sucked," Lilly announces, tossing her purse on the counter with more force than is perhaps strictly necessary. "Did you know Charlotte is sleeping with Colin?"

She's fully expecting her sisters to gasp in piercing horror but instead neither one of them says anything for a moment, like they're a pair of elder matchmakers taking the union under consideration. "Did you know?" Lilly presses, suddenly filled with deep suspicion.

"No," Olivia says thoughtfully, "but it makes sense, right? They're both, like, nerds."

Lilly whirls on her. "Charlotte isn't a nerd," she says witheringly.

"I mean, she kind of is," Olivia counters without malice. "Not in a bad way."

"She won a James Beard Award two years ago!"

"Okay, so she's a nerd with a James Beard Award."

Lilly sighs loudly, holding her hand out for the ice cream. She doesn't know why nobody seems properly outraged here. "Are you listening to this?" she asks, turning to June. "Colin! I would literally rather be alone for the rest of my life, rattling around this house with pantyhose on my head like Little Edie, than have sex with Colin."

"That's good," Olivia puts in helpfully, "since it would be incest."

Lilly rolls her eyes, frowning down at the cardboard carton. "What am I even eating right now? PS, it's disgusting."

"Kit and I are doing a partnership," Olivia tells her, peering curiously at the label. "I think it's mostly just air."

"It tastes like lint."

"Does she seem to like him?" June asks, pulling one leg up

onto her stool and resting her chin on her knee. "Charlotte, I mean."

"I—" Lilly breaks off. She thinks of the way Charlotte was looking at Colin out on the patio the night of Charlie's premiere, as if she was actually interested in whatever boring, pedantic thing he was talking about. She thinks of the dozens of bad Tinder dates Charlotte has endured in the last five years. She thinks of the way she reached for his hand in the hallway at the restaurant earlier this evening—instinctive, like she's already gotten used to the way it feels in hers. "Kind of," she admits grudgingly.

"Well then," June says, shaking her head when Lilly holds the rest of the poison ice cream out in her direction. "Maybe it's not such bad news after all."

"Why are you like this?" Lilly asks her. June only grins.

Lilly says her good nights and shuffles crabbily upstairs to the bathroom, where she brushes the fake-sugar aftertaste from her mouth. She should have known June was the wrong person to talk to about this. She should have brought it to Mari, who never has a nice word to say about anybody. She should have brought it to Kit. Still, the more she thinks about it the more she realizes she doesn't actually want to complain to Mari or Kit.

As a matter of fact, the person she actually wants to complain to is—

Well.

She pushes Will's face from her mind and crawls under the covers, stares at the sliver of moon hanging in the purple sky outside the window. She doesn't fall asleep for a long time.

CHAPTER NINETEEN

CHARLIE

For the record: he definitely doesn't ghost June *intentionally*.

He just gets so busy. Which, okay, sounds like a bullshit excuse, and truthfully it is kind of a bullshit excuse, but also, it's true! It's true. Who is busier than him right now? Well, the president, probably. Maybe the head of Sony Pictures. But after that: Charlie Bingley, who is appearing on three different magazine covers and four network talk shows this week alone, and who held his pee for four straight hours yesterday afternoon because Caroline was in meetings and in her absence he didn't know who to ask for permission to go to the bathroom, is the most overexposed person in Hollywood. It says so right there on the Sinclair.

Anyway, he leaves for New York fully intending to text June when he gets there, but then it's a circus and every time he remembers there's a reason he can't do it in the moment—one time Caroline is holding his phone in her purse while he does a photo shoot for *Vanity Fair* in a vintage Camaro; another time he's snorting cocaine off a conference table with the head writer of *SNL*—and then suddenly it's four days later and the whole thing stops feeling quite so urgent, the memory of her muffled from three thousand miles away. This happens to Charlie sometimes, though he doesn't like to admit it: a certain kind of distractibility, like that fish from

Finding Nemo. A habit of accidentally forgetting whatever isn't right in front of his face.

Still, he's going to call her. Tomorrow, probably. If not, definitely the day after that.

And in the meantime—

"Charlie," Caroline says, her hand whisper-light on his shoulder, "there's somebody I want you to meet."

CHAPTER TWENTY

LILLY

Her head is still jangling when she wakes up the following morning, so she laces up her sneakers and takes herself for a long, rambling walk to the Topanga Canyon overlook. Lilly loves it out here—the sunshine and the sagebrush and the black walnut trees, the odd mule deer nosing quietly along the side of the trail. The year after Joe died, she wore through the soles of two different pairs of shoes.

When she gets back to the house she finds June sitting in the media room with the blinds drawn, watching one of those competitive cooking shows where the contestants have to sabotage each other by hiding each other's paring knives or replacing all the salt with ricin. She hovers in the doorway for a moment, watching as June glances at her phone, then tosses it onto the couch with a sigh that seems to come from deep inside her chest cavity. A minute later, she picks it up again.

Lilly chews her bottom lip. "He still hasn't texted?" she asks.

"Don't you think I would have told you if he'd texted?" June fires back. Then: "Sorry," she says immediately, even though her tone was completely mild for anyone besides June. She yanks distractedly at the end of her ponytail. "No, he still hasn't texted. Caroline messaged me this morning, though. It sounds like they're not going to be back in LA for a while. I guess they're going to spend the holidays with some family in Boston."

"Boston is terrible," Lilly declares immediately and with great conviction, though in fact she has never actually been there. Still, the very thought of it conjures a mental tableau of Ben Affleck hoovering Dunkin' Donuts in a beer-soaked depression while grown men paint their faces in the team colors of the New England Patriots and it's always twenty-seven degrees Fahrenheit. "Who purposely spends winter in the Northeast, anyway?" Lilly continues, perching on the arm of the sofa. "It's like bragging that you're going to pass a relaxing summer nestled behind Satan's nutsack."

"Evocative."

"Thank you."

"I'm almost thirty years old," June moans, flopping backward against the mountain of rooster-print throw pillows their mother had custom-made during her brief but memorable French country period. "I live at home with my parents. I'm a dried-up party girl whose entire claim to fame was being third banana on a now-defunct reality show that once dedicated an entire episode to whether or not my medical aesthetician could successfully shrink a whitehead in time for Demi Lovato's birthday party. This is humiliating."

"Oh, that's not true," Lilly counters. "You were second banana at least."

"Mean!" June cries, but she's laughing, which was the point. "I'm serious. We used to be at least a little bit fabulous, weren't we? I'm pretty sure we used to be at least a little bit fabulous."

Lilly considers that. It feels like this lately, if she's being honest with herself: Like all of them speak a disappearing language, like none of the old rules apply. Like any day now a team of archaeologists is going to show up at Pemberly Grove and sink an informational plaque into the ground: ON THIS SITE WAS LOCATED THE HOME OF DOMINIC BENEDETTO AND HIS FIVE DAUGHTERS, BOURGEOIS LAUGHINGSTOCKS, TWENTY-FIRST CENTURY BCE. They're a civilization in decline, her family. If it isn't already over, it sure as shit will be soon.

"Well then," Lilly suggests, because she cannot bear the thought of it for one more moment, "let's go out and be fabulous."

She's expecting June to turn her down but instead her sister looks immediately interested. "Really?" she asks.

Lilly shrugs. "Sure," she says, though in truth she's not even sure what that would entail at this point. She stopped going out so much after Joe, the shine worn off the whole scene like costume jewelry passed through too many hands. Still, fundamentally Lilly feels about clubs the way she imagines moms of three from the Upper Midwest feel about Target, which is that as soon as she enters one—no matter which or where or whether she's been there before—she is instantly, utterly at home. She can think of worse things to do tonight.

She rounds up Kit and Olivia, who are out on the patio pretending to meditate as part of a sponsored campaign they're doing for a mindfulness app. Tony clicks busily away. "We need to go out and be fabulous," she reports.

Olivia cracks one eye open. "When are we not?" she retorts, but she dutifully whips her phone out of her shorts pocket and three minutes later has them on the list for a table at a club opening in West Hollywood, a bottle of champagne icing in anticipation of their arrival. "Fabulous enough for you?" she asks pointedly, and Lilly grins.

That night they crowd into June and Lilly's bathroom to get

ready, Kit and Mari jostling each other for sink space and the whole house smelling of product and burning hair. Junie sits on the closed toilet lid and tilts her chin up so that Kit can do her eyeliner while Lilly sticks her dress to her boobs with body tape leftover from Olivia's burlesque-themed eighteenth birthday. When that old Montell Jordan song comes on shuffle Kit turns it up until it's shaking the floor of the house, all of them singing along like a bunch of goobers at a middle-school dance. What do people *do* who don't have sisters? Lilly feels heartbroken for them.

At last they're all dressed and plucked and painted, ambling down the hallway in a cloud of perfume. "Wait!" June calls urgently, stopping so short that they all bang into each other on the landing like something out of *Looney Tunes*. "We need a picture." She holds her phone up, the five of them clustering together as June purses her lips and clicks. "Okay," she says, once she's satisfied. "Let's go."

Lilly knows what people say about her family—that they're crass or that they're grasping, definitive proof that money cannot buy good taste. *Those people can go fuck themselves*, Lilly thinks happily, then piles into the car behind her gaggle of chattering sisters, all of them zooming off into the balmy desert night.

* * *

The club is hot and loud and crowded, the wallpaper vaguely baroque; they get their drinks and settle in, Junie drifting off to say hello to some girls she knows who sell expensive condos on the Hollywood Channel while Kit and Olivia pose for selfies in front of a neon sign that says FOR SHAME. "This is good," Lilly announces, downing her champagne perhaps more quickly than necessary. Isobel is here, perched on a balcony up in the VIP area, her shoulders bare and sharp-looking. "I'm glad we did this." Mari nibbles her hair in reply.

Lilly waves to Isobel, who smiles tightly before turning her attention elsewhere. She pulls out her phone and pretends to send a text. The truth is now that they're here the whole errand feels deeply and abruptly ridiculous: the dresses and the crowd and the angling to be photographed, the bottle service they certainly cannot afford. Probably she should have suggested a movie night instead.

Finally she peels off to go to the bathroom, slipping neatly past two girls doing lines off the backs of their manicured hands and shutting herself safely inside a stall. She's just about to flush when she hears the door swing open, a cloud of Dior wafting in. "—the most pathetic," a woman's voice is saying. "Did you see that, like, all five Benedetto sisters are floating around out there?"

"Oh my god, yes," a second voice agrees, this one vaguely familiar. "In Forever 21's most glamorous evening wear."

The first one snorts. "There goes the neighborhood, et cetera."

"It's fine," a third voice says—Isobel's, Lilly realizes suddenly, high and musical and the slightest bit French for no discernable reason. "I mean, you know it's only a matter of time before one of them does something to get kicked out and banned for life. Just make sure you don't wind up in any photos together for them to splash on every conceivable social media site as supposed proof of how people still tolerate them and you'll be good."

Lilly frowns, sitting down fully dressed on the toilet and trying to ignore the familiar drop in her chest. It's not so much that her feelings are hurt. Sure, they are, a little, but she's heard plenty of way meaner stuff before, both in the bathroom at Saint Ann's before homeroom and in the opening monologue of the Golden

Globe Awards. It's not a big deal. It's just that it gets tiring some-times, being a national punch line. It's just that there was a time when she thought Isobel was her friend.

For a moment she thinks about bursting out of the stall like the Kool-Aid Man and embarrassing them, granting herself the small pleasure of watching their contoured faces go white, but in the end it feels like a lot of work for nothing. It's her own fault, probably: it was silly of her to come out to begin with, to think this would solve June's broken heart or her own restless bore-dom, the feeling that she forgot to do something important and now it's too late.

All at once Lilly is exhausted—the noise and the warm crush of bodies, the thump of the bass in her spine. She thinks she might beg off, get an Uber and spend the rest of the night at home, but when she goes to let her sisters know she's leaving, she can't find them. They're not at the bar or camped on the low cluster of couches or behind the rope in the cordoned-off VIP area—which, not for nothing, she doesn't think they'd actually be allowed into anymore. They're not fighting a minor pop star and her entourage in the alley outside the club.

Where are you??? she texts the group chat, a strange flush of panic buzzing through her. For one truly unhinged moment, she feels like she might be about to cry. *Did you leave???*

Finally she spots them in the center of the dance floor: all four of them clustered together, luminous in the strobing lights. They look like a frolic of fairies, a tangle of sequins and limbs.

"There she is!" June hollers as Lilly approaches, unsteady with relief at the sight of them. "Come dance!"

Lilly shakes her head, jerking a thumb toward the exit. "I think I'm actually going to—"

"No way!" Kit interrupts, grabbing Lilly by both hands and pulling her into the circle. "Stay with us."

So: Lilly stays.

They dance for a long time, sweaty and breathless: their arms wrapped around each other, their hair in each other's mouths. For a while Lilly forgets how little she has to show for herself, after everything. For a while she just feels . . . glad.

"Hey," someone says, pointing his finger in their direction; when she turns to look it's an actor she recognizes vaguely from a handful of Christmas movies on Netflix, handsome and affable and drunk. "Aren't you—?"

"Sisters?" Lilly supplies, gathering them tight around her as she bares her teeth in a smile. "How'd you guess?"

* * *

Their uncle Lou and aunt Veronica come from New York for Christmas, descending on Pemberly Grove with a panettone fresh out of a Bay Ridge bakery and a dozen brown paper shopping bags from Bloomingdale's. Lou and Dominic grew up together back in Newark; Lou was a silent partner in the Meatball King back in the early aughts, but instead of spending the returns maintaining the lifestyle to which his daughters had quickly become accustomed, Lou quietly invested his portion in some tech startups out of Silicon Valley, and now neither he nor Veronica have to work ever again. Instead the two of them spend most of the year traveling in Europe and South America, splitting their time at home between a Craftsman in Carmel and a tony apartment in Brooklyn Heights.

It's a cozy, boozy holiday, Veronica dragging them all to the seafood market so she can make the Seven Fishes and everyone staying up late to watch *The Godfather*, a Benedetto family tradition. They get dressed up and go to the Festival of Carols, drink champagne from juice glasses around the pool on Christmas morning. Olivia posts a photo of herself in a red and white bikini and a Santa hat on Instagram, and it gets four hundred thousand likes. It's the first Christmas Lilly's felt like herself in a long time, and if there's a tiny part of her that can't help but wonder if it's the last one they'll spend in this house, well, she does her damnedest to put the idea out of her mind.

She pulls June into the pantry beside a couple of forgotten meal kits, which have begun to emit an odor all of them have tacitly decided to ignore: "How you doing?" she asks, plucking a bag of red and green M&M's off the shelf and holding it out in June's direction. June's been shining it on, bingeing Hallmark movies and making pizzelles with the rest of them, though Lilly can't help but notice that she hasn't actually eaten any of them.

Now she waves off both the candy and the question. "I'm fine," June insists, and her smile is almost convincing. "I promise. Honestly, we were barely even dating. If I were Taylor Swift I probably wouldn't even bother writing a song."

"Okay." Lilly takes a breath, and then she says it. "Junie," she begins quietly, "you're getting a tiny bit thin."

Right away June's shoulders straighten, her eyes flashing wary and hot. "I said I was fine, Lilly."

"June—"

"I'm the big sister, all right?" she asks, brushing past Lilly and out into the kitchen. "I know neither one of us acts like it, but it's true."

Lilly isn't buying it, and apparently neither is Veronica: "Why don't you come back East with us after New Year's, Junebug?" she suggests later that evening. They're drinking Manhattans around the fireplace, which keeps flickering out intermittently and filling the room with the unmistakable smell of a gas leak. "Do some shopping, see some theater."

"Eat at a restaurant that doesn't have microgreens on the menu," Lou puts in, patting his gut.

"It's not like we don't have the room," Veronica continues, raising her voice so that June can hear her over the sound of Cinta and Colin warbling an extended version of "Baby It's Cold Outside" at the top of their voices. "Louie's going to be traveling. You'd be doing me a favor. I get weird when I'm alone too long. I start talking to the cats."

"You talk to the cats regardless," Lou says mildly.

Lilly smiles. Veronica and Lou have always been a stark contrast to her own parents: how much they seem to like each other, the two of them always holding hands and teasing each other with little inside jokes. Lilly remembers staying at their apartment in New York back when she was fourteen or fifteen and realizing one of them had written a dirty little note to the other in the magnetic poetry kit on the stainless-steel fridge.

"Anyway," Veronica says now, "you should think about it. You too, Lilly."

Lilly shakes her head. "That sounds amazing, but I should stay here and get some work done," she says, which is true, though it's not the only reason: She likes to have everyone in one place, where she can see them. She likes to be able to make sure everyone is whole.

"I'll go!" Olivia pipes up from the other end of the couch, still in her red and white bikini. Veronica, reaching for her wineglass, politely pretends she didn't hear.

* * *

Lilly gets up early the day after Christmas and drives to Charlotte's house in Silver Lake, a cheery yellow bungalow with a riot of lavender and rosemary growing in a wild tangle outside the front door. "I fucked up," she announces when Charlotte answers.

"You did," Charlotte agrees, stepping back to let her in.

They look at each other for a moment, wary. Charlotte is wearing a Johnson & Wales tank top and a pair of reindeer antlers, her bright red hair a thick rope of braid slung over one freckled shoulder. "Come on," she says at last, antlers bouncing as she nods toward the kitchen. "There's coffee."

Lilly follows her down the hallway. She loves Charlotte's place: the airiness of it, the arched doors and clay tile and hundreds of cookbooks lining the shelves in the living room. A bright pair of screen prints hangs above the sofa; a quilt Charlotte's mother made at a women's retreat in Taos slouches over the back of the chair. Lilly thinks she'd like to have something similar, if she ever manages to get it together enough to move out of her childhood bedroom again—not the specific décor of this place so much as the feel of it, like an actual adult woman lives here complete with her own set of wineglasses and several potted plants.

"I'm sorry," she says, once Charlotte has handed her a mug—smooth, heavy pottery, hand-thrown by a ceramicist Charlotte knows through work. "You're my best friend, and I love you, and you deserved better than my shitty behavior. No matter what baggage I have around Colin, there was no reason for me to be . . ."

She trails off, waving her hand vaguely, but Charlotte only tilts her head to the side.

"Go on."

Lilly sighs loudly. "A cranky old bitch, okay? Is that what you want to hear?"

"Yes," Charlotte says immediately. "That's actually exactly what I want to hear."

"Fine," Lilly replies. "In that case, I'm very sorry I was a cranky old bitch to your boyfriend and also, you know." She winces. "Accused him of sexual assault."

Charlotte presses her lips together, like possibly she's trying to hide a smile. "You did do that, didn't you."

"I did," Lilly says grimly.

"Yeah." Charlotte sits down on a stool at the kitchen island, wrapping both hands around her mug. "He's going to Joshua Tree after New Year's, and he asked me to go with him," she confesses, her voice quiet and almost shy. Then, without waiting for Lilly to comment: "I told him I'd love to."

Lilly blinks. "Wow," she says, struggling to absorb that information without making a retching sound like the bratty little brother in a 1980s family comedy. "What about the restaurant?"

"We usually close for a couple of weeks in January anyway, remember? It'll be fine without me for a little bit." Charlotte shrugs. "You should come out and see us for a few days," she suggests. "The place Caitriona's assistant found for him has a little guest cottage out back by the pool, so you'd have plenty of privacy." Her lips twitch, mischievous.

Lilly snorts. "Noted." The idea of purposely subjecting herself to a desert vacation with Colin is only slightly less appealing than that of curling up in a sand pit and waiting for a lonely rattlesnake to find her and make her his bride; still, the naked hope on Charlotte's face makes her feel like the worst person in the universe. They've been friends for a long time. "Maybe," Lilly hedges.

"No maybe," Charlotte counters. "If anybody could stand to blow this town for a little while, you could. Besides, Colin's teaching a writing seminar while he's out there that I really think you'd get a lot out of." Then, when Lilly only stares at her: "I'm kidding! Oh my god, Lilly." She sets her coffee down and takes Lilly's face in two hands, planting a smacking kiss on her cheek. "I'm kidding. I forgive you. And I'm happy, okay? Try to be happy for me, if you can."

Lilly nods. "I'm sorry," she says again—putting her hands over Charlotte's, feeling herself flush. "I am. I'd love to come out."

"Thank you," Charlotte says, letting go. "In the meantime, I'm going to get dressed and you can come to the Grove with me. My mom did all her Christmas shopping with Rebecca Barnes this year and I have like four different ruffly Victorian nightgowns I have to return."

Lilly grins. "I'd love to," she repeats, more truthfully this time, and finishes the rest of her coffee.

CHAPTER TWENTY-ONE

OLIVIA

Olivia's frenemy Jocelyn is dating a guy who works as a sound tech at EastWest, which is how Olivia and Kit wind up at a hipster pickleball court in Santa Monica late Friday night celebrating the album release of a tatted-up underwear model from Michigan who's currently reinventing himself in the ethical reggaeton space. Olivia is nibbling a vegan grilled cheez the size of a postage stamp and wondering about the feasibility of doing something in music, or at the very least music videos—do people even still make music videos anymore? Olivia hadn't thought so, but they're projecting the ethical reggaetonist's latest offering onto the wall at this very moment, so she guesses she was wrong—when all at once she catches sight of a familiar face across the room. "Shit," she says, gesturing with her chin in the direction of the bar, "isn't that Nick?"

"Lilly's Nick?" Kit asks distractedly, barely looking up from her phone. She's been seeing this new girl from Eagle Rock who makes bespoke lampshades or some other unbearably boring thing, and the two of them have been texting nonstop all night long.

Olivia scowls. "He's not Lilly's anything," she corrects. "They hung out for like two seconds literally last year." She pops the rest of the grilled cheez into her mouth, wrinkling her nose at the plasticky aftertaste. He looks different from all the other guys in here in his plaid button-down and work boots, she notices, unfashionable in a purposeful way. She wonders how he got on the list. "She said they didn't even bang."

"Oh, well, in that case," Kit says, in the voice of someone who thinks she's a lot more than just fourteen months shy of being the youngest. "I mean, now that it's January and all." She finally deigns to look up from her phone, lifting one thick, drawn-on eyebrow. "I guess he's fair game."

"Whatever." Olivia hates when Kit does this, acts like she's so much more mature and sophisticated just because she's had a marriage annulled and recently announced on Instagram that she's pansexual. "I'm going to get a drink."

She orders herself a mojito and waits for him to come over and say hello to her, but he doesn't, so finally, after two cocktails and twenty minutes wasted listening to Jocelyn's long, convoluted story about how she's thinking of doing a threesome with the sound guy and a drummer he knows with a Prince Albert piercing, Olivia fluffs her hair and throws her shoulders back and marches over to where Nick is leaning against the bar. He's drinking a whiskey with no ice cubes; there's a cigarette tucked behind his ear. Olivia can kind of already hear what Lilly would say about that—that it's a prop, stored there specifically for semiotics or whatever the fuck—but still there's something about it that kind of does it for her, that feels romantic in an old-fashioned James Dean kind of way.

James Dean was manufactured by executives at a lunch meeting, same as the rest of us, Imaginary Lilly reminds her. Olivia drains the rest of her drink.

"I thought that was you," she says, reaching out and putting one hand on his bicep. His skin is very warm through his shirt.

Nick turns to look at her, recognition taking a moment to settle over his features; his smile, when it comes, is equal parts lazy and pleased. "Olivia Benedetto," he says, ducking his head to kiss her on both cheeks. Something about the gesture feels very adult to her—the faint scruff on his face, maybe, the way it rasps against her skin—and Olivia barely manages not to shiver. She's been in the public eye at least in part since she was ten years old, and if she's being honest there's a part of her that still secretly feels like she's still in elementary school most of the time: running as fast as she can after her sisters, *Hey, guys, wait for me!* Never mind the fact that by the time she was finally old enough to go anywhere the rest of them had decided the party was over, that none of them ever wanted to do anything fun ever again. It sucks, to come of age in a declining empire. It sucks to feel like you missed out on all the best parts.

"What are you doing here?" Olivia asks now—popping one hip just slightly, her tongue finding the straw in her mostly-empty glass. It's not against the law to have a good time, she reminds herself, ignoring the skeptical burn of Kit's gaze on her from the other side of the party. It's not against the law to talk to a friend.

Nick's lips twist. "A buddy of mine owns this place," he explains, with the casual shrug of a guy who's got a lot of buddies. "Asked if I wanted to tag along." He glances over her shoulder, just for a second, and Olivia can't quite read the expression on his face. "Are all you guys here?"

"Just me," she says, hoping she sounds confident in the enough-ness of it. Hoping she sounds confident enough in herself. "Well, and Kit."

"That tracks," Nick says thoughtfully. "Somehow I can't imagine your sister is big into ethical reggaeton."

Olivia shakes her head, slow and teasing. "Lucky for you," she tells him—liking the tiny cleft in his chin and the way his hair is a little grown over his collar, liking that he didn't mention Lilly's name. Lilly is their father's favorite, maybe, but she doesn't have a claim on the whole entire universe. And judging by the way he's looking at Olivia right now, that warm flicker of interest—she doesn't have a claim on Nick, either. "I'm nothing like my sister."

Nick doesn't answer for a moment, reaches for his glass on the bar. "You know," he replies, and there's a split-second flash of his tongue behind his teeth as he grins at her, "I am starting to get that impression."

CHAPTER TWENTY-TWO

WILL

He spends Christmas Eve alone in Pemberly Grove, eating takeout and watching a *Lord of the Rings* marathon on cable. Georgia made some noise about coming to visit—"I want to decorate a palm tree, damnit! I want to see a Santa Claus in shorts"—but he told her not to bother. "I'll be back in New York in a couple of months," he reminded her. "There's no reason for you to schlep all the way out here."

Still, slouched on the couch surrounded by plastic take-out containers, stomach gurgling warily away, it occurs to Will that possibly he overestimated his own tolerance for melancholy holiday solitude. He could get a red-eye, he thinks, reaching for his phone to book a ticket. Be back home by Christmas morning. But then—what? Georgia's with some friends in Connecticut, the kind of place where they sing carols around a piano and everyone has a personalized stocking. She doesn't need her mopey older brother shuffling along like the Ghost of Christmas Past. He tosses his phone back onto the coffee table and reaches for the scallion pancakes, feeling embarrassed even though he's the only one here.

It's a relief to get back to work. Will's only on the call sheet for a couple of hours the Monday after New Year's, but there's a problem with one of the cameras, and in the time it takes to fix it

Sextus Pompey's wig catches fire, two of the chickens escape, and Johnny loses his temper and storms off set, spending the better part of the afternoon slouched in his trailer snorting various substances and listening to Benny Goodman. He refuses to return until his assistant plies him with promises of an enthusiastic round of applause from the crew and half a dozen Doritos Locos Tacos.

By the time Will is done for the day it's right smack in the middle of rush hour. He grits his teeth as he pulls onto Malibu Canyon Road and traffic slows more or less immediately, brake lights flaring like hot coals as far up ahead as he can see. He's a nervous driver to begin with, though he doesn't like to admit it—it feels fundamentally unmanly somehow, like confessing to fainting spells or waxing his legs—and sitting at a standstill makes the inside of his skin itch, the anxiety of wasted minutes trickling away. If he was stuck on the subway back at home at least he could read or work the crossword; here there's nothing to do but stare at the Darwin fish bumper sticker on the car in front of him and flick through Charlie's satellite radio presets with rising desperation. It makes him feel claustrophobic, even though the evening sky is enormous. It makes him feel trapped.

He's been inching along for the better part of an hour before he finally reaches the source of the jam—an ancient sedan broken down on the excruciatingly narrow shoulder, other drivers rubbernecking by at a crawl. Will blinks, then frowns, squinting out the windshield: sitting perched on the hood of the stalled-out Honda, sharp face tilted up like she's angling for a suntan in the rapidly fading light, is Lilly Benedetto.

Will swears. Before he knows what he's doing he's flicking his blinker on and pulling over in front of her, killing the engine and sliding awkwardly out of the driver's seat while trying his best not to get creamed by passing cars. "What are you doing here?" he asks, ignoring the irritated honk of a pickup truck, its driver's middle finger raised in salute.

If Lilly is at all surprised by the sight of him, she doesn't show it. "Hoping to get discovered," she deadpans immediately. "What does it look like I'm doing?"

"Did you call a tow truck?"

"No," she says, tilting her dark head to the side, "why do you ask?" Then, even as he's holding his hands up in sheepish self-defense: "Of course I called a fucking tow truck!"

"Okay. Well, good for you." Will keeps his palms out, like he's trying to stave off an angry coyote. Still, "Aren't you, like, glamorous?" he can't help but ask her. "Isn't that your thing?"

Lilly's eyes narrow. "I'm sorry?"

"I just . . ." He looks at the Honda, then back at her. She's dressed like a grad student in jeans and a beat-up leather jacket, a pair of cheetah-print sneakers on her feet. He hasn't seen her since the night of Charlie's premiere and she's gotten her hair lopped off in the interim, messy waves just brushing her shoulders. He wants to put both hands in it and tug. "This is not the car I pictured you driving."

"When you sat around picturing me driving my car?"

"You know what I mean."

"I truly don't."

"Okay, can we just—" Will blows a breath out. He's stunned by her, truthfully, her skin and her scowl and the proud, delicate set of her jawline. Every single time, she somehow catches him up short. "Hello," he tries again, his voice coming out fake and formal. "Sorry to see you're having trouble. I can give you a ride home, if you want."

Right away, Lilly shakes her head. "Thank you for the offer," she says primly, "but I'll be fine."

Will nods. "I'm sure you will be," he says, sounding mostly like himself again, then sits down beside her to wait.

Lilly sighs loudly, but she doesn't tell him to go fuck himself, which is probably about as close as he's going to get to a letterpressed invitation. They listen to the roar of the traffic for a moment, though it's not quite enough to drown out the weird, thick silence between them. "How's the movie going?" she finally asks.

"It's fine," Will says half a beat too quickly, surprised that she broke first. Even through the car exhaust and asphalt she smells the same as she did the first night they met, like citrus and herbs and manifest destiny. Like the state of California itself. "I mean, I'm lying. It's kind of a disaster."

"Really?" Lilly perks up visibly at that, turning to him with interest in the hazy pink twilight. "Say more."

Will snorts. "I don't think I will, actually."

"Oh, come on," she prods, nudging him in the rib cage. "Don't be withholding. If there's one thing I've been clear about in the time that we've known each other, I hope it's that I'm always absolutely dying to hear any story about you embarrassing yourself or doing poorly in any way."

That makes him laugh. "Yeah, you've been pretty forthcoming on that front," he agrees, rubbing a hand over his face. "I don't know. I mean, it's not like I have a ton to compare it to, right? Maybe all film sets are wildly dysfunctional. But I had it in my head that coming out here and doing this movie was a way to like, try and reset my life after the whole—" He waves a hand. "You know."

"I don't, actually." Lilly lifts an eyebrow. "After the whole what?"

Will hesitates. He's always weirdly surprised when there are people in the world who don't already know about this, though of course it's not like he's famous or even really known at all outside an extremely specific niche group of East Coast theatergoers. Sometimes he forgets the entire universe isn't New York. "I had kind of a . . . situation," he says finally, looking down at his hands. "Back at home."

"Public urination?" Lilly guesses immediately. "Jerking off in a subway car. Flashing a bunch of little old ladies attending an afternoon lecture on Basquiat at the 92nd Street Y."

"Can I ask you something?" Will glances at her sidelong. "Is there any particular reason I have my dick out in front of strangers in all of these scenarios?"

Lilly smiles sweetly. "Just spitballing."

"Uh-huh." He gazes out at the horizon for a moment, trying to decide how honest he wants to be here. Trying to decide if he trusts her or not. "I played Hamlet on Broadway last spring," he finally begins. "Which was, like . . . a big part."

"Oh!" She nods earnestly. "Is he the star?"

"Fuck you," Will replies with a smirk. "You know what I mean. It's a lot of pressure, that's all. It's such a famous play, it's been done so many times, on top of which there were a couple of real names in the cast, people from out here, so. It was getting a lot more attention than something like that might ordinarily get." He shrugs. "The *New Yorker* sent a writer to do this whole long process story about rehearsals. We were on the front page of the Arts Preview in the *Times*."

Lilly nods. "Okay," she says again, though he can tell it's taking significant effort for her not to repeat the words *Arts Preview* back at him in a mocking tone of voice. "And?"

"And . . ." He trails off, watching a hawk turn lazy circles in the distance. He wants to tell her about New York at the beginning of March, everything cold and wet and stained with salt from late-season snowstorms. He wants to tell her about the backbreaking grind of rehearsing for a play. He wants to tell her about the hours he spent lost inside the lush green hedge maze of the language, and he wants to tell her about the moment he realized he couldn't get out.

"I started dreaming about my dad," is where he begins.

Lilly's eyebrows lift, infinitesimal. "Ah."

"Yeah." Will swallows at the remembering of it, a taste like copper and panic at the back of his mouth. It was only a couple of times at first—violent, twisting nightmares that left him sweaty and shaking, gasping awake in the dark. Sometimes his mom was there; sometimes she wasn't. Sometimes Will was trying to stop the accident. Sometimes he was the one driving the car.

By the time they got to tech it was happening every night, Will avoiding his bedroom like a crime scene, like the bloody final act of the show. He meditated. He stopped eating gluten. He saw a doctor, who wrote him a prescription for sleeping pills, and when that didn't work he just . . . stopped sleeping altogether. He got lost on the way home from his final dress rehearsal. By the time the show opened he'd lost eighteen pounds.

"I should have talked to somebody about it, probably," he says now, elbows on his knees and head bent toward the pavement. "But—and I'm sure this will come as a deep shock to you—that kind of thing can be sort of a nonstarter for me."

"Really?" Lilly murmurs. "I'm floored."

"Instead I just kind of . . . kept going. Which—again, earth-shattering, can't imagine anything that would have been more of a surprise—didn't work out so well in the end, for me or for the show."

"How bad was it?"

Will sits up. "Bad," he tells her honestly. He's never said any of this out loud before and the telling of it makes him feel light-headed and untethered, like he might come flying off the face of the Earth entirely and wind up drifting outside of gravity for all eternity. "Opening night, I just . . . choked. I couldn't remember my lines or my blocking or what I was doing up there to begin with. The reviews were eviscerating. The whole thing closed up shop after six performances. And it was . . . entirely my fault."

Lilly wrinkles her nose. "Yikes."

"Yikes," Will agrees. "It wasn't great." He flexes his fingers, scrubs a hand over the hair at the back of his head. "Anyway. I got back to my apartment the night after the last show, and I was so fucking tired. I took a couple of Ambien, and I waited like half an hour and I was still awake, and I was really kind of freaking out by that point, so. I took some more."

All at once he feels Lilly get very still beside him. "How many more?" she asks.

Will shrugs, looking out at the traffic one more time. He thinks for a moment about people who commute to office jobs, people who drive monster trucks and enter bake-offs and live completely normal, healthy, theaterless lives. He wonders how they do it. He wishes he could be more like them.

"I wasn't trying to . . . whatever," he says finally, and taps his foot twice on the bumper. "I don't think. Not really. But when you wake up in the ICU of Lenox Hill on a seventy-two-hour psych hold, it's sort of hard to convince them you were just trying to catch some Z's."

Lilly nods slowly, her face impassive. "I can see how that might be the case."

"Anyway," Will continues, "I had already turned down the offer from Johnny by that point, but after everything happened, the idea of staying in the city started to feel kind of . . . untenable? On top of which it's not like a bunch of producers and directors were exactly banging down my door. So I called him back to see if the part was still available, and here I am."

"Here you are," Lilly echoes. They're quiet for a long time, watching the line of traffic snake by. "I'm glad, for what it's worth. Not that you wound up in the hospital, obviously. But that you wound up in the hospital instead of . . ." She trails off.

"The probable alternative?"

Lilly laughs at that, low and quiet. "Yeah."

"Yeah." Will looks at her in the quickly falling darkness. There's a spray of coppery freckles across her cheekbones, just faint ones. You'd have to be looking to notice, which he guesses he is. "Is that the nicest thing you've ever said to me?"

"What, 'I'm glad you didn't die from an accidental-or-not overdose of sleeping pills'? It might be," Lilly concedes. "You should be sure to write it down in your journal."

"Joke's on you," Will says, "I don't keep a journal." He taps the side of his head. "Store it all right up here."

Lilly nods, then doesn't say anything for a long moment, leaning back against the hood of the Honda and exposing the long, graceful line of her neck. Will doesn't say anything, either. He's thinking he'd be happy to stay here in silence with her all night, the lights of the city blinking like neon stars in the distance, when all of a sudden she clears her throat. "The car was Joe's," she tells him quietly. "My ex—my fiancé." She frowns, sitting up a little straighter. "Is it an ex if he dies? I can never figure out what to call him."

Right away, Will has never felt more like an ass. "I'm sorry," he tells her. "When I said—I didn't realize."

"Of course you didn't." Lilly shrugs. "I never talk about it. Anyway, I got it after he died because nobody else wanted it, and it's not like I don't know it's a piece of shit. It breaks down more or less constantly. The A/C hasn't worked in a full year. And it's clearly not doing a whole lot for my personal brand, which any of my sisters would be happy to tell you. But I can't make myself give it up, either."

Will thinks about what it must have been like for her, to lose someone like that with neither warning nor privacy. He thinks about the night his parents died. He thinks about all the different ways the past bleeds into the present, and finally he leans over on the hood of the Honda and nudges her denim-covered knee with his. "I'm sorry about that day at the restaurant," he says. "I was a weirdo. I'm a weirdo sometimes, clearly. What I said to you, about getting it out of our systems . . . that wasn't what I wanted to say."

That gets her attention. "Oh no?" she asks. "What did you want to say, exactly?"

Will gazes at her for a moment, their pinkies just barely brushing. Lilly's lips part. Will is about to lean in closer when all at once a tow truck clanks up behind them, a gruff-looking lady driver hopping down out of the cab. "Somebody call for a tow?" she asks.

Lilly jumps down off the hood of the car like it's on fire. "Me!" she calls, waving madly. "I did."

The driver nods, then turns to Will. "That your car?" she asks, nodding at Charlie's Land Rover. "You're in the way."

Will nods. "Often," he confirms grimly.

Lilly smiles. "I think I can probably handle myself from here," she says. "Thanks for the company."

"Anytime," he tells her, and he's surprised to find he means it. Then, before he has time to think it through: "Text me when you make it home, will you?"

She looks at him archly. "If you want my phone number, you could just ask for it."

Will blanches, embarrassed. "I— That's not—"

Lilly rolls her eyes. "I'm teasing you, William." She holds her hand out for his phone, nimble fingers skipping across the screen. "No pictures of your penis, all right?" she says as she hands it back. "I get enough of those as it is."

"That's just for my OnlyFans," he says. "Exclusively paying customers."

"He doesn't know basic reality television, but he knows Only-Fans."

"I contain multitudes."

"So I am beginning to understand." She lifts her hand in a wave. "Nice running into you, Will Darcy."

"Nice running into you, Lilly Benedetto."

He gets back in his car and pulls out into traffic, the night air warm on his face through the open window. He watches her in the rearview until the car disappears out of sight.

CHAPTER TWENTY-THREE

LILLY

The house is empty when she finally gets home, which is surprising—the house is never empty; there's always someone rummaging through the refrigerator or beaming TikTok videos to the TV or loudly scheduling an appointment with their gynecologist—and the quiet feels almost luxurious, the only sounds the echo of her footsteps on the tile and the beat of her own heart. She changes into shorts and a hoodie, then cobbles together a dinner of cold roasted veg and some almost-stale focaccia left over from one of the restaurants before dutifully carting her laptop out into the backyard, trying to tamp down the bright flicker of dread at the idea of opening the screenplay again. It's felt like this lately, every time she sits down to try and get some work done: the underwater sensation of getting absolutely nowhere, the dull knowledge that she's wasting her time. *Famous for being famous*, she thinks grimly. Lacking a single marketable skill.

She's not sure how long she's been staring at the cursor when her phone chirps on the table beside her, a text from a New York number she doesn't recognize.

You make it home okay?

It takes Lilly a moment to realize she's smiling, the gesture so sudden and sincere and involuntary that she reaches up and touches her own mouth to feel the curve of it underneath her fingers.

Still in the tow truck with Lorraine, actually, she replies. *We're considering hitting the road like in* Travels with Charley.

Don't take any wooden nickels, Will fires back immediately. *Write if you find work.*

Lilly ducks her head even though nobody is watching, her entire body warming with a goofy, middle-school blush. She'd be lying if she said her stomach hadn't thrilled a little bit at the sight of him climbing out of his car earlier, his dark jeans and V-neck T-shirt and wry, half-bashful expression. She thinks of the long, architectural lines of his body, like possibly he was designed and assembled using the golden ratio. She remembers the knowing rasp of his tongue against her skin.

For one insane second she nearly picks up the phone and texts him again: *I'm alone here*, she imagines typing, her fingers aching faintly with longing. *What are you doing right now?*

Instead she looks back at her screenplay for another long beat before closing out the window. Then she grits her teeth, opens a brand-new document, and gets the hell to work.

* * *

Junie FaceTimes from New York, where she has not in fact taken in any theater but has ruined a $400 pair of suede booties by stepping off a curb into a six-inch-deep puddle of slush. "I ran into Caroline at Bloomingdale's yesterday," she reports miserably, curled up on the couch at Lou and Veronica's; there's a Hockney half-visible on the living room wall behind her, Miles Davis wailing away on the sound system in the background. "So Charlie definitely knows I'm in town now, if he didn't already."

"Assuming your super-chill and low-key Instagram posts hadn't already tipped him off, you mean?" Kit leans over Lilly's shoulder, her long hair migrating up Lilly's nose as she squeezes into the frame.

"What, like the one of me wearing my I Heart NY shirt while riding on the Circle Line and eating a soft pretzel?" June asks, grinning ruefully. "Or the one of me outside the stage door of *Hamilton* that I captioned 'The Room Where It Happens'?"

"She actually meant the one you geotagged 'New York City' in case he couldn't put it together himself from the context clues," Lilly teases, "but we do admire the way you've covered all your bases." She smiles. "I mean, who knows, right? He might turn up yet."

"Or not," Mari mumbles from her perch in the armchair across the living room. Lilly shoots her a murderous look in reply.

"What did I even think I was going to accomplish by coming out here?" June asks, leaning her head back against Lou and Veronica's green velvet sofa. "You were right about Caroline, PS, if you want to take this well-earned opportunity to say 'I told you so.' From the look on her face when she saw me you would have thought I caught her pawing through the clearance rack at Express."

"I don't want to say 'I told you so,'" Lilly promises, which is true. Mostly she just wants to knock on the door of whatever elegant, minimalist hotel room Caroline is staying in and punch her directly in the vagina. "I never want to say 'I told you so.'"

June waves a hand in front of her face, like her own heartbreak is a cloud of smelly subway steam she can bat away. "How are things with Nick?" she wants to know.

"Wait," Kit says, turning to look at Lilly a little strangely, "are you still hanging out with Nick? Because—" She breaks off.

Lilly frowns. "Because what?"

"No, nothing." Kit shakes her head, goes back to her embroidery. "Just wondering. You hadn't mentioned him, so."

"I had not," Lilly agrees, turning back to Junie. "Honestly, I think that whole thing kind of ran its course pretty quick."

June wrinkles her nose. "That sucks," she says. "I'm sorry."

"It's fine," Lilly promises, and she's surprised to discover she's telling the truth. She's been busy since June's been gone, working almost nonstop on the novel she started the night her car broke down: staying up late and getting up early, fingers flying over the keyboard and eyes gone sandy from staring at the screen.

Also, as much as she hates to admit it, she's been having a lot of fun texting with Will.

It started a couple of days after he waited with her for the tow truck, her phone buzzing on the counter as she was putting together a weird lunch from a couple of meal kits that hadn't gone bad yet: *How's the open highway?* he wanted to know.

Lilly bit her lip, even though there was nobody around to see her smile. *Not bad*, she wrote back, thumbs moving slowly over the keys. *Really making the most of the all-you-can-eat breakfasts at the Hilton Garden Inn.*

Lining your pockets with mini croissants?

Stuffing my purse full of Danishes.

Since then they've been volleying back and forth a dozen times a day, talking about all kinds of random things: an editorial in the *Times* and their favorite movies from when they were teenagers, where to get a decent bagel in LA. She's found herself listening for the sound of her phone vibrating, an illicit little thrill zinging through her every time she sees his name on the screen.

It doesn't mean anything, obviously.

But she's not sure if it means nothing, either.

"Come home soon," she says now, blowing a kiss in Junie's direction. June blows one back, says goodbye.

* * *

"I'm going to need an advance on my allowance," Olivia announces that night, sliding pertly into her seat in the dining room. Cinta put a huge dinner together, meaning she ordered $150 worth of food from an Indian place in Agoura Hills and harangued them loudly into sending extra naan. "A friend of mine has VIP passes to Moon Landing, so." Olivia tilts her head to the side like, *You all know how it is.* "I need bikinis."

Lilly winces. "Seriously?" Moon Landing is a three-day music festival out in the desert, the cursed love child of Coachella and Burning Man. She went herself once, a few months before Joe died; in her memory it's a blur of champagne cocktails and MDMA, everything in her suitcase caked with a fine pale layer of grit. She and Joe got into a screaming argument in the lobby of the Ace Hotel in Palm Springs that showed up on social media before they were even finished having it, the two of them hurling accusations at each other across the glittering terrazzo tile. The thought of it makes Lilly's chest ache, like her lungs are full of sand. "That shit makes Revolve Fest look fun."

"I mean, it's no postmodern feminist Quebecois paleo dinner at Lodge that's over by nine p.m., I'll grant you," Olivia replies sweetly, "but you gotta take your excitement where you can get it, I always say."

"Didn't, like, four different people get roofied there last year?" Lilly presses, looking around the table for assistance and wishing uselessly for June. It's coming back to her now in queasy neon flashes: Joe strung out and mean and sweaty, the unceasing shriek of synth. She hasn't let herself think about it in a long time. "And there was that thing with the porta-potties—"

"None of that happened in the VIP section, Lilly!" Olivia's voice is shrill. "On top of which, I don't actually remember asking for your opinion." She turns back to their father. "Anyway! The bikinis. You can just Venmo me if you want."

"Of course we will," Cinta agrees immediately, even as Dominic is shoving his chair back and marching off in the direction of his rowing machine. "Do you need cover-ups, too?"

Lilly bites her tongue, reaching across the table for the korma and trying to ignore the weird, amorphous dread blooming like cactus blossoms in her chest. Her relationship with Olivia has always been like this—smooth and then prickly, hot and then cold. She thinks it's possible Olivia reminds her too much of the person she was before Joe died—too sure of herself, too confident in the notion that nothing truly bad could ever happen. She thinks about that person sometimes and wants to shake her. Wants to say, *You idiot. Take better care of what you already have.*

* * *

After dinner she finds her dad in the gym on the second floor of the pool house just like always, the clank of dumbbells and the wail of the classic rock station echoing out across the backyard. Lilly climbs the steps and watches him for a minute before he notices her: tufts of gray chest hair poking out of his tank top, the veins in his biceps bulging as he lifts. He's in fantastic shape—of course he's in fantastic shape, he literally spends four and a half hours a day pumping iron—but still he's starting to look a little bit older to her lately, though she'd never say that to him in a million years.

He'd prefer to be stabbed in the heart. "Brought you a protein shake," she says, holding up the plastic tumbler.

Her dad smiles at her in the mirror without breaking his rhythm. "You're a sweetheart, Elisabetta," he tells her, motioning with his chin toward the bookshelf. "You know you've always been my favorite daughter."

Lilly smiles back as she sets the shaker down beside his impressive home library of workout DVDs, ignoring a tiny pang of something uneasy behind her ribs. She used to love it when her dad singled her out as special—the smartest, the most talented, the one with the best head on her shoulders—and if she's being honest with herself there's a part of her that can't help but want to be his #1 girl. Still, lately something about it reminds her of what Will said that night at the premiere of Charlie's movie. *I am exactly like my sisters*, she thinks again.

"Listen," she says, sitting down on the edge of the weight bench. "About Olivia and this festival. I just don't think it's a good idea for you to let her—"

Right away her dad shakes his head. "Have you met your sister?" he asks pointedly. "If I tell her she can't go she'll just make my life a living hell until finally I give in. Better to save myself the effort."

Lilly doesn't know that *Better to save myself the effort* is a parenting motto to which one should necessarily aspire, but she doesn't say that out loud. "Oh, she'll have us all longing for the sweet embrace of death, absolutely," she agrees. "But—"

"Besides," her father interrupts, setting down his thirty-fives and reaching for his fifties, "Olivia is twenty-one. My role is strictly ceremonial, same as with the rest of you girls. I'm like Stanley Tucci in *The Hunger Games*."

"And just as nattily dressed," Lilly promises; her father is nothing if not susceptible to flattery. She thinks of Caroline inviting June over to Charlie's hoping she'd somehow embarrass herself. She thinks of Isobel DesRoche in the bathroom at the club. She thinks of the money they don't have, the house they're about to lose, and thinks she'll be damned if she's not going to try her hardest to protect Olivia and all the rest of her sisters from everything she can, up to and including their own bad decisions, whether they like it or not. "Your opinion still matters, though. She listens to you more than you think. I mean, we all do."

"That's very sweet of you to say, Elisabetta," Lilly's father tells her cheerfully, "though I think we both know it's bullshit." He grins at her then, winking like they're in on something together before gesturing with a dumbbell in the direction of the stairs. "Get the hell out of my gym, would you? I've got thirty-eight more reps."

Lilly hesitates. Back when they were kids they all used to clamber out of bed and run to the front door in their pajamas when he got home from the restaurant late at night; he'd swing them up in the air one by one like something out of the opening credits of a vintage TV show, all of them barefoot and giggling. *I need you to remember you care about us for a second*, she almost tells him. *I need you to be our dad.*

"Sure thing," she says instead, then offers him a crooked smile. "Don't hurt yourself, all right?"

"Brat," he says, turning back to the mirror. Lilly can hear him laughing all the way back down the stairs.

CHAPTER TWENTY-FOUR

WILL

A week passes. The movie grinds along. They lose one full day to a freak grasshopper infestation in the craft services tent and another two when Johnny is arrested for urinating on a police car outside a gentlemen's club in North Hollywood and spends the night in Los Angeles County lockup. Will keeps his head down, shoots his scenes.

Charlie is somewhere in Europe, though Caroline calls to tell him she's back in LA: "I've got meetings," she reports breezily, and Will purposely doesn't ask if that's the only reason. They go to dinner at a seafood place in Malibu, a big outdoor patio and the smell of the ocean, a band playing jazz standards underneath a white sliver of moon. It's a fun time, actually—wine and oysters, Caroline complaining about all her friends from back in New York who are moving to the suburbs to have a million babies; still, Will can't get over the feeling that something isn't right.

"Do you remember the first summer we met?" she asks him, plucking a cocktail shrimp from the platter. Her hair is long and loose, the white-gold of summer corn at the Union Square greenmarket.

"Of course I do," Will tells her. She was in town from Chicago to visit Charlie; they drank their way from Lincoln Center all the way down to the Brooklyn Bridge. "I was terrified of you."

Caroline grins at him across the table. "Good," she says. "That's how I like it."

It's after midnight by the time they pay the bill and make their way to the valet stand; the back of her hand brushes his as they're waiting for their cars. "You coming over?" she asks, and she is so, so casual. "Or do you want me to meet you back at your sumptuous accommodations in Pemberly Grove?"

Will takes a deep breath, and then he says it: "I don't think we should do this anymore," he blurts, which is of course the moment the valet pulls up with Charlie's Land Rover. He resists the urge to dive in and peel off into the darkness, but barely.

Caroline doesn't hesitate, her gaze like a nuclear missile. "Is this about Lilly Benedetto?" she asks.

"What?" Will feels himself blanch. "No."

"It is!" she accuses. She looks utterly astonished. "You're throwing me over for Lilly Benedetto. I cannot believe it."

"I'm not throwing you over," he says miserably. God, he hates conversations like this. "It's not like—I mean, we always meant for this to be casual, right? We always said no strings."

"I—" Something steadfast and fundamental slips in Caroline's expression then, a look on her face he's never seen in all the years they've known each other. He wildly underestimated what was happening here, Will realizes suddenly. This whole time he had no idea what she felt.

"Caro," he starts, reaching for her across the pavement, but Caroline is already correcting, drawing herself up like a duchess. "You're right," she agrees; just like that she's herself again, cool and unflappable. Just like that she's a person who would never let him break her heart. "No strings."

CHAPTER TWENTY-FIVE

LILLY

~

She takes one more run at it the night before they both leave, Olivia off to the festival and Lilly headed to Charlotte in the desert: "Look," Lilly says, finding Olivia tweezing her secret unibrow in the magnifying mirror above the sink in the upstairs bathroom, "about Moon Landing."

Olivia smirks. "Oh, Lilly," she says gently, her reflection almost beatific, "I can't even tell you how much I am not interested in hearing you lecture me about this."

"I'm not lecturing you about anything," Lilly argues. All week the weird bad feeling has been growing, clanging around like a rock in a dryer deep inside her chest. "I just think—"

"Can I ask you a question?" Olivia interrupts her. "Who exactly died and made you the boss of everyone?"

"I—nobody," Lilly says, wounded in spite of herself. Still, she grits her teeth and tries again. "I just don't think it's a good idea for you to go and do Molly in the desert while wearing an Indigenous headdress so it can be on *TMZ* twenty minutes later, that's all."

"I'm not going to wear a fucking headdress!" Olivia's tweezers clatter into the sink.

"It remains not a good look."

"Your *face* remains not a good look," Olivia counters. "For fuck's sake, Lilly, lighten up for once, will you? Just because you have PTSD from Joe sticking one too many needles in his arm doesn't mean the rest of us are never allowed to go do anything fun."

For a second Lilly just blinks at her, reeling. Right away, Olivia seems to realize she's gone too far. "That's not—" she starts, then breaks off and tries again. "Lilly, honey, I didn't mean—"

"No." Lilly holds a hand up. She doesn't know why it feels like Olivia has punched her. It's not like Olivia is saying anything she doesn't know. What does she even think she's trying to accomplish here, telling Olivia not to make the same mistakes she herself made with flair and abandon? Who is she to tell Olivia not to do anything at all? It's useless to try to stop whatever's going to happen. It's useless to keep trying to hold it all together with her two shaking hands. "You're right, you're a big girl. Do whatever the hell you want."

"Lilly," Olivia says again, reaching for her, "come on."

But Lilly is already gone, down the stairs and through the foyer, out into the yard where the air is cool and blue. She walks the whole development, past Charlotte's parents' place and Rebecca Barnes's absurd English Tudor and Charlie Bingley's house where the windows are empty and dark.

She's still standing there, hands in her pockets, when the porch light flicks on and the front door opens wide. "Lilly?" Will asks, squinting at her in the darkness. He's wearing jeans and a thin-looking hoodie, his feet bare against the brick of the stoop. "Is that you?"

Lilly freezes. ". . . No?" she tries, then shrugs a little helplessly. Of course the truth is she came here looking for him. It's ridiculous to pretend she wasn't hoping for this exact thing at the back of her brain. "Hi."

She's prepared for something scathing, but instead Will just grins. "Hi," he says, reaching up to scratch one shoulder. "Do you want to come inside?"

Lilly blinks at the directness of it, the sight of him touching himself so casually doing something to her stomach. "Now?"

Will nods. There's a stillness to his body she's never noticed before, a palpable calm. "Now," he says.

Lilly glances over her shoulder in the direction of her parents' house, hears an owl hooting somewhere in the distance. Looks back at Will and nods.

CHAPTER TWENTY-SIX

WILL

"Okay," she says twenty minutes later, laughing at him over the bowl of her wineglass, "that's not real." She's perched on his kitchen counter in ripped jeans and a tank top, the heels of her bare feet bumping lightly against the cabinet doors. "I refuse to believe that even you would—"

"The ad said they needed an actor!" Will defends himself, arm brushing hers as he reaches for the bottle. "Technically, I was acting."

Lilly snorts. "Standing outside a tax place dressed as the Statue of Liberty is not acting."

"Says you, maybe." Will grins, ducking his head a little. "Anyway, that was how I learned that one cannot circumvent the need for an agent by booking one's own jobs on Craigslist dot org."

"A real coming-of-age moment for you." Lilly's lips twist.

"Basically the plot of 'Don't Stop Believin',' yes."

"Is that your karaoke song?"

"Uh, sure is not." Will snorts. "I'd rather shave off both my eyebrows than sing karaoke."

"Oh, right," Lilly says, nodding seriously. "Sorry, I forgot for a second how terminally opposed to a good time you are."

"I'm not opposed to a good time," Will protests, leaning back against the island with his ankles crossed. "I just, as a general rule, prefer to humiliate myself accidentally instead of on purpose."

"How's that working out for you?"

"I mean, nobody's going to accuse me of not being committed to the bit." He lifts an eyebrow. "What's yours?" he asks, lifting his chin in her direction. "Your karaoke song, I mean."

Lilly doesn't hesitate. "'Scenes from an Italian Restaurant.'"

Will laughs, then realizes she's serious. "Wait, really?" he asks. "That song is, like, twelve minutes long."

"Seven and a half," Lilly corrects him. "It's actually my favorite song of all time, period. My mom used to sing it to us all the time when we were kids."

"That . . . tracks," Will says, then catches himself, remembering what happened at the movie premiere: the angry flash of her expression, the stubborn set of her jaw. "I just mean—"

Lilly cuts him off. "Fuck you," she says, but there's no heat behind it. "I know everybody thinks my mother is warped, and, like, fine, she is, but she was a good mom when we were kids."

Will nods. "I can see that," he says, and he's surprised to discover he actually means it. "I bet she was fun."

"She was." Lilly shakes her head. "Anyway. That song always makes me want to cry a little bit, honestly, even though it's not actually sad. Or maybe it is a sad song, and people just don't realize that because it's so fast? I don't know."

Will thinks about it for a minute, trying to remember the words. "'Brenda and Eddie would always know how to survive'?"

"Exactly." Lilly's smile is slow and luminous. "Equal parts delusion and grit, that's what I always say."

He's not sure who she's talking about, the people in the song or her own mother, but either way Will nods. "She must have done something right," he says. "Your mom, I mean. Look how close you and your sisters are. How much you all—" He breaks off, gesturing vaguely. "You know."

Lilly makes a face. "Are obsessed with each other?" she supplies.

"I'm serious!" Will defends himself. "I do actually think it's nice, the way you guys are. It's not like that with Georgia and me. It never has been."

"You don't keep each other company while you pee?"

"Only on special occasions." Will shrugs. "I don't know. I'm just . . . not a very good brother, I guess."

"Well, that's bullshit," Lilly says immediately.

Will blinks, caught up short by the baldness of it. "Excuse me?"

"I said," she repeats, hopping down off the counter and splashing more wine into both their glasses, "it's bullshit. I hate when people say things like that, like the way you act as a human is some binary thing you're born with or not. You want to be a good brother, just . . . be a good brother." She shrugs, gesturing in his direction with her wineglass as she walks backward in the direction of the living room. "Call her up and ask her how she's doing. Invite her out here. Reassure her that she doesn't need to have her buccal fat remediated by a professional."

"It's not like that for me, though," Will protests. "Also, I don't know what that last thing is."

Lilly ignores him. "You don't know how to use the telephone?" she asks, sweeping an armful of throw pillows off the sofa before curling up at one end of it. "You have way too many of those, PS."

"I didn't buy them," he says, following her into the living room. "They came with the—whatever. The point is, I'm not the kind of person people trust with their secrets. And I don't always know how to trust people with mine."

Lilly shakes her head. "I don't think that's true," she insists, tucking her long legs underneath her. "You told me about what happened back in New York, right?"

"Yeah, well." Will watches her for a moment, feeling the back of his neck get warm. He likes seeing her here, is the truth—likes how comfortable she looks, the way she has of making herself at home wherever she goes. His heart has been thrumming since the moment he saw her outside, a feeling like a curtain rising. "You're a special case."

"Because it doesn't actually matter what I think of you?"

"That's not what I—" Will shakes his head as he sits down beside her, his knee just bumping hers. "Can I ask you a question? Why do you always have to immediately jump to the most dickish possible interpretation of whatever it is I'm saying?"

"Habit," Lilly says immediately, mouth curving as she turns to face him. "Experience."

"Rude."

"Yeah, well." She knocks her knee against his one more time, not quite gentle. "I'm rude." She grins. "Is that what happened with you and Nick, in the end?" she teases. "He wanted you to bare your soul to him, and you were too emotionally unavailable?"

"Me and Nick?" That surprises him, and not in a good way; all at once, Will's whole body goes tense. "What does Nick have to do with anything?"

"No," Lilly says quickly, "nothing. I'm curious, that's all. You're saying you're not good in relationships, and you guys obviously had some kind of"—she waves her hand—"intense relational malfunction, so—"

"Why is that something you care about?"

Lilly lifts an eyebrow. "Easy," she says, laughing a little. "It's not, particularly."

"It sounds like it is." At the very back of his head he knows he's probably overreacting, that the very mention of Nick's name turns him hotheaded and irrational; still, he can't quite turn it around. "Like, is that why you came over here? To pump me for information about Nick? Because that's cheap, Lilly. Even for—" He breaks off.

"Watch yourself." Lilly's eyes narrow, her own temper flaring. "I'm just saying, if you're going to go around making vague insinuations that someone is a dirtbag—particularly if you're going to get him fired from his job—at the very least you ought to be able to back it up with some data."

"Fired from his—" Will has no fucking idea what she's talking about. "Are you sleeping with him?" he blurts, then immediately wishes he hadn't. "Is that what's going on here?"

"Wow." Lilly barks a laugh. "That is emphatically none of your business."

"You make it my business when you show up at my house in the middle of the night to grill me—"

"It's like nine thirty p.m., Will!" Lilly throws her hands up. "How old are you, a hundred?"

"That's not the point. The point is—" Fuck, he can't think. He can never think, when it's her. "The point is—"

"The point is you talk a big game about who I might or might not be sleeping with when you're hooking up with your literal best friend's sister," Lilly interrupts. "And I'll tell you, Will: I'm not really interested in hearing it."

All the blood drains out of Will's face at once. "How did

you—how do you know about that?" he asks, then realizes half a second too late that she didn't; she was fishing, that's all, and there he was openmouthed at the other end of the line. "There's not—I mean, we aren't—" He winces. "I ended it."

Lilly rolls her eyes. "Uh-huh," she says primly. "I'm sure you did." She sets her wineglass down on the coffee table, then stands up and brushes her hands off on the seat of her jeans. "I should get going," she announces. He can't decide whether or not she looks hurt. "I'm leaving for Palm Springs tomorrow, so. I won't see you."

"No," he agrees, which isn't what he means to say at all. "I guess you won't."

Lilly sighs. "You know what, Will?" she starts, then seems to think better of it. The door slams shut behind her as she goes.

Once he's alone again Will forces himself to finish what he was doing before he saw her out there in the darkness: loading the dishwasher, making his coffee for tomorrow morning. Finally he picks up the phone. *You had no idea what you were talking about*, he starts, then deletes it.

I think we misunderstood each other— No, that's not right, either.

He flops down onto the couch, closing his eyes for a moment. Listens to the fridge clicking on and off.

He met Nick his last year at Juilliard, at a bar on 71st Street with a dart board and a perpetually burned-out neon sign. It was Charlie's favorite bar and eventually it became Will's favorite bar, too—the dark paneling and the high-backed wooden booths with thirty years' worth of names and numbers carved into the seats, cheap beer and endless pickles and enormous baskets of fries. They closed it down after every performance, spilling out onto the sidewalk as the sky turned gray over Amsterdam.

Georgia came to stay with him the March of his senior year. She'd graduated early from boarding school in Connecticut and was taking a year off before she started at Princeton to do an internship with a cousin of theirs at Wells Fargo; she stayed at his apartment near Lincoln Center, almond milk and Greek yogurt and three different kinds of hot sauce appearing in his fridge overnight. Charlie was living with a girlfriend that year and Will was surprised by how much he liked having someone else around again: the sound of the coffee grinder in the morning, someone to watch TV with on the weekends. They hadn't lived in the same place in years. She'd found an old Polaroid camera at a thrift store in Brooklyn and ordered a bunch of film for it online; when Will thinks of that spring he can hear the whir as the camera spit out its pictures, the way Georgia pinned them to the walls of the bathroom and the hallway. She wanted to go to warehouse parties in Bushwick. She wanted him to take her out to bars.

"You're seventeen," he said, and she laughed, not unkindly.

"I've had a fake ID for three years," she informed him. "Let's go."

So. They went. A decade and a half later and Will still blames himself for this part—that he let his guard down, didn't pay closer attention. That he didn't take her to Shake Shack instead. That when she started hanging around near the bar, head tipped close to the wry, wisecracking bartender, he didn't put a stop to it then and there. *Families look out for each other*—at least, they're supposed to. And Will is the one who dropped the ball.

It was Charlie who told him. He did it as delicately as possible: Polaroids, he explained. Half a dozen of them, tacked to the wall in the men's room at the bar. "I took them down, obviously," he reported, looking extremely miserable. "Threw them in a trash can a few blocks away. But I just . . . thought you'd probably want to know."

He was hoping that Georgia didn't know anything about it but when he got back to the apartment he found her sitting on the couch watching reruns in a pair of grubby sweatpants. The camera was sitting broken in the trash.

"Georgia," he said. Even as the words were coming out of his mouth it was like he couldn't help himself. "I mean, did you *give* him—"

But Georgia shook her head. "I swear to god, Will, if you lecture me about this I'm going to walk out of this apartment and you're not my brother anymore."

Right away, Will held his hands up. "I'm not going to lecture you," he promised. "I'm going to take care of it."

When Nick got off work the following night, Will was waiting for him. He can remember how cold his feet were inside his boots, the faint smell of garbage from the alley. A yellow cab speeding by. He remembers feeling faintly ridiculous: he was an actor, for fuck's sake. Not even an actor, an acting student. He'd never been in a fight that wasn't staged.

Nick, for his part, didn't even have the decency to look surprised: "Dude," he said, his smug face twisted in lazy self-satisfaction. "Relax. It was a joke."

Will's never admitted this part to anyone, but it felt good to hit him, years of pent-up anger and loneliness in a mess of spit and blood. It was about Nick and what he'd done to his sister, yeah. But there's a shameful part of him that knows it wasn't ever only about that.

Somebody called the cops, in the end; Will performed the

second week of *Orpheus Descending* with pancake makeup thick enough to cover the black eye and split lip. When he walked back into the apartment Georgia looked at him for a moment, then shook her head slightly. "You are so fucking dumb," she said, but she went to the freezer and got him a box of Eggo waffles to put on his face, and they sat and watched *Criminal Minds* on her laptop and didn't talk about it again after that.

They still haven't, even all these years later: it's in a locked box with their parents, he guesses, and the morning Georgia found him on his bathroom floor. Some things don't need to be opened up again. Some things don't need to be shared.

Now Will gazes out the living room window in the direction of the Benedettos', his whole body restless and achy. Then he goes upstairs and puts himself to bed.

CHAPTER TWENTY-SEVEN

LILLY

She speeds south toward Joshua Tree the following afternoon, salty and seething: At Charlie Bingley, who was photographed canoodling with Sera Foye at a club last night in Paris. At Olivia, who's on her way to Moon Landing in stubborn defiance of all good sense and judgment. At her parents, for every financial decision they've made since 1994.

At Will most of all.

Lilly lay in bed all night replaying their argument over and over, something about it snagging like a pair of cheap tights in the very back of her brain. He was wrong that she showed up at his place sniffing around for gossip. He was wrong that she didn't want anything more.

Charlotte comes running out of the house as Lilly pulls the brake at the end of the long, winding driveway, her red hair streaming behind her like a flag. "You're here!" she hollers delightedly, and when they hug Lilly kind of forgets all the weirdness that's been calcifying between them lately, the feeling of squeezing into shapewear a full size too small. "Thank you for coming."

"Of course I came," Lilly says, breathing in the vanilla-jasmine smell of the same shampoo Charlotte has been using since high school and feeling 100 percent like a jerk. So what if Charlotte is dating someone Lilly herself finds deeply irritating? If she's happy—and, god love her, she keeps saying she is—isn't that all that matters? Lilly wants to be the kind of friend Charlotte can count on. She wants to be the kind of friend Charlotte deserves.

Then Colin comes strolling out the side door in a pair of skinny jeans and an oversized, short-sleeve button-down shirt screen-printed with a neon rendering of the Notorious B.I.G., clutching a Karl Ove Knausgård novel in one pale hand, and Lilly has to give herself the entire fucking pep talk all over again.

"Lil!" he says, opening his arms magnanimously. "Welcome to our humble abode."

Lilly plasters a smile onto her face. "Thanks for having me, *cugino*."

Charlotte beams at them. "Come on," she says, swinging an arm around Lilly's shoulders and steering her across the driveway. "Let me give you the tour."

Colin's got a work deadline, and he makes himself gratifyingly scarce while Lilly and Charlotte spend the better part of the next two days lying by the pool, gossiping and reading magazines like they did back when they were teenagers. The property is incredible: the trees and the garden and the mountains soaring high in the distance, the sky clear and blue and enormous overhead. Lilly is staying in a tiny guest cottage that's connected to the main house by a covered breezeway, the bright white walls hung with neon posters advertising the Rolling Stones at the Greek and Stevie Nicks at the Hollywood Bowl. The whole place smells like oranges and sandalwood, the tile baked warm under Lilly's feet.

"He's making noise about staying here through the winter," Charlotte confides, hulling an avocado for guacamole as Edith Piaf bellows on the expensive sound system. It's impossible to deny how at home Charlotte seems here, how very much herself—making complicated meals in the outdoor kitchen and padding around barefoot, her whole closet full of flowy white caftans. "Colin, I mean."

Lilly raises her eyebrows; she can't help it. "Would you stay with him?" she asks.

Charlotte tilts her head, considering. "I need to get back to the restaurant eventually," she says. "But I'd stay for as long as I could."

Lilly nods without comment. The truth is that since she's been out here she can't help but notice how Colin is with Charlotte: pulling her chair out and refilling her wineglass, exclaiming ebulliently over every bite of food he puts in his mouth. He kind of makes Lilly want to barf, though not in precisely the same way he usually does. She digs her phone out of her pocket, scrolls to Will's name: *Don't you think the worst thing in the world is when someone you hate turns out to be sort of decent?* she types, then abruptly remembers they aren't doing this anymore and deletes the message letter by careful letter.

"You okay?" Charlotte asks, handing Lilly a bowl of tortilla chips and shooing her out in the direction of the patio.

"Never better," Lilly lies in reply.

* * *

Colin invites some friends for a dinner party on Friday—including, he tells Lilly breathlessly, Caitriona de Bourgh—so Lilly tags along with Charlotte to the farmer's market that morning, nibbling a corn muffin while Charlotte inspects greens and tomatoes with the keen-eyed intensity of a 1950s bride-to-be selecting a pattern for heirloom china. Back at the house she slips into a stretchy floral dress that used to—or possibly does still—belong to June, then slicks on some mascara and heads across the yard to the main house, where Charlotte is mixing an enormous batch of palomas while Colin fusses with the turntable in the living room.

"How can I help?" Lilly asks—at least, she starts to, but she's interrupted by the sound of a mechanical rumbling so loud and insistent it shakes the very plates on the counter, and she whirls around in sudden alarm. "What the fuck is that?"

"That," Charlotte says, the tiniest smirk appearing on her round, catlike face as she rests her wooden spoon against the side of the pitcher, "is Caitriona de Bourgh."

Lilly follows Charlotte out into the driveway, where a tall, lean woman in her forties is dismounting an enormous motorcycle. She's sporting a leather jacket and combat boots and no helmet, plus the exact same pair of aviators Colin is always wearing. Lilly wonders, briefly, if she bought them for him and told him he had to wear them or else.

"Cait!" Colin calls, his voice cracking a bit as he darts out of the house behind them like a little kid spotting the ice cream man. "You made it!"

"I never pass up a chance to stretch this girl's legs out in the desert," Caitriona announces, stroking the chassis of the bike like it's a beloved horse on an old episode of *Dr. Quinn, Medicine Woman*. "Collie. How the hell are you?"

Lilly misses his answer as the rest of the guests begin to arrive, a surprisingly eclectic mix of friends and neighbors: a woman who runs a gallery in Twentynine Palms and a lesbian couple who keep a hobby farm outside of Palm Springs, the actor who played the brother in Colin's last movie and a trio of chefs Charlotte knows from back in LA. A fundamental truth about Lilly is that she both

likes parties and is very, very good at them; it's always come natu-
rally to her, the call and response of a good conversation, the game
of drawing someone out. She's endlessly curious about other people. She's happy to eat and drink and dance.

Tonight, though, her heart isn't in it. It's a lovely dinner, warm
and raucous, chatter and candlelight bouncing off the white stucco
walls; still, Lilly's mind drifts. She misses her sisters. She misses
Will. It's not like her to be so lonely in a big group of people. It's
not like her to feel so ill at ease.

She's finishing her panna cotta and telling herself not to be
such an insufferable sad sack when Colin plucks the spoon from
her hand and sets it on the table, even though she's still got another bite left to go. "Gotta make sure two of the most creatively
talented ladies in my life get a chance to talk to one another!" he
announces, ignoring Lilly's scowl as he tugs her across the living room to where Caitriona is smoking a cigar on the sofa, ashes
burning a tiny hole into the white canvas arm. "My cousin Lilly is
a screenwriter, as well."

Caitriona looks at Lilly archly. Her hair has a certain overpro-
cessed coarseness to it, her skin turned slightly leathery from years
of shooting on location in various American deserts filtered yellow
to look like the Middle East. She smells like leather and like hemp.
"Are you?" she asks.

But Lilly shakes her head. "I'm trying something else right
now, actually," she admits. "A novel."

"You are?" Colin asks, sounding genuinely interested; Lilly
remembers what he said back at her parents' pool that morning, *if
there's something you'd rather be writing.* "You know, I've got a friend
who's an agent in New York—"

"I hate working with women screenwriters," Caitriona announces, ashing her cigar into one of Charlotte's Diptyque candles. "Of course, god forbid you say that now, you'll get run out of town with a pitchfork, but the reality is they're just so fucking sensitive. When I was coming up, at the very least we could recognize that sometimes you just have to hold your nose and suck a—"

"Caitriona!" interrupts Charlotte politely, popping up bright and sudden as a spring tulip. "Come on into the kitchen and I'll grab you another drink."

Lilly slips outside for some air as Charlotte leads Caitriona in the direction of the bar, Caitriona regaling her with a long, convoluted story about playing Russian roulette with Ryan Gosling in the parking lot behind a Dollar General in a suburb of Tucson, Arizona. The evening is still and cool and blue. The stars are wild out here, a million more than you ever see back in the city; every single night since she's been here Lilly has snapped a picture to send to Junie, and every single morning when she's scrolled through her camera roll it's all just looked blurry and vague.

She imagines going back inside the house and pitching her book to Caitriona. She imagines getting in her car and driving home to Pemberly Grove. She imagines tromping out into the middle of the wilderness and screaming as loud as she can for as long as she can manage, but when she glances over at the driveway Will Darcy is standing there in jeans and a soft-looking T-shirt, his hands hanging loosely at his sides, and for a moment she can't imagine anything else at all.

"Oh my god." Lilly stops so fast she almost trips—gaping at him in the moonlight as her wineglass slips from her fingers, the sheer mathematical impossibility of him here in this place in this moment turning her shaky and shrill. She feels like she took peyote when she wasn't paying attention. She feels like her knees might give. "Are you—I mean. What are you doing here?"

Will kisses her instead of answering, crossing the distance between them in two big steps and wrapping a hand around the back of her neck, pulling her flush against him. Lilly gasps into his mouth. She kisses him back, though, arms winding around his neck and fingertips sifting through his hair, quick and frantic. She's never been more relieved to see someone in her entire life.

"Okay," she manages finally, even as she's tilting her head back so he can nip at the thin skin underneath the hinge of her jaw, sharp teeth and the warm slick of his tongue over the bitten place. "Okay, okay, stop, I just—"

Will lets go of her immediately—too fast, if Lilly's being honest. Her whole body is aching with want. He's breathing hard, his eyes wide and startled, like possibly he drove here in his sleep and is only just waking up right this minute. He takes a wild, unsteady step back.

"No, don't—" Lilly shakes her head, frustrated, fingernails zipping along the fabric of his T-shirt as she yanks him back against her. His chest is always more solid than she expects. "Just—come with me." She turns him around and shoves him in the direction of the guesthouse, sliding her hand down the front of his jeans as they go; Will sklonks his ankle hard on the doorframe, and Lilly laughs. "Careful," she chides, shutting the door behind them. "Winding up with a grievous bodily injury while fooling around with a Benedetto sister at a party in Palm Desert is exactly how a person winds up on the Sinclair."

Will ignores her, rucking her dress up; his hands are warm and enormous, touching her stomach and her rib cage, reaching back behind her to cup and squeeze her ass. He drops to his knees in the hall-way, hooking his fingers in the elastic of her underwear and looking up at her for permission. Lilly's head thunks back against the wall.

It doesn't take long for him to get her there, his hands and his mouth and how long his eyelashes look from this angle, her whole body blooming bright and sudden as a desert flower. Will reaches up and takes her hand.

"Fuck," she says when she's finished—the last dregs of the orgasm still buzzing through her, her legs water-wobbly and weak. She curls her hand around Will's shoulder for balance, scratching through his shirt as she yanks him unsteadily to his feet. "Okay, okay, come up here."

In the bedroom she fishes a condom out of her suitcase, push-ing him backward toward the mattress: She wants to make this good for him, suddenly. Wants to be the best he's ever had. "I missed you," he admits, his voice barely more than a whisper. It's the first thing he's said since he showed up.

"Yeah," Lilly says, and tilts her face up to kiss him. "I missed you, too."

It's surprising at first, the size and the stretch of him. She hasn't done this in a very long time. Lilly shifts her hips against the mat-tress, looking for a better angle; right away Will frowns, his body stilling on top of her. "No?"

"You're fine," she promises, using her knee to nudge him in the side. "Don't stop."

"Bullshit," he says. "What can I—?"

"I mean it," she says. She feels keyed up and a little hysterical, all these stops and starts. "Keep going."

But Will shakes his head, almost imperceptible. "Lilly," he says quietly, "tell me how to make this good."

Lilly sighs, squeezing her eyes shut and then opening them again. "Switch," she tells him finally, pushing gently at his shoulders. "Let me—"

Will's eyes widen. "Yeah," he says, pulling out of her so carefully. "Of course."

As soon as she gets up there she can tell it's going to work like this, him flat on his back underneath her: "Touch me," she says once she's settled, bracing herself against the solid planes of his chest.

Will doesn't move. "Show me how."

Oh, she thinks, abruptly getting it. Her stomach swoops low and dangerous. "Give me your hands," she instructs, pressing one of them down between her legs and dragging the other one up her body, sucking two of his fingers into her mouth. Right away, Will pulls back.

"Can't do that," he says, shaking his head urgently, his whole body gone tense underneath her. "You can't—"

"Or what?" she asks with a grin, rocking herself against his hand. "Sorry, just—what's going to happen if I—?"

Will scowls. "You know what," he says. "I don't wanna—I mean, you gotta let me—" He takes a breath. "We're only gonna do this the first time once, all right?"

Lilly swallows hard. "Well then," she says, raising her eyebrows. "Do something else."

Will's eyes darken but he takes the direction, catching both her breasts in his free hand, working one nipple between his thumb and index finger. Lilly gasps. "Better?" he asks.

"Good," she allows, her head dropping forward. Will's grin is sharp and bright in the dark.

It doesn't take long like that. It happens for them more or less simultaneously, Will's face going vulnerable and open just as the orgasm crests inside her. *Of course*, Lilly thinks, and then for a moment or two she doesn't think a single thought at all.

"I'm sorry about the other night," he tells her later, the two of them lying there in the darkness; she texted Charlotte to say she's got a headache, grabbed a couple of beers from the guesthouse fridge. "I didn't mean—"

But Lilly shakes her head, pressing the chilly bottle against the bare skin of his side to cut him off. "I don't want to talk about the other night."

Will looks at her for a long moment, like he's debating something. "Fair enough," he finally agrees, lying back against the pillows. "How's it going with your cousin?"

"Fine," Lilly admits, "although he keeps asking if I want to get up at five a.m. to do morning pages."

"Five a.m. is the best time to walk the spiritual path to higher creativity," Will says, and for a moment Lilly is completely unsure if he's kidding. "And the book?"

"It's good." Lilly ducks her head, trying not to smile. The truth is it's been going so well she's been almost afraid to talk about it, the words pouring out of her from an inside deeper than she knew she had. "I mean, nothing's going to come of it, but . . ."

Will frowns. "You don't know that."

"I do know that."

"You seem like the kind of person who's harder on herself than anyone else is."

"You seem like the kind of person who's never read the comments on Instagram."

"I don't have Instagram."

"I know you don't," she blurts without entirely meaning to.

Then she shrugs. "Joe used to say that too, though. Like, 'Come on, Lilly, who's gonna believe in you if you don't believe in yourself?'" She frowns, hearing it out loud; she hardly ever talks about Joe, especially without meaning to. "Sorry. Is that weird?"

Will raises an eyebrow. "That you somehow have not arrived at almost thirty years old with no romantic history whatsoever?" he asks. "I think I can give you a pass."

Lilly makes a face. "To talk about him, I mean. When we're—" She gestures between them.

"It's not weird." Will's voice is quiet. "What was he like?"

"Really?"

He shrugs. "If you want to tell me."

Lilly sits up on the mattress as she thinks about it, tucking the top sheet around her and drawing one knee up to her chest. She can hear the rumble and hum of the party spilling onto the patio outside, the sound of someone laughing. "He worked at the original Meatball King," she says finally, "back in the Valley—he ran the fryer, did the prep work, that kind of thing. And by senior year I was the only one of us who was still going over there after school sometimes to see my dad. That's how we met." She remembers it now, noticing him—his muscles moving inside his T-shirt, the tiny burn marks speckling his arms all the way up past his elbows. He'd been nineteen at the time.

"I think about it sometimes," she tells Will, "what would have happened to us if things had been normal. If I hadn't been who I was. But right away, we were just . . . everywhere, you know? On the blogs, in magazines. We were photogenic, I don't know."

"You were," Will agrees. "I can use Google."

"So, then. You know what happened next."

"The broad strokes, yeah." Will nods. "I'm sorry."

"It's not your fault," Lilly says, and admittedly her voice doesn't sound quite as casual as she'd like. "You didn't give him the drugs. I didn't give them to him, either, not that it made any difference in the end." She shrugs. "It always made me so mad, you know? All those articles that came out after he died. Not because I didn't think I deserved the blame—of course I deserve the blame—but because it made Joe sound like this oblivious dumbass who was too simpleminded not to be ruined by someone like me, like I dragged him down into some glamorous underworld full of fast cars and bottle service and cast a spell to keep him there. But he was smart, you know? He could argue LA politics with my father and fix an industrial range and smell bullshit from a mile away. He just . . . got sick, is all."

"Yeah," Will says. "I think that's how it goes sometimes."

"I didn't know he had a problem. Or no, that's a lie, of course I knew he had a problem, there was no way to miss the fact that he had a problem; I just didn't realize I wasn't going to be able to fix it before it killed him. I just . . . thought I had more time." Lilly sighs. "Anyway," she says, picking at a loose thread in the sheets. "I didn't."

"You couldn't have," Will says, reaching out and lacing their fingers together, squeezing once before letting go. "And you don't, actually. Deserve the blame."

"Well." Lilly doesn't believe him, not really, but she lies back down beside him anyway, her ankles brushing his under the covers. They're quiet for a while, just the sound of his heart beating; she thinks she must drift off for a minute, but when she opens her eyes next he's still awake, keeping watch, one arm tucked beneath the pillows. She looks again at the freckles on his nose.

"You," he says, "are. Extraordinary."

Lilly snorts, she can't help it. "Are you trying to pick me up?" she asks. "Because frankly it's a little late for—"

"Uh-huh." Will cuts her off. "Just take the compliment, you fucking monster."

Lilly thinks about it for a moment. "Okay," she says eventually, and yawns.

CHAPTER TWENTY-EIGHT

WILL

Lilly's still sleeping when he wakes up the following morning. Will gazes at her in the warm light spilling in through the curtains, transfixed in spite of himself: her dark tangle of hair splayed all over the pillows and the long, graceful ladder of her backbone, one tan arm slung up over her head. At some point during the night she yanked all the covers off him and onto herself, and the artic blast from the A/C is blowing more or less directly onto his dick; still, to Will's surprise, he finds he doesn't actually want to wake her up by stealing them back.

After a moment she stirs, though, lean muscle moving underneath her smooth, unblemished skin. "It's creepy to watch someone while they're sleeping, weirdo," she mumbles into the pillows.

Will startles, feeling himself blush. "How do you know I was watching you?" he asks, taking the opportunity to pull the sheet back up over his junk. He's been hard since before he opened his eyes, her smell and her body and the heat of her lying here beside him; he's never felt this helpless with a woman before, like she could take him apart with both hands.

"I could sense you hovering." Her voice is gruff, but when she rolls over and pushes her hair out of her face she's smiling. "Hi."

"Hi yourself." Will grins back, he can't help it, only then she's reaching down and wrapping her hand around him, squeezing roughly; he growls when she lets go again almost immediately, his head whoofing back against the pillows. "Cute," he accuses.

"Thank you," she replies sweetly, "I am." She props herself up on one sharp elbow. "I'll go get coffee in a minute," she offers. "Tell Charlotte you're here, apologize for bailing early on dinner."

"Think she'll forgive you?"

"She once abandoned me with a cart full of groceries in the middle of the Whole Foods in Calabasas because she saw one of the guys from *Supernatural* buying tricolore pasta salad at the deli counter and followed him right out into the parking lot and all the way home," Lilly recalls. "So, I suspect she'll get over it." She grins. "Do you need to get back to LA right away?"

Will shakes his head. "I can stay for a little bit," he tells her. "They don't need me on set until tonight. We're in the home stretch, anyway. We've only got another couple of weeks 'til we wrap."

Lilly hums. "And then?"

"Back to real life, I guess." The realization is startling: all he's wanted since he got here was to go the fuck home where he belongs, but now . . . He runs the pad of his thumb over the piping on the top sheet. "New York's not so bad, you know."

Lilly lifts an eyebrow. "It's not, huh?"

He shakes his head. "Museums. Galleries. Plenty of places to write."

"You realize we also have all those things in LA."

"Seasons."

"We have those here too, asshole," she protests. "They're called Hot and Fire. Get with the program."

"Sorry, sorry." Will grins. "I'm just saying, you ever want to come spend some time . . ."

"I might."

"You should," he says. "My place doesn't have a guest room, but I could probably borrow a blow-up mattress from one of my neighbors, set you up in the hallway or something."

Lilly laughs out loud. "Fuck you," she says, clambering inelegantly on top of him. "Kiss me."

Will does: gently at first and then a little bit deeper, licking his way into her mouth. Lilly kisses him back. She braces her hands against the mattress and drags herself along the length of him, her body hot and slick and ready; the tip of his cock catches, and both of them gasp.

"Hold that thought," Will manages, reaching down and digging a condom out of his jeans pocket, nudging her onto her back. It's like reading a new play for the first time, being with her: the possibilities unfolding in front of him, the thrill of not knowing what's going to happen next. She makes him feel like he could do eight shows a week with no understudy. She makes him want to try *Hamlet* one more time.

They go slower than they did last night, his mouth on her neck and her ear and her sternum. He wants to learn everything she likes. Lilly makes a quiet, approving sound as he reaches down in between them, shifting her hips to take him deeper: "You're better at sex than I thought you'd be," she tells him, and Will coughs a short, nervous laugh.

"Uh." He peers down at her for a moment, not sure exactly how to take that particular declaration. "Thank you?"

"You're welcome." Then, seeming to register his sarcasm a

beat too late: "It was a compliment. It was!" she insists, off his dubious expression. Her smile is teasing and fond. "At the very least it means I thought about it."

"Uh-huh," Will says, but it doesn't come out quite as dryly as he means for it to. Then, because she's still looking at him, and because she's blushing a little across the bridge of her nose, and because it's not like it isn't true: "I thought about it, too."

Lilly likes that: "Oh yeah?" she asks, rolling her hips slow and deep underneath him. "What'd you think?"

"None of your business." Will bites at her jaw.

"I mean, it's a little bit my business," she protests, raking her nails lightly over his rib cage. "Come on, tell me one thing."

Will considers that for a moment. "Your hair," he tells her finally, dropping his head to murmur low and quiet into her ear. "Your smile. Your shoulders. Your ass."

Lilly eyes him, running the sole of one bare foot up and down the back of his calf. "Are you an ass guy?" she asks, sounding interested in spite of herself.

"Not really," he admits. He feels shy all of a sudden, though not necessarily in a bad way. "Mostly just with you."

Lilly grins and rolls them, bracing her palms on his chest and boosting herself upright.

She looks like the queen of an ancient civilization. She looks like a Renaissance painting in the Met. She looks like an old-fashioned movie star, but more than any of that she just looks like herself, and as soon as he thinks it Will feels something so surprising and unfamiliar and dangerous that he forgets to move for a second, hips stuttering as he loses the rhythm entirely.

Lilly's eyes narrow. "Hey," she says, reaching down and flicking his chest with two fingers, not especially gently. "Pay attention."

"I am," he promises, then rolls them one more time so he's back on top. "I swear to god I am."

He's still buried inside her twenty minutes later when her phone buzzes on the nightstand, one quick shrill vibration. "Ignore it," he advises, sucking a mark on the underside of her breast.

"That's the plan," she mumbles back, only a second later it buzzes again, and then again a moment after that, until finally it's just one long frantic drone like a swarm of bees. "Okay," Lilly says finally, pushing him gently off her. "Let me just—" She sits up and reaches for it, the morning sun golden along the planes of her back. Will reaches out to trace the knobs of her spine with one finger, and he can feel the moment when her entire body tenses.

"What?" he asks.

"I need to call my sister."

Will frowns. "What's wrong?" he asks again, but Lilly is already hitting the screen to dial, waving him off.

"Olivia and who?" she asks whoever answers—jamming the receiver between her neck and shoulder as she pulls on her underwear, digging around under the bed until she comes up with her bra. "Junie. Olivia and who?" Then she's shutting herself in the bathroom where her voice is low and muffled, the door clicking tidily behind her.

She's in there for a long time. Will stays in bed for a while, then finally gets dressed because he doesn't know what else to do—he doesn't know what's happening in there, but he has a feeling that whatever it is he's not going to want to confront it with his dick hanging out. He's just scooping his T-shirt off the floor when the door to the bathroom opens and Lilly comes out, the expression on her face sincerely rattled for the very first time since he's known her. All at once Will thinks of the night the police showed up at the house to tell Georgia and him about their parents: he remembers focusing on the raindrops on the younger officer's uniformed shoulders, counting them to avoid doing anything else. "What?" he asks again, and it sounds a lot more like pleading than he means for it to.

Lilly sits down on the edge of the bed. "There's a video," she says slowly, "of Olivia at Moon Landing. With Nick Harlow."

The sound in Will's head is the rushing of water. The feeling in his chest is pure dread. "Olivia with Nick Harlow doing what, exactly?"

Lilly shrugs, but barely. "All the things you might expect."

"And she . . . she released it?"

"What?" Right away she's on her feet again, whirling on him like a boxer. "Of course not. Nick sold it to the Sinclair."

"I—right." Will nods. It's like he's trying to hear her from the other side of the freeway. "I—of course. Right."

"What the fuck is wrong with you?" Lilly demands, pacing like a lioness across the carpet. She's still in her bra and underwear, wrenching open a dresser drawer and pulling out a pair of jeans. "You think she would sell a video of herself—"

"I don't," he backpedals quickly. "Of course I don't." He twists the T-shirt into a rope with both hands, guilt and dread blooming inside him like the algae on the pond back in Pemberly Grove. "Lilly," he says, and oh, already he knows he is going to regret this. Already he knows this is going to be bad. "About what happened between me and Nick."

* * *

She's still as the desert at night the whole time he's telling it, Georgia and the Polaroids and *Orpheus Descending*. Then all at once she's nothing but motion. "Are you kidding me?" she demands, sitting down hard and then immediately jumping up again, wrenching open the closet door. "I mean—how can you possibly have—are you kidding me?"

Will flinches. "Lilly—"

"I asked you," she interrupts, her eyes glowing coal-dark with fury as she flings her empty suitcase onto the bed, nearly hitting him square in the chest. "I fully asked you what the deal was with that guy and you called me cheap for wanting to know. You let me send my baby sister off to that stupid fucking festival with a literal sex predator—"

"You never told me he was taking her to a festival—"

"I didn't know!" Lilly explodes. "I didn't know, because I didn't think to ask, because I didn't know he was someone I needed to protect her from. Because you didn't tell me."

"I explicitly said he wasn't a good guy!" Will protests. "I'm sorry I didn't provide you with the salacious detail you so obviously require—"

"Oh, right," Lilly says, stalking over to the dresser and yanking open the middle drawer. "When it was your family he was messing with he deserved a beatdown in an alley, but when it's my family it's just, 'Eh, I don't like him, can't tell you why, but odds are good it's just because I'm a giant fucking snob who hates everybody—'"

"It had nothing to do with me being a snob!"

"How the fuck was I supposed to know that?" Lilly demands. She flings an armful of clothes into the suitcase, then bangs into the bathroom, returning a moment later with an armful of expensive-looking cosmetics. "You let me be a target, Will. You let my sister be a target."

"Wait a second." Will blinks. "Are you saying this is my fault?"

"I mean." She dumps the makeup into her bag with a noisy clatter. "It's not *not* your fault, that's for sure."

"That's insane," Will counters, his mouth falling open at the unfairness of it. "That's insane! I warned you, Lilly. I warned you, and I'm not about to take responsibility for your shitty taste in guys, and I'm definitely not about to take responsibility for your sister's shitty taste in guys. Like, not to put too fine a point on it, but this kind of thing is, like, pretty on-brand for her, isn't it?"

All at once, Lilly stops moving, her sudden stillness taking his breath away. "I'm sorry," she says, and her voice is dangerously quiet. "What?"

Right away, he realizes that was exactly the wrong thing to say. "I didn't mean—" he starts, then completely fails to follow it up in any meaningful way. "I'm only making the point that—"

"It's on-brand for my sister to have an incredibly personal, private, vulnerable moment broadcast all over the internet without her consent?"

Her voice is calm and deadly. Will scrubs his hands through his hair. "Of course not," he tries. "That's not what I'm—"

Lilly shakes her head. "This was a mistake," she says, leaning hard on the suitcase as she struggles to zip it shut. "I mean, of course it was a mistake, I knew it was a mistake from the literal first time we met when you were objectively very rude to me, but—"

"Lilly—"

"I need to go be with my family right now," she announces sharply. She turns a frantic circle around the bedroom, yanking at the bedsheets and tossing throw pillows onto the floor until she finally finds her phone sitting on the edge of the dresser. She stuffs it hastily into her pocket, then heaves the suitcase up with two hands even though it's a roller and clomps awkwardly toward the door. "I'll catch up with you later. Or . . . not, I guess. I mean." She drops the suitcase, yanking at the handle until it extends. "Probably not."

"What does that mean?" Will asks. "Lilly, you can't just—at least let me help you—"

But Lilly is already gone.

CHAPTER TWENTY-NINE

LILLY

She says a hasty goodbye to Charlotte as she throws her bag into the trunk of the Honda, her blood thudding wildly in her ears. "I'm sorry specifically and generally," she promises, wrapping her arms around Charlotte and squeezing, "and I am so sincerely happy for you guys." She slides into the driver's seat, turns the key in the ignition. "Also, um. It's possible Will Darcy might or might not be squatting in your guesthouse."

Charlotte's eyes widen, whipping her head around to look. "Wha—?"

"I love you!" Lilly hollers. "I'll call you from the road."

She steps on the gas, lower lip trembling, her thoughts a noisy, poisonous whirl inside her head: Will. Joe. Olivia. Junie, rail-thin in New York City. The house slipping away in front of her eyes. She can't keep a single bad thing from happening. She can't save a single person she loves.

Kit and Mari hopped a last-minute flight from Burbank; Lilly scoops them from the airport before speeding across town and fetching Olivia from the Parker, where she's checked into a suite they 100 percent cannot afford while a dozen paparazzi camp on the street outside. She wears the robe and a pair of sunglasses right out to the car.

"I'm not talking about this," Olivia announces, sliding into the passenger seat.

"That's fine," Lilly promises. "You don't have to."

"But I don't regret it, for the record. I'm a modern woman, and I own my sexuality. Anyone who has a problem with that is just in shackles to our Puritan, patriarchal culture."

"I'd hardly call performing a sex act on a bartender at a culturally appropriative music festival a feminist act," Marianne volunteers from the back seat.

"Fuck you, Mari!" Olivia whirls on her. "Nobody asked you!"

"Easy," Lilly says, holding a hand up. "We're going to figure this out together. As a team."

"There's nothing to figure out," Olivia insists. "It's not a big deal. I don't even care."

Lilly and Kit exchange looks in the rearview. On the one hand, if this is how Olivia wants to handle it, Lilly's not about to tell her otherwise. She knows the value of the stories you tell yourself as much as anyone else.

On the other . . .

"Olivia," she says, as gently as she can manage, and that's when Olivia starts to cry.

"I liked him," she admits in a small voice, throwing her hands up like she's disgusted by the very thought of it. God, she is so impossibly young. "I thought he liked me, too."

"I know," Lilly says, reaching across the gearshift and squeezing Olivia's shoulder. Mari reaches forward, stroking a hand through her hair.

* * *

By the time they finally get back to the house Olivia is snoring in the passenger seat and there's an unfamiliar sedan parked in the driveway; as Lilly's pulling her bag from the trunk of the Honda the front door opens and a man in a suit comes striding down the walk—her father glowering behind him, Cinta following at his heels. The stranger nods once at Lilly, and she lifts a hand in automatic greeting, then immediately lowers it, glancing back at Dominic and feeling pretty sure she just did something wrong.

"Who was that?" she asks.

"Nobody," her father announces, loud enough that the guy can certainly hear him even as he's pulling out of the driveway. "An empty suit, that's who!" He stomps back into the house, the door slamming behind him hard enough that Lilly can feel it in her jaw.

"An appraiser," Kit says quietly.

Lilly frowns. "From, like, the bank?"

Kit nods. "I heard them talking about it while you were gone," she explains. "Something to do with the foreclosure." Lilly feels the word drop through her body like a marble.

Olivia startles awake. "Are we home?" she asks, pulling off her sunglasses. There's a crease on her cheek from where the plastic was digging in.

"Yeah, honey," Lilly says, opening the door and holding a hand out. "We're home."

* * *

June flies in from New York that night. "I shouldn't have gone," she says. "I felt like such a sad sack the entire time I was there. And I didn't see a single play." She frowns. "How's Olivia?"

"She'll be okay," Lilly promises, trying not to stare. In the weeks they've been apart June's lost what must be close to ten more pounds, her collarbones jutting like fiberglass, her skin gone faintly gray. Lilly opens her mouth, then closes it again, looking around wildly to see if anyone else has noticed, but her mom and sisters are busy nosing through Junie's luggage, looking for gifts. She imagines being the first person to spy an invading army. She imagines being the first person to smell the smoke at Pompeii.

* * *

Late that night she finds her mother in the kitchen squinting at her computer, Olivia all over the homepage of the Sinclair; if Cinta thinks it's strange to be perusing media coverage of her youngest daughter's sex tape, she gives no indication.

"I'm going to kill him," Lilly says, reaching out and snapping the laptop closed. She means it, too: she's going to find Nick and dismember him and leave his body in the desert for the vultures to pick apart like a chicken dinner. Caitriona de Bourgh can find some man to write the screenplay. "I'm going to make him wish he was never born."

"Oh, don't be so dramatic, darling," her mother says with a wave of her hand. "I think there's a way we could spin this to our advantage, don't you? After all, all publicity is—"

"Mom," Lilly interrupts, holding a hand up. "Please don't."

"Well." Her mother sniffs. "You're not thinking very creatively, if you ask me."

They're quiet for a moment. "Can I ask you something?" Lilly asks, leaning back against the kitchen island. "Why did you decide to marry Dad?"

If her mother thinks it's strange that Lilly wants to know, she doesn't show it. "He had the best head of hair I'd ever seen on a man," she says immediately, no equivocation at all. "Lustrous, spectacular hair."

Lilly snorts. "Mom," she says. "Be serious."

"I am being serious!" her mother protests. "I looked at him and thought, 'One day I'm going to have sons, and when I do, I want them to have hair like that.'" She shrugs. "Then I had you girls, one after another, and your father went bald, and now here I am."

"Our hair is very good," Lilly admits.

"You're welcome." Cinta opens the laptop again, and Lilly swallows down a small wave of disappointment at the knowledge that no other answer will be forthcoming. The worst part is that she doesn't even think her mother is being facetious: when Lilly thinks about what her parents could possibly have seen in each other thirty years ago, thick, gleaming hair seems about as good a reason as any. How are you supposed to know who someone is going to be in three decades? How can you even know who they are right now?

Lilly takes a deep breath. "Listen," she says, "about the appraiser."

"Oh, Lilly," her mother says, not looking up from the screen. "Drop the rock, will you?"

"Drop the—?" Lilly frowns. "I mean, sure, but also the rock is our house, Mom. The rock is the place where we live. So if we're going to lose it, then I want to at least—"

"Contrary to what your father might have you believe, Elisabetta," Cinta interrupts her, "you are not actually the woman in charge in this house."

Lilly blinks, feeling briefly like her mother has slapped her. She leans back against the lounge chair, swallowing down a burning sensation that is, she tells herself firmly, definitely not tears. It's just that she's tired, maybe. It's been a crazy couple of days. "Okay," she says quietly. "Well. Sorry."

"That's fine," her mother replies. "I'm glad you could go get your sister."

"Yeah," Lilly replies, once she's sure her voice is steady. "I'm glad I could go get her, too."

CHAPTER THIRTY

CINTA

They're going to lose the house, obviously.

Oh, Cinta knows it; of course Cinta knows it. She's known it for years, somewhere in the back of her brain's bargain basement: that the money wasn't coming in like it used to, that there was no way it could possibly last. She grew up eating margarine sandwiches, her pants always two inches short at the ankles. She can smell lack a mile away.

Still, she thinks, hushing the low whoosh of panic like a child misbehaving in an expensive department store: they're not going to lose the house tonight, are they?

So. Nothing to worry about, then.

She slathers on her potions—*A hundred and fifty dollars an ounce*, she can hear Dominic grumbling, but you just go ahead and ask him if he wants to be married to a wrinkled old crone—and slips into a fresh pair of pajamas, pads down the hall toward the stairs. She loves this house, truly, almost as much as she loves to complain about it: its high ceilings and the wide arches of the windows, terra-cotta tile and creamy white paint. She always imagined throwing dinner parties here, the dining room finally full of the right kinds of people: the tinkle of their brilliant conversations. Some proof that she finally belonged.

Well, she thinks again. *Not tonight.*

In the living room she finds the girls heaped in a Turnpike Pileup, all five of them fast asleep like something out of a fairy tale. Cinta watches them for a moment: the long lines of their calf muscles, their faces smooth and relaxed. Olivia's hair across June's shoulder. Kit's head in Lilly's lap. Mari is curled on her side, turned away from the others; still, Cinta can't help but notice, one seeking hand reaches back.

They'll land on their feet, she thinks in the moment before she forces herself to stop imagining it, heads back up to bed with a mind gone perfectly, peacefully blank: her girls, her dark-eyed wonders, her miracles each and every one. After all, they're Benedettos. After all, they always do.

CHAPTER THIRTY-ONE

WILL

He finishes the movie, but barely. He skips the wrap party, spends the next four days on the couch watching back-to-back reruns of *Castle* on Charlie's expansive cable package. He was supposed to fly back to New York this week, but opening up his laptop and booking the ticket feels fucking impossible. Everything feels impossible all of a sudden, doing the dishes piled in the sink or washing the dirty clothes draped over the furniture. Cooking food that isn't jelly toast. He feels bad—he's a guest here, technically, it's Charlie's house even if Charlie is in Paris or Jakarta—but not bad enough to do anything about it. He runs out of paper towels. He runs out of steam.

Charlie calls and he sends it to voice mail. Georgia calls, and he doesn't pick up. He remembers this feeling, he thinks, from the days after *Hamlet*. How easy it is not to take a shower. How easy it is to just . . . sink.

Lilly doesn't text, not that he's expecting her to. Will doesn't text her, either.

It's been a little over a week when the bell rings, an insane Baroque chime that lasts roughly forty seconds and rattles his teeth in his head. God, Will hates this house so much. He thinks it's probably a delivery person—Georgia keeps on sending things from

Amazon, like she's worried he's still sitting standing in Target unable to make any decisions—but when he finally opens the door Will is stunned to see his sister herself, a duffel in one hand and a massive shopping bag from Zabar's in the other.

"LA is terrible," she announces. "It took me forty-five minutes in an Uber just to get out of LAX."

"It's a nightmare," Will agrees reflexively, then blinks. "What are you doing here?"

Georgia shrugs. "I missed you," she says lightly, bustling past him in the direction of the kitchen. "And then Caro said you were acting like a total psycho when she saw you, so. Figured I'd come and do a wellness check."

"And you didn't think maybe a heads-up would have been appropriate?"

"I like to preserve the element of surprise," she says, then stops short, taking in the state of the house: the blinds shut tight and the gunk caked to the counters, the unwashed funk hanging grossly in the air. "Oh, Will," she says softly, and she sounds so disappointed. It makes Will feel about two inches tall.

"Not now, okay?" he mutters, taking the Zabar's bag from her hand and setting it on the island. "I can't deal with your judgment on top of everything else."

Georgia frowns. "My judgment?"

"You know what I mean."

"I don't, actually."

Will sighs. They don't have this kind of relationship, where they fly across the country unannounced to solve each other's problems. Where they fake their way through with rugelach and good cheer. All at once, he's furious: At Georgia for coming all the way out here in the first place. At Nick for being an unrelentingly predatory prick. At himself most of all. Fuck, it's like none of his clothes have fit properly since he got to California. It's like his life hasn't fit properly in months. "Can you spare me the guilt trip, please? You show up here with no warning, you expect me to drop everything—"

"I flew out here because you tried to kill yourself, you absolute dipshit!" Georgia drops her duffel onto the floor with a thump. "What part of that don't you get?"

Will blinks at her, feeling—there is no other word for this—gobsmacked. "I—"

But Georgia is just getting started. "Quite seriously, Will, what in the actual hell is wrong with you that makes you like this?" she demands, pacing across the dusty hardwood. "You're the only family I have, do you get that? You're it. Do you have any idea what it was like, to walk into your apartment and find you lying there in the bathroom? Do you have any idea how afraid I was? How afraid I was coming here today? Have you ever even stopped to think about it?"

"Of course I have," Will protests.

"I don't believe you." Georgia shakes her head. "Look," she says, "I know that whatever you're going through isn't about me, and that I'm supposed to be gentle with you and give you a wide berth and act however you feel is the right way, but honestly, fuck that. You think I just love buying you shit off Amazon? Patronizing some billionaire's conglomerate marketplace, exploiting low wage workers and destabilizing the entire American economy? Of course not!" She huffs a breath. "I send you that stuff because I don't know how to take care of you or have a relationship with you! Because you won't let me."

Will looks at her for one helpless moment, totally at a loss for what to say. "There was a woman," he confesses finally. "And I fucked it up."

Georgia laughs at that, a sharp surprised cackle that doesn't sound anything like her normal laugh. Then, all at once, she starts to cry.

Will gapes. He hasn't seen his sister cry in the better part of two decades and the sight of it cracks something open inside him, leaking in his chest like a broken egg. "It's okay," he says, lifting his hands in her direction, wanting so badly to reach out and touch her. Not entirely sure how. "It's not a big deal, really. We weren't seeing each other very long."

Georgia looks at him like he's too stupid to breathe air. "I'm not crying about your breakup, Will!"

"Oh." Oh. Will processes that for a moment. It would sound insane to say he didn't know she cared about the rest of it—of course he knew she cared about the rest of it, she's his sister; but still, it's like the full force of what happened isn't hitting him until now. The full force of what he almost did. She was so young when their parents died, Will thinks suddenly. Both of them were so, so young. "Georgia," he tries—completely unsure how to follow it up, but wanting to. *"Georgia."*

Georgia sighs and sits down at the island, wiping her face with one palm. "There's smoked salmon in the Zabar's bag," she informs him. "It needs to go in the fridge."

CHAPTER THIRTY-TWO

GEORGIA

Will takes her to lunch, and then to dinner at Dan Tana's; the following morning they get around to the bagels, slightly stale now but still tasting definitively of the Upper West Side. It occurs to Georgia, as she reaches for the cream cheese, that it's possible they'll spend the entirety of her visit this way: leapfrogging from one mostly silent meal to another, their mouths too full to talk.

In the end Will surprises her, though: "When did you see Caroline?" he asks, splashing milk into his iced coffee. His voice is so casual Georgia almost laughs.

"She was in New York a couple of weeks ago," she explains. "We met for a drink." She and Caro have always been friendly, though Georgia has never been stupid enough to imagine it has anything to do with her personally. "You know, a few days after you dumped her."

"I didn't—" he protests immediately. "I mean, we weren't—" He stops. "You know about me and Caroline?"

Georgia snorts. "Everybody knows about you and Caroline, dumbass."

"Even Charlie?"

"Even Charlie." Georgia munches a sprig of dill from the garden, truly enjoying herself for the first time since she got here. "I gotta tell you, William: you are not, nor have you ever been, quite as low-key as you like to imagine you are."

Will winces. "Please believe me when I tell you I have never imagined myself to be even remotely low-key." He stirs the coffee for another moment, though all he's actually doing at this point is melting the ice. "She was really mad, huh?" he asks quietly. "Caroline, I mean."

"Caroline doesn't get mad," Georgia reminds him. "She gets a media strategy. Let's just say I probably wouldn't consider putting myself forward for anyone's consideration this award season if I were you."

"Yeah," Will says. "I guess that tracks."

"Was that the breakup?" she asks, fanning a couple of slices of tomato across the surface of her bagel. "The one you were talking about yesterday?"

Will drops his head back, sighing. His neck badly needs a shave. "No," he admits grudgingly, talking up at the citrus trees instead of looking directly at her. "Do you know who Lilly Benedetto is?"

Georgia almost chokes on a caper. "Are you kidding me?" she says, once she's recovered. "You're hooking up with *Lilly Benedetto*?"

"First of all, please don't say it in that tone of voice," he begs, closing his eyes forbearingly. "Second of all, no. I hooked up with her, I guess, though I want to go on the record as saying I really hate that language. Past tense."

"First of all," Georgia imitates, "you're a prig and a grandpa. Second of all, no wonder Caroline lost her shit. I'm surprised her brain didn't come flying out of her head and careen into the ocean like one of those whirligig fireworks." She twirls a finger to demonstrate. "I do love how you said that, though: 'Do you know who Lilly Benedetto is?'" She pitches her voice low and dopey. "Like, 'Have you ever heard of an astronaut called Neil Armstrong?'"

Will scowls. "That's not what I——"

"'Are you familiar with an American politician by the name of George Washington?'"

"Okay."

"'Have you ever encountered the cuisine of celebrity chef Guy Fieri?'"

"Can you stop?" Will asks, but he's laughing, the sound of it deep and loose and genuine. He has a nice laugh, Georgia's brother. She only ever gets it out of him like once a year. "I'm just saying, I didn't know who she was when we met."

"I am . . . sure you did not, actually," Georgia agrees. The thought of it makes her feel very fond of him. "So what happened?"

Will shrugs. "There was a thing," he says, "with her sister and Nick Harlow."

"Ah." Georgia nods, picking at a bit of smoked salmon. "I may have heard something about that." She doesn't keep track of Nick, as a general rule, but Olivia Benedetto's sex tape has been more or less everywhere the last few days, talk of it hanging in the air like a noxious cloud. Georgia would be lying if she said that wasn't part of the reason she finally just booked a ticket and came out here, a restless energy she couldn't shake. She was running from something, maybe. But she thinks she was running toward something, too.

"I handled it badly," Will confesses now. "When the tape came out. I was a donkey about it, I don't know. And, like, if you pick a fight with one Benedetto——"

"—you better be ready to fight all the Benedettos," Georgia finishes with a small smile. "I always kind of liked that about them."

"Yeah," Will says. "I like it about them, too."

They're quiet for a minute, both of them eating their bagels, the birds chittering wildly in the bushes around the pool. "You know, we never really talked about the thing with me and Nick," Georgia says cautiously. "I kind of feel like there are a lot of things we've never really talked about."

Will bristles, she can see it, the way his back visibly straightens inside his shirt. "Uh-uh," he protests. "You explicitly told me you didn't want to talk about Nick. That wasn't some fucked-up thing where you were, like, dying to confide in me and I—"

"I explicitly told you I didn't want you to lecture me," Georgia counters immediately. "There's a difference."

"Semantic."

"Hardly." She blows a breath out. "You're my brother, Will," she tells him, setting her bagel down on her plate, "and I know that your instinct is to stutter and bluster and immediately bail when things get weird or awkward or feelings-y, but I gotta tell you, it's not exactly a recipe for lasting relationships and robust emotional health. Actually, not to put too fine a point on it, but it's how you wind up passed out alone on your bathroom floor with an empty bottle of sleeping pills on the counter."

Will doesn't answer for a moment, his jaw set and stubborn. He fidgets with the edge of the butter knife beside his plate. "Okay," he says finally, and it sounds like a challenge. "Well. Let's talk, then."

"Okay," Georgia agrees. "Let's talk."

So, they talk: about Nick and about Caroline and about the

years they lived with Marcy; about what they're reading and watching and the woman Georgia's dating back in New York. She stays for the better part of a week, the two of them strolling the grounds of the Getty and staying up late playing a battered game of Scrabble she picks up at the Rose Bowl flea market. She hasn't been back to LA since her parents died and being here is sort of wild, like walking around in a dream from when she was a little girl: They drive by the breakfast place their parents used to take them to on Saturday mornings. They drive by their old house in Toluca Lake.

"Do you think he did it on purpose?" Georgia asks.

"Yes," Will says immediately. They're idling in the car a little ways down the block, the engine humming. He doesn't bother to ask what she means. "I think he probably did it on purpose."

Georgia nods, gazing out the windshield: rusty red roof and bright white stucco, a trio of kids playing freeze tag in the yard. "Yeah," she says, reaching for Will's hand across the gearshift and squeezing. Letting go. "I think he probably did, too."

On her last night in town they pick up dinner from the Meatball King: a pepperoni pizza and an order of garlic knots, Will pulling a couple of beers from the fridge. He looks better since she got here, Georgia notices with some satisfaction. At the very least he's showered and shaved.

"You think you'll see her again?" she asks, a cloud of steam rising around her face as she slides a couple of slices onto a plate and hands them over. "Lilly Benedetto, I mean."

Right away, Will shakes his head. "Nah," he says, no hesitation. "She doesn't want to hear from me."

Georgia bites her lip. He makes her so sad sometimes, her brother, his stubbornness and his solitude and his pride. He breaks her fucking heart. Still, she's supposed to fly out first thing in the morning, and she doesn't want to fight with him right before she leaves, after everything that's happened, so in the end she just shrugs and lifts her slice in a cheesy salute. "Well," she says, "at the very least you should tell her this pizza is a revelation. Like, say what you will about these people, but they make a delicious fucking pie."

Will smiles at that, a breeze rustling the leaves of the trees high above them. "Yeah," he agrees quietly. "You wouldn't expect it, probably. But the pizza's the real deal."

CHAPTER THIRTY-THREE

LILLY

The coverage is . . . not great. "Benedetto Bares All," proclaims the headline on the Sinclair, with a link to the video itself plus a slideshow of Olivia's most revealing outfits. "Liv's Festival Fiasco," *Us Weekly* reports. *In Touch* is blunter about it: "Olivia's Moon Landing Sex Tape Scandal," they promise, in a font bright enough to hurt Lilly's eyes.

"Where's all the feminist outrage?" she fumes, stomping down to the kitchen for a bag of pretzel rods, though of course she already knows the answer, which is that she and her sisters are not exactly the kind of women most feminists particularly care about. Though no one has said it explicitly—well, no one outside of the *Meet the Benedettos* subreddit—the general consensus seems to be that Olivia had this coming. Lilly remembers that feeling from after Joe died: the creeping suspicion that she lived a kind of life that invited spectacular calamity and so had no right to be anything but unsurprised when it came calling. It doesn't feel any better this time around.

Days pass. Lilly walks the neighborhood, committing the curve of the road to memory. She finishes her draft, sends a dozen hopeful emails to literary agents. Gets a dozen form rejections almost as fast. She takes a deep breath, reopens the document. Takes a second look and tries again.

On Saturday morning she finds her dad up in the gym, where he's lying on the bench joylessly pressing two hundred pounds over and over. "Need a spotter?" she asks.

Dominic shakes his head, jaw clenched. "Finishing up," he grinds out, setting the weight back on the rack with a noisy clank before sitting up and reaching for his towel. "How's your sister doing?"

Lilly hesitates. *Which one?* she wants to ask him. *The one with the sex tape, the one with the eating disorder, the one with all the talent nobody cares about, or the one who doesn't want anything to do with the rest of us?* "I think she's been better in her life," she finally allows.

"Yeah." He rubs the towel over the top of his head before draping it around his neck. "Did you come up here to say 'I told you so'?"

"What? No," Lilly says, stung. "When have I ever said anything like that to you?"

"Well, maybe you should," her father says. "You did tell me so. Or you tried, at least."

Lilly opens her mouth, closes it again. It's her instinct to make him feel better—to tell him it's not his fault, he tried his best, that Olivia's a grown woman—but in the end she doesn't say anything, and after a moment her father continues.

"I wanted to give you girls more than I had," he says quietly. "The house, the pool. That's what every father wants, right? That's American. But now that it's all said and done . . . I don't know if it was the right thing."

Lilly doesn't know if it was the right thing, either. She wonders sometimes what their lives would look like now if they'd stayed in the house in the Valley—if maybe they'd have grown up and moved out and found identities apart from one another. If maybe Joe would still be alive. Still, when she thinks about it for any length of time she doesn't think it would have changed anything, not fundamentally. She thinks fundamentally they'd all still be themselves. "I don't know if it was the money that got us here."

Her father shrugs. "What, you mean because of your mother?" he asks with a shake of his head. "That's what I'm saying. The money turned your mother into—"

"I'm not talking about Mom right now, Dad!" Lilly's surprised by the heat in her voice, the surge of defensiveness she feels on her mother's behalf. "I'm talking about you. You just . . . gave up on us. At some point you decided we were spoiled and ridiculous and ungovernable, same as everyone else did. And you just gave up."

"Meaning what, exactly?" Her father's eyes narrow; the two of them haven't argued in years. "I've been here every day—"

"Here," Lilly says, gesturing around at the gym. "Up here working out by yourself, getting stronger and stronger—for what? What battle are you preparing for, exactly? Because I'll tell you, there have been a hell of a lot of them in our house the last few years, and you left us to fight them pretty much on our own."

"When have you ever needed me?" her dad explodes. "When have any of you ever, ever wanted my help?" He shakes his head. "You girls have always been your own nation, all to yourselves."

Lilly has no idea what to say to that, exactly; she knows she's not going to get what she wants from him, that he abdicated his responsibility to them a long time ago. Still, "Every nation needs a leader," she can't help but remind him. "Ours included."

Her father smiles at that, just faintly. "Well," he says, and lifts his chin in her direction, "lucky for your sisters, yours has one."

Lilly shakes her head, something that feels dangerously like tears rising at the back of her throat. "Dad," she starts, but Dominic shakes his head.

"I've got two hundred push-ups to do," he tells her, tossing his towel in the hamper. "I'll see you girls at dinner."

* * *

Back in the house her sisters are draped across the sofa in the living room, the quartet of them all scrolling their phones in silence like some kind of bizarro Renaissance painting. "Listen up," Lilly announces, with as much authority as she can muster. June is the only one who bothers to lift her eyes from the screen.

Lilly sighs. She's not an idiot. She knows what people see when they look at her family. Her father's failing business and obsession with his own pectorals; her mother's swollen, flattened lips. Olivia's mostly one-sided feud with Lorde, who to this day refuses to acknowledge her in interviews. Lilly guesses she can't blame them. After all, that's what the Benedettos have shown to the world—in brilliant, blazing Technicolor—for over a decade. Still, those people weren't there the nights her father brought home a tall stack of pizzas for taste-testing, all of them crowded around the table at the old house; they weren't there when he collapsed on the patio in the middle of a diatribe about their mother's landscaping expenses and needed nine hours of emergency surgery at Cedars. Those people don't know that after Joe died all four of her sisters holed up in her bedroom with her for five full days without leaving, June stroking her hair and Olivia reading her magazines out loud and Kit rubbing lotion into her feet. Even Mari stayed close, curled in the armchair like a cat with her computer in her lap, the sound of her endless typing like one of those white noise machines people use to shush babies to sleep. Every once in a while Lilly still creeps into her room if she's restless in the middle of the night, dozing off in the cool blue glow of the screen. Marianne has never once told her to leave.

She doesn't notice she's crying, but she must be, because all at once Kit catches sight of her and sits up on the sofa, a half-empty bag of Smartfood popcorn sliding off her lap and onto the floor. "Lilly?" she asks. "What's wrong?"

Lilly shrugs helplessly. "I can't fix any of it," she confesses. "I don't know how to make the video go away. Junie is sick again and I can't get her to talk to me. I fucked things up with Will. And I have no idea how we're going to save the house. It feels like the end of everything, and I don't know how to stop it from happening. I don't know how to solve any of it by myself."

For a moment none of her sisters say anything, a quick silent conversation happening among the four of them. In the end, Mari is the one who speaks first.

"Lilly," she says, holding her hand out so she'll join them. "Why the fuck would you ever think you had to?"

* * *

A week passes. They hunker down. Their phones ring endlessly, calls rolling in from every gross, unsavory corner of the Hollywood-industrial complex: An offer from Joe Rogan. An offer from *TMZ*. An offer from a producer at Big Dipper Adult Enterprises—who, Cinta is validated to learn, did in fact rent Charlie's house on Netherfield Place for a period of time several years ago. "They used it to film *Oceanfront Orgy*," she reports when she hangs up, sounding satisfied. "Also, *Oceanfront Orgy 2*." She gestures knowledgeably with her wineglass. "They added the ocean in post."

Kit throws her phone into the pool in protest, then changes her mind and dives in to fish it out again. Lilly doesn't check her email for eight days. "Maybe I should just do it," Olivia says, working her sharp nails beneath the skin of an orange at the table on the patio. "I mean, not the porn, obviously. But the podcast."

Kit makes a face, plucking the peel from Olivia's hand and draping the long curly strip of it over her lips like a mustache. "Honestly," she advises, "at this point I think you'd be better off doing the porn."

Lilly's phone buzzes, skittering nervously across the table like a tropical bug. She grits her teeth and moves to send it to voice mail, then changes her mind at the last possible second and lifts it to her ear instead, punchy and brave. "Whatever it is," she announces, "she's not interested."

"Oh. Uh, sorry," a voice says—young and female and perky, though not quite as young and female and perky as most of the assistants who've been calling. "I think I might have the wrong—is this Lilly Benedetto?"

Lilly frowns, glancing around the table at her sisters' curious glances. She pushes back her chair. "Yes," she says, slipping around the side of the house for some privacy. "This is Lilly."

"Oh, good," the woman says. "Lilly, this is Marissa Tasco, with Ravenwood Literary Associates in New York." She pauses then, the noise of a city faintly audible in the background. "I'm calling to talk to you about your book."

CHAPTER THIRTY-FOUR

MARI

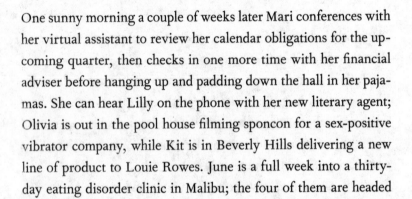

One sunny morning a couple of weeks later Mari conferences with her virtual assistant to review her calendar obligations for the upcoming quarter, then checks in one more time with her financial adviser before hanging up and padding down the hall in her pajamas. She can hear Lilly on the phone with her new literary agent; Olivia is out in the pool house filming sponcon for a sex-positive vibrator company, while Kit is in Beverly Hills delivering a new line of product to Louie Rowes. June is a full week into a thirty-day eating disorder clinic in Malibu; the four of them are headed there to visit her later this afternoon. Charlie Bingley, according to the high-resolution photos on the landing page of the Sinclair, was spotted bringing flowers yesterday morning.

Mari pauses for a moment at the top of the grand, winding staircase, tracing one finger along the family photos there. It took her a long time to love her sisters without being jealous of them: She's not the smartest Benedetto girl, the most talented or clever or vivacious. She's not the one who gets photographed, or even noticed when she walks into a room.

She is, however, as far as she knows, the only one of them who has been regularly investing in the stock market since she was thirteen.

She finds her father at the table on the patio, eviscerating a grapefruit with a serrated spoon. Mari sits down across from him without bothering to wait for an invitation, folding her pale, freckly hands in her lap. "I have a proposal for you," she announces. "About the house."

Her father rolls his eyes. "You sound like your mother," he tells her, still sawing ineffectually away at the pink flesh of the citrus. He's making it much more difficult than it needs to be, Mari observes idly. He ought to just use a sharp knife. "What do you want to do, install a soundstage in the basement?"

Mari smiles at the sound of her sisters' voices drifting out the open windows. Their father's main problem, she's always thought, is his lifelong insistence on underestimating them. "No," she says calmly, opening her folder and pulling out her offer letter, sliding it across the table so he can finally see. "Actually, I'd like to buy it."

CHAPTER THIRTY-FIVE

WILL

It's just past twilight when he rings the Benedettos' doorbell, the chimes echoing out across the empty development. It's Lilly herself who comes to the door. She's wearing a vintage Meatball King T-shirt, a crude likeness of her dad in a chef's hat doodled on the front of it; her feet are tan and bare against the baked tile floor. "Hi," she says, and her voice is very quiet.

"Hi," he says.

They stand there for a moment, Will gazing at her in the half dark. Somewhere behind her he can hear the sound of her sisters laughing, one of them singing the chorus of a Celine Dion ballad with great conviction. Somebody's bra is draped over the banister like a flag. The walls in the foyer are dinged and smudgy, a pair of running shoes slumped next to an orphaned stiletto in the doorway. It looks like a place where people live. "I'm flying out tomorrow," he tells her finally. "I just came to say goodbye."

Lilly nods slowly, her face impassive. "Back to New York?"

"A guy I know from the Public is doing *Twelfth Night* downtown," he admits. "He called me a couple of days ago, asked if I wanted to take a crack at it."

"Imagine that," Lilly says archly. "Almost as if your career on the stage was never actually over to begin with."

"Almost as if."

"Well," she says with a shrug. "Maybe I'll see you out there. I've got a meeting with my agent in SoHo in a couple of weeks."

Will's eyes fly wide open. "Seriously?" he asks, feeling the smile spread across his face, easy and true. "For the novel?"

"Yeah, well." Lilly shrugs, but he can tell by the way her gaze flicks briefly downward that she's proud of herself, that she's excited. "Can't be famous for being famous forever."

"You know," he says, "you never actually told me what it was about." He pauses as whoever is singing gets to their big finish, someone else bursting into raucous applause. "The novel, I mean."

"No," Lilly says, "I guess I didn't." She glances over her shoulder in the direction of the clatter. Glances back. "It's about sisters."

Will grins at that, sudden and honest. He wants to tell her that he's different since he met her. He wants to tell her she deserves every good thing. He wants to tell her that he's sorry, that she's luminous, that he loves her, but when he opens his mouth to say it Lilly holds up a hand to cut him off.

"Come inside and say hi to my family, will you?" she asks, stepping back to let him into the foyer. "We're just about to eat."

ACKNOWLEDGMENTS

One particular joy of having done this job for so long is the way there are new people to be grateful for, every single time: thank you to Mary Gaule, who was excited about this book from the very beginning, and to Millicent Bennett for taking our girls over the finish line with grace and aplomb.

To Elizabeth Bewley for everything, always.

To everyone at Harper Perennial for your hard work and good humor, especially Liz Velez, Michael Fierro, Megan Looney, Suzy Lam, Kelly Doyle, and Jamie Kerner. To Robin Bilardello and Jessica Brilli, for that stunning cover. To Olivia Burgher and Sanjana Seelam at WME for your enthusiasm and smart ideas.

To my sisters, Jackie, Kate, and Sabina, and all the rest of my family and friends and colleagues. To Tom, Annie, and Charlie for the most beautiful life.

ABOUT THE AUTHOR

Katie Cotugno is the *New York Times* bestselling author of *Birds of California* as well as eight novels for young adults. She is also the co-author (with Candace Bushnell) of *Rules for Being a Girl*. She lives in Boston with her family.